"J. K. Beck delivers exciting paranormal romance with a sharp, suspenseful edge."
—*New York Times* bestselling author LARA ADRIAN

"A red-hot page-turner. I can't wait to read more from this author!"
—*New York Times* bestselling author KRESLEY COLE

"J. K. Beck takes you on a dark, twisty ride that will leave you breathless. Smart, suspenseful, and jam-packed with startling twists, *When Blood Calls* is pulse-pounding pleasure. Gripping and utterly compelling! J. K. Beck brings it!"
—*New York Times* bestselling author LARISSA IONE

"Buckle up. *When Blood Calls* is a dark and sexy ride!"
—*New York Times* bestselling author GENA SHOWALTER

BOOKS BY J. K. BECK

When Blood Calls
When Pleasure Rules
When Wicked Craves

WHEN WICKED CRAVES

J. K. Beck

BANTAM BOOKS
NEW YORK

A Bantam Books Mass Market Original

Copyright © 2010 by Julie Kenner

Excerpt from *When Passion Lies* copyright © 2010 by Julie Kenner

Published in the United States by Bantam Books, an imprint of The Random House Publishing Group, a division of Random House, Inc., New York.

BANTAM BOOKS is a registered trademark of Random House, Inc., and the colophon is a trademark of Random House, Inc.

ISBN 978-0-440-24579-7

This book contains an excerpt from the forthcoming novel *When Passion Lies* by Julie Kenner. This excerpt has been set for this edition only and may not reflect the final content of the forthcoming edition.

Cover art: Cliff Nielsen

Printed in the United States of America

www.bantamdell.com

2 4 6 8 9 7 5 3 1

To the Whine Sisters. Thanks for making me smile.

ACKNOWLEDGMENTS

Thanks to everyone at Bantam without whom these books wouldn't have been possible: Shauna, Scott, Jessie, Margaret. Everyone in art and production and sales and marketing and editorial . . . and the entire team. Y'all rock!

PROLOGUE

The vampires moved through the night, their unconscious cargo even more deadly than they—who had seen much throughout the centuries—could imagine.

"We need a secure location," Nicholas said. He had an angel's face and a scientist's mind. But nothing in his studies had prepared him for the transformation he had just witnessed in his friend.

"I know a place." Lucius, practical and methodical, steered the truck through the Los Angeles night. They had escaped a fierce battle, but this wasn't over. Both of them knew that for their friend Sergius—tranqued in the cargo bay—it might never be over. Once a tormented vampire whose daemon had fought for release, he was now so much worse, his reality shifted by nothing more substantial than a touch.

The girl's curse had transformed him into something unnatural and terrifying. Something monstrous even by the broad standards of a world that lived in shadows and hovered on the fringes of human nightmares.

"They will look for him," Nicholas said. "If we want to have any chance of reversing this thing, I need time to investigate. Time to think."

"The girl said there was no way to reverse the transformation."

"The girl is human. She may well be wrong."

Lucius nodded. "We don't have time, especially once word of what happened spreads. The Alliance will search for Sergius. And eventually, they will find him."

"Not if they believe there is no reason to look."

Lucius took his eyes off the road long enough to glance briefly at Nicholas. "You have a plan."

"Yes," Nicholas said, his voice heavy with purpose. "I do."

CHAPTER 1

Petra Lang did not want to die.

Too bad she didn't have even the slightest say in the matter.

A specially convened Alliance Tribunal had indicted her, an Alliance prosecutor had outlined the evidence against her, and the high examiner had sentenced her. Now she awaited her punishment from within a coffin-size portable holding cell, her hands bound tightly in front of her despite the space being so tiny there was no way she could have even shot someone the finger, were she so inclined.

And, frankly, she was definitely so inclined. As far as she was concerned, the preternatural assholes who'd sentenced her to die deserved one hell of a lot more than a rude gesture.

Never mind that she was willing to submit to whatever restrictive and oppressive rules the Alliance wanted to subject her to. Because of her curse, she'd been deemed a danger to both the human and the shadow communities, and in less than an hour, she would be dead.

She closed her eyes, trying not to think about it. Trying not to wonder if it would hurt or if she would slip softly away into the black. Trying not to wish she'd had the chance to lift the curse, to touch a man, to see the friggin' Eiffel Tower or the Great Wall of China. Hell, she'd never even made it up to San Francisco to see the Golden Gate Bridge. She was only twenty-six. She wasn't supposed to die.

She hoped she wouldn't cry; if she could make it without tears, at least then she could take some small victory with her to the grave.

Mostly, she thought about Kiril. Worried about him. Her brother who'd dedicated his life to protecting her. The boy who wrote such beautiful poems and could spend hours searching for the proper word for one of his short stories. The sorcerer who'd exploded in a frenzy of wind and thunder when the elite Covert Alliance Apprehension Squad had burst through the door of their house in Studio City.

The squad members had gone for Kiril first, with such swiftness that Petra had assumed they'd come for her brother and had no interest in her. She'd tried to help him, but though the family's magic flowed in her veins, too, the curse had always interfered, and summoning her meager power during a crisis had never been easy for her.

Instead, she'd watched, horrified, as the officers fired tranquilizer darts at him, the magic fading as Kiril collapsed unconscious onto the floor. She'd raced to him but hadn't made it to his side. Instead, a burly officer had lassoed her—*lassoed!*—then dragged her back toward the door.

She'd fought, digging in her heels, tugging on the rope, screaming for her brother. But she had never once run toward her captor. Never tried to rip the cloth that covered his body from nose to toes. Never yanked her own glove off or tried to touch skin upon skin.

She hadn't used the curse to fight back—she hadn't even tried.

And yet it was for that very curse that she would die tonight. She'd intentionally pushed the curse once. Only once. And it had been Serge's decision as much as her own. The vampire knew what would happen—what he would become. But they'd had no choice. They'd been trapped, and time had been running out.

It had been a total Hail Mary ploy, but it had paid off. She'd touched, he'd transformed, and the monster he became had wreaked havoc on their captors.

Serge had sacrificed his sanity, his soul, and even his life to save countless more, but did the Alliance care? Not one damn bit. They didn't look at the reason or the result; they looked only at the curse, at what she could wreak with nothing more substantial than the slightest brush of skin against skin.

She closed her eyes, clenched her fists, and wished she had the power to turn back time. If she had, she wouldn't hesitate. She would touch them all and take her chances with the vicious monsters she unleashed. She would do that very thing for which they were now executing her. She would turn them all, torture them all, and, dammit, she would fight to live.

She didn't deserve this.

Tears pricked her eyes, spilling out over her lashes, and she tried to lift a hand to wipe them away, then shook with fear and fury when her arm wouldn't move. She couldn't even dry her own damn tears! Dear God, she didn't ask for this. Didn't want it, would walk away if she could. So how was it fair that she died tonight, when she'd spent her whole life apart and alone, protecting the entire world from what she was?

Stop it! Stop thinking!

She almost wished the guards would hurry up and come. Right then, locked in the small concrete cell, she had no company other than her thoughts. And those thoughts were tormenting her.

"Prisoner!"

A tremor ran up her spine, and she took back the earlier wish. She wasn't ready, not at all.

"Prisoner!"

"Yes." Her voice was soft, but she took a small bit of pride from the fact that it didn't shake.

"It is time."

"What about my brother? My advocate? Can't I see them?" Didn't the condemned have the right to say good-bye to their families? To speak one last time to their legal representative?

"Your brother's request for visitation has been denied."

"Oh." She squeezed her eyes shut, not quite able to believe she wouldn't get the chance to say good-bye to Kiril, that she'd never again hold his hand when a blue moon filled the sky, or read one of his stories, or harass him about kicking up a whirlwind inside the house. Her chest tightened. There were too many things left undone. Too many things she still wanted to say. Now she'd never be able to.

She swallowed, forcing thoughts of her brother out of her mind. "What about Montegue?" she asked, referring to Nicholas Montegue, the vampire advocate who had represented her during the proceedings. Following the verdict and sentencing, he'd filed an appeal with the Alliance, specifically addressing it to Tiberius, the governor of the Shadow Alliance's Los Angeles territory.

Petra still hadn't heard the outcome, but Nicholas had been hopeful. Tiberius, he'd said, owed her one.

"The appeal was denied," the voice said. "The Tribunal has ordered that your execution proceed with all due speed. And Montegue filed no request to visit or be present at the execution."

She tried to draw a breath as the walls of the already tiny cell seemed to crowd even closer against her as she processed what the voice was saying. Nicholas had fought for her—spent hours researching centuries of shadow law and drafting brief after brief, his intensity and determination so thick that she'd actually dared to hope.

He'd been her courage during the weeks leading up to the hearing, and she'd relied on his quiet strength and sharp reputation. He was Nicholas Montegue, after all, the advocate who represented all vampiric interests on behalf of the Alliance. Who had a hand in the affairs of Tiberius himself.

If anyone could see her safely out of this mess, it was Nicholas. And each day, she'd anticipated his visit, eagerly working beside him, poring over the cases he'd copied and the statutes he'd dug up from faraway jurisdictions, so desperately grateful that he'd given her the gift of hope.

But that hope had died with the sentencing, and now he couldn't even face her?

How completely pathetic.

"Prisoner!" The sharp voice brought her back to the

present, to the small cell and the reality facing her. "Do you willingly accept your fate?"

"No!" The word seemed to burst from her mouth without any forethought.

There was nothing but silence around her, and she took some small bit of satisfaction in having apparently mucked up their formality, even if only a little bit.

"You may proceed," the voice said, only this time, it wasn't speaking to her. Within moments, the air in the cell grew thicker, as if it was pressing in against her head, and after a few seconds of that, the air seemed to be actually drilling into her. She wanted to reach up and clasp her skull in her palms, wanted to press her hands hard against her cranium and hold her head together before it exploded, but her shoulders were jammed against the concrete walls and there was no moving—she could only scream, and scream, and scream.

Something creeping.

Something looking.

Something moving like a worm through her mind. Digging and twisting and turning. Searching.

Searching . . .

It hurt. Oh dear God, it hurt, and as the pain spread out through her body—as bile rose in her throat and her chest heaved in acid-filled gags—she realized what it was. A Truth Teller—a rare creature in the shadow world. Although she'd spent years poking around in the shadows trying to find the truth for her clients, she'd never once met anyone who'd experienced the mind meld of a Truth Teller. It was horrible, and the more the creature poked around, the worse it became.

What the hell was it looking for?

The claws of the Teller's grasp scraped through the dark spots of her mind, riffling through long-forgotten memories, stirring up lost scents and fears and small joys along with the raw, red pain of the search.

And then, as fast as it had entered, the intruder withdrew. Her head felt strange, as if there were cotton inside it, and she had to struggle not to sink into herself and to listen instead to the low voices outside her small concrete prison.

"Clean," announced the baritone voice. "There are no plots. No plans for escape. She will take no secrets to her grave. Her mind is prepared to die."

No, she wanted to shout. *No, it isn't.* Her mind wasn't any more prepared than she was. But it didn't matter. They didn't care.

This wasn't about her; it was about the ceremony.

It was about the result.

With a jolt, the concrete cell into which she was locked started to rise. She was being lifted to the execution chamber. This was it. Time's up. Arrivederci, au revoir, and auld lang syne.

Petra tried to swallow, but her throat was too thick. She couldn't do anything anymore.

All she could do now was die.

CHAPTER 2

The small cell rose through the floor, then came to a stop with a sudden jolt, shaking Petra and kicking her pulse back up, her body primed for flight even though there was nowhere to flee. Without warning, the front and side walls of her tiny cell fell away, crashing to the ground with a thud that reverberated through the small chamber. She was on the stage of a very small theater, her back still strapped to the standing concrete block, on display for the three Tribunal members who sat in the plush chairs and stared at her, their faces impassive.

She'd witnessed executions in the Preternatural Enforcement Coalition's theater before, but those were always following a criminal conviction and took place in a cavernous room with dozens upon dozens of witnesses. Her termination might be taking place within the walls of the PEC, but this was an Alliance execution, not punishment rendered following a crime.

She was not being executed for what she'd done to the vampire, but because they were afraid of what she might do in the future. She scared them, and they were going to kill her.

She forced her chin high. It was their shame, not her actions, that had her dying in this dingy little room; the shame of knowing that what they did was unjust. Vile. And as she looked out upon the three of them, she hoped her expression telegraphed what she didn't have the guts to voice: *Screw you all.*

She recognized the three, of course. Dirque, Trylag, and Narid. A jinn, a para-daemon, and a wraith, and all three members of the Alliance.

She'd seen them every day during the charade they'd called a hearing. She'd hated them during the trial, and she didn't feel any more charitable to them now. They were the last people she wanted to watch her die. She wanted Kiril. Hell, she wanted Nicholas. But the guard had been right—neither her brother nor her own advocate would be with her at the end. She'd been isolated her entire life, and she'd learned to accept that. This, however . . . this bruised her heart.

A door in the center of the back wall opened, and as the theater had only two rows of seats, she could easily see the face of the person who stepped in. Or she could have seen him, had he not been covered in head-to-toe black, swathed just as she was. Her, they'd covered so that an accidental brush against her skin could bring no harm. He was covered not for safety, but for anonymity.

The executioner.

Dirque, acting as the high examiner, stood, a brooding jinn who ruled the territories he governed with an iron hand. The executioner lifted a bow, then notched an arrow into it. Petra tried to breathe and realized she couldn't.

"Petra Lang!" the executioner called in a low, harsh voice that seemed almost familiar. "This Tribunal has determined you to be a dangerous entity and subject to termination pursuant to the Fifth International Covenant and the common law of the shadow world. I ask the high examiner, is this so?"

Dirque's eyes glowed yellow in the dimly lit room, and his mouth stretched into a thin, smug smile. "The punishment is just and good."

"Petra Lang, do you have any last words?"

Did she? She wanted to talk and talk. To babble her way back to life. But she didn't. What was the point? All the talk in the world would change nothing, and in the end, she'd be six feet under.

"Then let us proceed."

In the audience, the high examiner returned to his seat. In the back of the room, the executioner positioned the bow, the tip of an arrow aimed straight for her heart. Slowly, he pulled the string back. In front of her, not one spectator moved. No one in the room even breathed.

Don't shut your eyes. Don't shut your eyes.

She didn't want to give them the satisfaction of knowing she was scared. But she was . . . she was so damn scared . . .

She closed her eyes.

The *twang* of the bow as the arrow flew filled the small theater, and Petra flinched, wishing she could raise her arms over her heart before the arrow hit home.

It didn't hit.

Her mind was working so hard to compute that anomaly that for a moment she didn't register the cries of agony and howls of disbelief.

Confused—and still very much alive—she opened her eyes, then added her own screams to the cacophony as her eyes burned from the blue-green smoke that now filled the room, her lungs joining in the agony as soon as she drew in the poisoned air. Once again, she tried to move her hands, and once again she failed.

She'd shut her eyes tight—the only thing she could do, bound as she was. But the darkness gave little respite from the pain, and she couldn't stand not knowing what was happening. Not understanding why chaos had erupted or, more important, why she was still alive.

Gingerly, she peered out through slitted lids, her body tightening as the mist burned eyes that she had to fight not to shut again.

Someone leaped in front of her—*the executioner*. His eyes were open behind plastic goggles, and he pressed against her, as close as a lover, his body demanding co-operation even though she was in no position to do anything but. The bow still hung from one shoulder, and now he lifted it and reloaded. But he wasn't aiming at the high examiner, who was rushing blindly toward the stage, his face covered with yellow pustules, his eyes red and swollen, and his hands glowing with the infamous blue fire of the jinn.

Instead, the executioner shot his arrow to the side. She turned her head, tears streaming, and the last thing she saw before her eyes swelled shut was the arrow striking a metal control panel on the far wall of the small theater.

Immediately, the concrete square on which she stood began to descend, dragging her and the executioner back down to the bowels of the building. Her heart pounded in her chest and she allowed herself the tiniest flutter of hope. *This was a rescue.*

"Kiril?" she whispered, but even as she spoke, she knew it wasn't her brother. The shapes were too different. Kiril towered over her, his height making him seem like a giant compared to the man who held her now, his firm body fitting perfectly against her during their swift descent.

And whereas Kiril smelled of incense and charms and mystical smoke, this man's scent seemed almost European. Nicotine and men's cologne, the aroma making her think of London or Rome, which was ridiculous since she'd never been to either city. But there was something so very old-world and sophisticated about the way the man smelled. Something familiar, too, and hope fluttered inside her.

The slab lurched to a stop, and she heard scraping above them that she assumed had to be the execution staff trying to pry open the hatch. Any moment now, guards would rush in from the single door through which they'd walked when the guard had led Petra to her tiny execution cell. She'd seen the room then, and now she tried to peel her eyes open and see it again, but it was no use. They were swollen shut, her lids glued together with a mixture of pus and tears.

She could hear well enough, though, and almost as fast as the thought had entered her head, she heard the motor of the door begin to whir. At the same time, the man's arms squeezed tight around her. She flinched automatically, then relaxed as she remembered. They were both fully clothed, every inch of skin covered with black.

There would be no physical contact.

Even as she sighed in relief, he pushed away with a sharp curse.

"What is it?"

"Goddamned hematite bands."

She wanted to gasp, but couldn't. How could she when her throat was so thick, her mind filled with confusion and wonder?

Because there was no doubt about the voice now.

Nicholas Montegue.

He'd come for her after all.

♦

Hematite. Why in the name of all that is holy had the goddamned guards bound her with hematite?

The question was an academic one, and one that Nick didn't have time to ponder. He'd taken the precaution of ensuring that the lock code for the door to the staging area was changed as soon as Petra's cell had ascended, but something as basic as a lock would not keep the guards out for long. The staging area for this particular theater of execution was one of the few places in the PEC's Division 6 complex that did not have a barrier of hematite, the vile mineral that prevented a vampire from transforming into mist.

That had been his plan, of course. To get Petra back down to the staging area, grab her, and transform them both to mist, a nearly invulnerable state for a vampire.

His asset had neglected to mention that the guards would bind Petra's hands with hematite. And Nick, damn him, hadn't thought to ask. She wasn't a vampire, so what was the point?

Had they anticipated him? Believed that he might try to rescue the girl?

It was a possibility he couldn't ignore, because it

would mean that the escape he had thought would be reasonably simple had transformed into a minefield of trouble.

"Change of plans," he said, and despite the pain that had to accompany her rapidly swelling eyes, Petra smirked.

"I didn't even know there was a plan."

He stifled a smile as he moved around the slab, grateful she wasn't cowering in fear, fighting him, or doing anything that would slow their escape. Behind her now, he pressed the latch to release the strap that bound her waist to the concrete and pinned her upper arms to her sides. "I can't do a thing about your hands." He reached for her arm to lead her, then grimaced when she stiffened at the touch. "Two layers of tight knit between us. I'm safe."

"Sorry. I'm not used to—"

"I know. Come on." He clutched her arm more firmly, and this time she didn't resist, though she did stumble.

"I could run a lot faster if you hadn't blinded me. What the hell did you do, anyway?"

He didn't answer, but instead reached into one of the pouches he'd knotted to his belt. He didn't want to take the time, but she was right. If she couldn't move fast, she was a liability.

He heard loud voices and scraping on the other side of the door. They were trying to break through. They wouldn't succeed, but someone must have radioed Security Section for the override code. His asset had buried it, but she wasn't able to completely delete it. They'd be through the door soon. And even if they weren't, that was the way he and Petra were going, too. His planned exit was useless if they couldn't transform to mist.

He'd removed a small jar from the pouch, and now he opened it, revealing a noxious-smelling, bile-colored cream. "Take some," he said, shoving it under her hand so she had no choice but to scoop some cream onto her cloth-covered fingers. "Slather it all over your eyes. That's the way." An inelegant job, but she'd managed even with bound wrists. "It takes a moment, but you'll recover soon. In the meantime, stick close. And swallow this," he added, reaching into the same pouch and pulling out a small pill that he pressed into her hand. "We're about to do this all over again."

"*What?*" Panic laced her voice, but he didn't have time to explain. Instead, he reached into another pouch, pulled out the second Du Yao Yan Qiu he'd created, and clutched it in one hand.

He'd launched the first one with the arrow in the theater above, releasing a temporary poison. This one he would hurl toward the guards—the same guards who were clambering through the now-open door. He waited, one hand tight on the girl, the other holding fast to the poison-filled orb, not a weapon of the shadow world, but of ancient China. With a few of his own modifications, of course.

"Take the damn thing," he said, noticing that she stood there, holding the pill, her wrists still bound together and her expression dubious. "I'm trying to get you the hell out of here, not kill you."

"Good point." She lifted the pill to her lips as the flood of guards started. Two burst through first, one firing a tranq dart that whizzed only inches from Petra's ear.

She screamed, then dropped to the floor, chasing the pill that had rolled away, disappearing down one of the gratings through which the ashen remains of the executed were swept for processing—the very grates through which he'd intended to escape with Petra as mist.

"Dammit!"

Mentally, he echoed her cry, but there was nothing he could do now. More guards had come through, seven total before the flood stopped and they were all in the room, a heavily armed contingent of creatures—all covered from head to foot in strike-team clothing, their eyes safe behind goggles, their skin safe behind cloth, and tranq guns held tight in their hands.

Nick shifted sideways before the guards fired, dropping to the floor next to Petra at the same time he let the orb fly. It burst on the ground, the small chambers within that had been keeping the components of the poison separate rupturing with the impact, and the magic of chemistry stepping in to aid their escape.

The room filled with noxious gas, but this poison didn't attack the skin. Instead, it formed a thick fog that made it impossible to see even a hand shoved straight in front of a face. More important, when breathed, the poison sucked the energy from the victim.

Unfortunately, since the antidote he'd tried to feed her had gone down through the floor vents, Petra succumbed to the poison as well, her low moans indicating just how hard the concoction had hit her human constitution.

Nick couldn't see the guards, but he could hear them slowing down, stumbling. All except one—and because he still stood, Nick knew it must be a vampire. Like Nick, the vampire guard could breathe, but didn't have to, and he'd apparently stopped at the first hint of poison, refusing to inhale the debilitating smoke. That guard alone remained a danger, and odds of one-on-one were perfectly fine with Nick, even with the baggage he was now hauling in the form of the lethargic girl.

Moving as silently as possible, Nick lifted Petra, then eased toward the door . . . and slammed right into the hard body of the vampire guard who, being a credit to the vampire community, had wisely moved to that exact location.

The vampire's reaction was immediate: a punch to Nick's throat that had him gasping in reflex—and inhaling the damn poison.

It didn't matter.

Nick had designed the poison himself, as well as the antidote, and he'd taken a dose before entering the facility. He coughed, the noxious fumes burning his lungs, but his strength wasn't sapped.

The vampire, however, wouldn't know that, and in a calculated risk, Nick allowed himself a long, harsh cry of frustration, then sank to his knees as if the muscles in his legs were suddenly incapable of supporting him.

As he fell, the vampire wrenched Petra from his grasp, and Nick grappled among the pockets and pouches at his waist for a weapon. He didn't want to kill the vampire—didn't want the death of a PEC guard added to his list of crimes—but he would do what it took to get out of this mess, and with the girl.

With a stake in hand, he gathered his strength, then lurched toward the vampire—realizing suddenly that he could see the guard clearly.

The vents.

Someone in Security Section had turned on the floor vents, and the poison was being sucked out of the room with amazing swiftness, replaced with clean air that filled the lungs of the lethargic guards, their strength returning.

Dammit, dammit, dammit all to hell.

He was surrounded, and the girl—the very reason he'd undertaken this absurd mission—was held fast by the vampire.

He could escape; he could turn to mist and escape the way he'd planned to all along. As of right then, his identity was still concealed behind the body-covering suit he wore. And considering the miasma of chemical smells in the air, he doubted any of the guards even realized he was a vampire.

But he couldn't leave without the girl. Security around her would be tightened, and she would be executed almost immediately. This was it. Now or never.

The answer had to be now. But now was impossible.

He hadn't counted on the security cameras. Hadn't counted on the vents.

Just as he hadn't counted on the goddamned hematite.

In front of him, the six guards were moving legs and arms. Soon they would rise again for battle.

"Surrender," the vampire said. "There is nowhere to go."

He stood still, his eyes on Petra.

He had only one option, and to take it would put his friends at risk.

He hesitated only a moment, and then he reached into his pocket and pressed a single button on his phone.

CHAPTER 3

♦ "The problem is that we don't have any witnesses who put our guy at the second crime scene," J'ared said, floating a few inches above the guest chair in Sara's office. "Our guts say it's him, but unless the investigators get us some solid dirt, we're going to have to charge him only with the first murder, and that would really suck dragon eggs."

Behind the desk, PEC Division 6 prosecutor Sara Constantine Dragos paced, her eyes on the desktop, but her mind on the execution. She glanced quickly at her computer screen, expecting to see the flash notification that Security Section sent following every successful termination.

There was no flash, just the brief she was working on regarding the current homicide investigation.

She leaned toward her keyboard, her fingers hovering there for a moment. There was really no reason to hesitate. As a prosecutor with the PEC, she had a perfect right to watch any execution, either in person or over the monitor.

Still . . . for this execution, she thought it was best to keep her distance.

She didn't know for certain that Nick was going to try anything. But that was only because her husband, Luke, would have Nick's hide if the advocate put her job at risk by telling her something that she would be obligated to report to her superiors.

And a plan to interrupt an Alliance-ordered execution and flee with the condemned definitely fell on the list of things her bosses would want to know.

She tapped one finger softly on the keyboard, considering. She wasn't worried that Luke was helping Nick out. He hadn't given up his old ways, but he would never do anything that might harm her. About that, she was absolutely certain.

To be honest, some small part of her actually wished he was involved. Between Nick and Luke, they could design a foolproof plan and get the girl out without any risk to Sara at all.

Hard to believe she was actually fantasizing about a prison break. Her, the woman who'd been weaned on the judicial system. But this wasn't justice in action, and the Alliance Tribunal had been a show without substance, not a courtroom in which facts were applied to the law. The idea that the Alliance could execute someone merely for being a threat made her think of the dystopian novels she'd devoured in high school. Not reality.

But months ago her reality had shifted dramatically, and she was still getting used to that.

"—and when we dance naked around the courtroom, the judge won't even realize that all our legal arguments are crap."

Sara jerked her head up and squinted at the poltergeist. "What?"

"Oh, so you are listening."

She tried to run her fingers through her hair, realized

it was pulled back tight into a ponytail, and shoved her hand into her pocket. "Sorry. Distracted."

His wispy shoulders shrank, and the spectral light that created his shape shimmered a bit around the edges. "The execution. You wanna put this off until tomorrow?"

She shook her head briskly and forced her attention back to J'ared. "No. No, I'm fine." As she spoke, her cell phone rang. She snatched it off her desk, checked the caller ID, and forced her expression to remain bland—because it was Nick's name flashing on her phone's tiny screen.

Panicked, she eased behind her desk, hoping she looked casual, then flipped open the phone.

Before answering, she covered the mic and mouthed, "Emily," referring to her best friend from her days as a human in the District Attorney's Office. She was just about to ask "Emily" what she needed, when she heard the sound coming through the phone's earpiece—a low, threatening voice telling someone to "get your hands away from that goddamn belt or we will drop you right here."

She stayed silent, her heart pounding so loud she was certain J'ared would hear it, then casually pushed the mute button on her phone, afraid that the security guard who was threatening Nick would hear if J'ared spoke.

Tossing aside her hesitations, she logged into the security system and viewed the feed for the execution theater. Empty. Frowning, she pulled up the grid of all active cameras, sucking in air when she saw the feed streaming from the execution staging room.

Petra was being held by a burly security guard.

Through the phone, she could hear him talking to Nick, telling him to take off the belt and drop all of his weapons. Nick, she realized, was the black-clad shape in the center of the room, now surrounded by a phalanx of guards who were pushing themselves up off the ground, clearly unsteady on their feet. Even over the monitor, she could see how tense he was, muscles prepared for flight.

So why didn't he rush the guard, grab the girl, and go? At this point, it damn well seemed worth the risk.

The question had barely formed in her mind when her eyes settled on Petra and she realized what Nick's problem was: hematite.

She shivered slightly, remembering the freakish sensation of being held in a vampire's arms and being broken down into particles of mist. The vampire had held her close, and they'd transformed together. But if she'd been wearing hematite . . .

"Hang on, Em," she said into the muted phone, hoping her voice sounded at least halfway normal. "I remember where I filed that phone number."

Across from her, J'ared rose from the guest chair and started doing lazy loop-the-loops in the air, obviously getting bored. At the terminal, Sara pulled up the Plan of Execution that had been logged that morning. If the Tribunal had ordered the hematite binders, there was nothing she could do—they would have to be removed from the terminal in the security office, and by someone with Alliance clearance.

But if one of the guards had made the decision himself . . .

She scrolled through the pages, finally finding the serial number of the cuffs, and the entry by Transport Officer Taaj Miran, who'd justified the binders since "her touch is transformative, and the binders ensure an additional measure of safety."

She copied the serial number, then logged into the resource program. All prosecutors had access to restraints that could be used during interviews and in the field. Put the restraints on potentially dangerous suspects, take them off potentially cooperative ones as a show of good faith. All part of the game.

This wasn't a game, though. This was her career. But more important, this was Nick, a friend, and one of Luke's best friends. And Petra, who had control and a respect for the curse that bound her, and yet she'd been unjustly condemned for crimes she had not yet committed.

Once upon a time, Sara had believed in black and white, but more and more she was seeing the world in shades of gray. And before she could talk herself out of it, she began to search the database for the release code to Petra's specific binders.

It was all she had the ability to do.

She hoped it would be enough. For that matter, she hoped she could do it in time.

◆

She was still going to die.

For a brief, fleeting, glorious moment, Petra had believed that her knight had come, not on a white steed, but in a black bodysuit, which didn't matter at all as she wasn't disposed to being picky about rescues.

This rescue, however, had fallen flat, and though she

wanted desperately to blame Nicholas—to hurl curses at him and scream that he was an idiot for getting her hopes up and demand that he figure out a way to fix whatever the hell went wrong with the plan—she couldn't even conjure enough brain power to do that.

Her mind was fuzzy from the poison, and her muscles weren't strong enough to hold her up, and all her support came from the vampire who clutched her with a firm grip on her arm as he spoke out loud, answering some security person who must be talking into his earpiece.

Behind them, the door had slid shut again, trapping her and Nicholas in the room with the guards. The vamp had called for backup, and soon she'd be returned to the coffinlike box, probably hauled back to the stage, probably executed right then.

These were her last moments, she was so close to freedom she could taste it, yet she couldn't do a single goddamned thing.

Around Nicholas, the guards were slowly climbing back to their feet. Apparently, preternatural creatures recovered faster from the poison than humans, because there was no way she was doing anything other than stand there like a damn useless noodle.

Her own rescue, and she couldn't even lift a finger. What a total freaking crock.

Magic?

She tried to think through the cotton in her head. Magic was hard for her—so hard—but she had to try. Had to do something. An electrical surge. A fireball. Some sort of distraction that would give Nicholas a moment to get to her. What he'd do then in a locked room with seven guards, she didn't know, but at least she'd have done something. At least she'd have gotten them back where they were before everything went to hell.

Squinting her still-tender eyes, she tried to focus her energy. Kiril had refused to teach her, insisting that the curse would interfere, and without the ability to control the magic it was too dangerous to wield.

About that, he was probably right.

At the moment, she really didn't care.

"Bind him," her captor said. He lifted his head, sniffed the air. "Hematite shackles."

"He be vampire?" a squat guard asked.

"I cannot tell. The suit masks his scent, as does the lingering poison. But we will take no chances."

Shit.

The guards began to advance on Nicholas—five of them keeping him covered, another approaching with the binders. "You fight, you die."

"I'll take that under advisement," Nicholas said. He kept one hand in his pocket, obviously holding on to something. His eyes stayed on Petra, his expression determined. She wished she knew what was going through his head, but she didn't, and all she could do was focus on the magic and hope, hope, hope that if it worked he would take whatever advantage she gave him and run with it.

The guard was almost at his side—if she was going to manage anything, it was going to have to be now.

Fire. Elements. The powers of the earth.

In her mind, she pictured a column of fire, rising up from the floor, the flames keeping the guard from Nicholas.

In reality, nothing like that happened. She was getting *something*, though, because she could feel the burn moving through her body—a slow, thick heat that seemed almost as languid as her uncooperative muscles, but *there*. And if she could only manage to focus it, she might—

"Witch!" The vampire howled, lashing out and knocking her to the ground and then clasping his arm. She gasped, confused, terrified, a whole flurry of emotions. But when she saw his arm—when she saw where the material had burned thin so that they had almost, *almost*, touched flesh on flesh—that was when the terror set in, because that same arm now wielded a knife, and it was coming right after her, procedure be damned.

"No!" The cry came from Nicholas, but when she instinctively turned that direction, he was no longer there, and before her mind could even process the movement, a thick mist rose up between her and the vampire guard, taking form and turning into Nicholas—his body falling under the blade meant for her.

Another scream of protest filled the room, and she realized it was coming from her. Her wrists might be bound, but in her mind, she lashed out, beating on the guard, ripping the damn suit, laying her hands upon him and taking her revenge for thwarting her escape.

She couldn't touch him, and yet he stayed away, and between Nicholas and the vampire guard, she saw the air shimmer, like heat rising from a desert highway, then burst into dancing tongues of flame. *She was doing that.* Which was, frankly, not nearly as cool as she'd hoped, because although her neat little wall of fire might keep the vampire guard away, the other six guards were racing toward them with hematite nets, ready to hurl them through the heat. Ready to trap Nicholas and take them both down.

"I'm sorry," Nicholas said, and she could only shake her head. He'd tried to save her, and for that, she'd always be grateful.

"It doesn't matter," she whispered. Without thinking, she reached for the knife he'd pulled from his chest. If she was going to die, she was going to do it on her own terms, and—

She stopped, her hand almost to the knife, her sore eyes widening as she met Nicholas's equally astounded expression. *The binders had fallen free.*

"The binders," she said, or she tried to. She couldn't get the words out, because as she spoke, Nicholas leaped upon her. Instinctively, she tensed as he clutched her, but she put her shackle-free arms tight around his waist even as the hematite nets flew through the air toward them.

And within the space of a heartbeat, she broke apart, her body and mind dissolving. No touch, no sight, no being.

Petra Lang was gone.

CHAPTER 4

Existing now only as mist and consciousness, Nick felt rather than heard the sirens that screamed out, announcing a total lockdown of the facility. It didn't matter—they'd successfully vaulted the bump in the road, and his plan was back on track. He'd done his homework and knew how the automatic lockdown worked—the doors slamming shut, the vents sealing tight.

The very vents they were now racing through as they headed toward the exhaust grid that opened into Los Angeles's Red Line subway terminal. They were, in fact, almost there now. He couldn't *see* it—the senses exist as part of the body, and he was currently operating without flesh—but he could *vision* it.

That exhaust terminal, a fourteen-inch mesh square, was designed to be sealed by a steel cover that slammed into place as soon as lockdown was instituted. Nick had no doubt the system worked as designed. And that was why he'd entered the building through that very portal, then transformed from mist into flesh inside the cramped tunnel. Now, when the steel door tried to seal, it would fail, the mechanism blocked by the insertion of a small metal rod that left a gap of approximately one-half inch between the metal flashing of the vent and the perpendicular steel seal.

Half an inch was more than sufficient for mist to slip through.

Swiftly, surely, he maneuvered them through the tunnels, and then—*yes*—through the small gap until they were soaring beneath the streets of Los Angeles, racing a speeding Red Line train, finally, gloriously, free.

They'd made it.

Thank the gods—and thank Sara—*they'd actually made it.*

Of course, the security team would register the breach and they would send agents to rectify. But it no longer mattered. They'd escaped the building, and the guards wouldn't find them. Not tonight. Hopefully not at all.

Too bad rescuing Petra had been the easy part. Now, the work really began.

But even the knowledge of all that lay ahead couldn't dampen his spirit. Within his consciousness, he smiled. Hell, he grinned like a fiend, his entire being overwhelmed by the euphoria of the moment—of the rescue, of having beaten a system that was supposedly unbeatable. Of simply winning. And even though he and Petra weren't cohorts—even though he'd pulled her from the execution floor for his own purposes—he wished that she could feel it, too.

Petra.

He could feel her, entwined with him, their beings mixed and meshed, an awareness of her running through him that seemed almost erotic. She might have no understanding of how her consciousness was reacting, but it *was* reacting. Strange that a human could retain any level of awareness in the mist. But she did. He could feel it.

Excitement. Fear.

Not arising from the dissipation of her body, but rather from the twining of their two beings. This wasn't touch, and yet it was intimate. Complete. More personal than sex, more erotic than a kiss, and as her consciousness moved through him, he felt the fear turn to understanding—there was no danger here. No flesh in which the curse could mount.

As the fear dissolved, the melancholy took over, a dark pit of sadness that turned his thoughts gray and slid like oil into the wisps of his being. This was it, he realized. This was as close to intimacy as she'd ever been, her touches limited and always, always protected by a barrier of tightly knit cloth.

She longed—by the gods he could feel the longing pulsing through her, her yearning so keen it conjured his own memories of Lissa, the only woman for whom his own need had been so intense it bordered on pain. Now they flooded back—memories he'd worked hard to push aside and that now sent desire coursing through him. Desire, and also the pain of loss.

He forced his mind to focus not on Lissa or himself, but on the girl. Her need cut through him, so desperately did she want that touch, that intimacy, and for a moment Nick felt shame that he so often took what women willingly gave. He'd been trying to erase the memories of Lissa, of course, but never once had he considered what a gift it was to feel flesh against flesh, heat against heat.

A flash of sympathy burned through him, and he pushed it brutally away. He could be sympathetic to her plight, yes, but he couldn't let the emotion rule him or influence his decisions. He hadn't rescued her out of kindness or out of anger that his carefully constructed legal arguments had been denied. He'd pulled off this stunt for one reason only—he needed her.

Whether it took her knowledge, her touch, or her blood, in the final analysis, Petra was the key, and Nick wouldn't rest until they'd unlocked the curse and set Serge free.

◆

"Sir," the med tech said, his voice unsteady. "Sir, if you could just stay still, the medicine—"

Dirque lashed out, the blue flame rising in fury from his fingertips visible despite the hazy veil that covered his eyes. "Give me the goddamned salve and I'll do it myself."

He could feel the tech's hesitation as he tried to avoid the flames dancing between Dirque's fingers, and it took all of his restraint not to lash out against the quivering brat. Not because the tech deserved it, but because Dirque's temper was running so high that he needed the simple, cathartic release that would follow the sound of an innocent's screams.

No.

This was a mission, not a vendetta, and he was too smart to give in to emotion. Too cunning to fall prey to fear.

But he was afraid. Dammit, despite everything he'd seen and done in over two millennia upon this earth, he was afraid of one goddamned curly-haired girl.

No, he corrected himself. Not the girl. He was afraid of what she could create.

More important, he was afraid of what she could destroy. Him. The Shadow Alliance. The whole fucking world.

Exhausted, he fell back against the pillow, the poison still working upon his eyes. He scooped up some salve and slathered it on.

"The others?" he asked. "Trylag? Narid?"

His eyes were closed now, the salve soothing and healing, but he could hear the med tech shuffle about near the foot of his bed. "They will recover," the tech said. "Member Narid is already almost fully healed, and the physicians anticipate member Trylag will be back to full strength within the hour."

"Good." Dirque's body relaxed. He'd feared the worst, but realized now that the poison the executioner had shot into the room was not meant to kill, only to hinder.

A mistake.

Had Dirque perished, his wrath would have died with him. As it was, he would spend the rest of his days—and as a jinn, they could be numerous indeed—seeking retribution for this crime against him, the Tribunal, and the Alliance itself.

"I must speak with them," he said.

"But—"

"Bring them here. As soon as they are able."

"I—" The tech lowered his eyes. "Yes, sir. Of course, sir."

"And the rest of the Alliance? They have been notified?"

"Yes, sir. I believe so, sir. I only work in Medical, and—"

"Send for Tiberius." The vampiric liaison to the Shadow Alliance hadn't sat on the Tribunal, but as the governor of the Los Angeles territory, he had remained on premises during the execution. Or, rather, during the attempted execution.

"He's already outside," the tech said, then scurried to the door. He opened it, and Tiberius strode in, and through Dirque's hazy vision he appeared even taller than his six and a half feet, his eyes as black as his clothing.

"Chairman," Tiberius said, referring to Dirque's position as the chairman of the Shadow Alliance. The vampire didn't incline his head, though, and the failure to display the proper deference was not lost on Dirque.

"We have had our differences, Tiberius," Dirque said, in an understated reference to his own attempts to oust Tiberius from the Alliance only a few months ago. "Now is the time to move past them."

"Indeed."

"It is not merely our positions on the Alliance that are in danger, Tiberius. It is the Alliance itself."

"Do not speak to me as if I were ignorant of these matters, Dirque. I was standing at your side when the Oracle spoke."

"I apologize," Dirque said, the words thick and unpleasant on his tongue. "You are right, of course." Of all the Alliance members, all but two had been present when the Oracle had made the disturbing announcement. And those two had been fully briefed by the five elder members.

Dirque slammed his fist down hard on the hospital tray. "Dammit, we should have simply sent a team in to destroy the girl the moment we learned of her existence. Going through the motions of this damned Tribunal was not only a waste of time, it has now proven to be unreasonably dangerous."

"This matter was voted on by all seven current members of the Alliance," Tiberius said. He aimed that hard stare right at Dirque. "All but one voted in favor of convening a Tribunal and executing the girl following the proper procedures."

"I'm sure the girl appreciated our efforts on her behalf." Dirque could not keep the sarcasm from his voice.

"Petra Lang is not like the others. She deserved more than to die in a dark alley with an assassin's bullet in her back," Tiberius said. "At least with an official conviction she could face death with some knowledge of why it was coming."

Dirque let out a long, harsh laugh. "You are a fool, Tiberius, to harbor any soft feelings for the human simply because of the role she played in saving your ass."

"The girl was a key player in proving that it was not shadowers who were murdering the humans in my jurisdiction," Tiberius said. "Were it not for her, I would no longer be a member of the Alliance and we would not be having this conversation." This time, he did incline his head. "I know, Chairman, how much that outcome would have disturbed you."

A slow burn rose up Dirque's back, and he wanted to lash out at the vampire for mocking him. He pushed it down, though. Now was not the time, and there were bigger things to worry about. "What's done is done.

You are correct that the full Alliance convened the Tribunal, and a judgment has been entered. We can at least agree that the death order was accurate? The girl poses an unacceptable risk to the shadow world and the Alliance?"

"We can agree to that, yes."

"I'm relieved to hear it." He sat up straighter, blinking, and realized that his vision had almost completely returned. A knock sounded at the door, and both he and Tiberius turned to look that direction. "Enter."

The door opened, and a tall, lean man stepped inside, clad in a black T-shirt and camouflage pants. He looked like a soldier returning from a human war, rough and dangerous, and he approached Dirque's bedside with a confidence that made Dirque proud.

"Uncle," the man said.

"Tariq." Dirque gestured toward Tiberius. "You know Governor Tiberius?"

Tariq inclined his head. "Sir."

Tiberius acknowledged the younger jinn, then turned his attention back to Dirque. He said nothing, but stood as if waiting for an explanation.

Dirque complied. "My nephew serves as a RAC team leader within Division 6," he said, referring to the Recon and Capture team. "As of today, he is on temporary loan to the Alliance as head of Search and Recovery."

"Sir?" Tariq said, and his diamond-shaped pupils constricted with surprise. And with ambition. Good.

"Perform your function well, and you may find yourself permanently assigned to the Alliance."

"Yes, sir. Of course, sir."

Tiberius stepped forward. "You have already begun investigating the escape?"

"Yes. All available Division personnel have been put to the task."

"And what have you learned?"

"The prisoner was aided in her escape by a vampire." Tariq straightened his shoulders and looked Tiberius directly in the eye. "The poison that was released in the air in both the execution and staging areas was not shadow-made. We believe that is a significant lead, sir."

"I see," Dirque said. "And do you have a suspect in mind?"

"Yes, sir."

Dirque held up a hand, silencing his nephew. Then he turned his attention from Tariq to Tiberius. "And you, my friend? Do you have a theory as to which of your kind did this thing?"

For a moment, he thought his rival wouldn't answer, then he saw the slightest straightening of Tiberius's spine, the firmness in those cold dark eyes. "Do not mock the enmity that exists between us," he said. "But yes. I have a suspect in mind."

"Who?" Dirque demanded.

"Nicholas Montegue." He spoke the name firmly, without hesitation, but Dirque heard the somber note of deep regret that colored Tiberius's voice.

He glanced toward his nephew, who nodded agreement, then turned his attention back to the vampire.

"You call Montegue friend." It wasn't a question.

"I did," Tiberius said. "I still do."

"And yet you condemn him here today."

"You know that I have no choice," Tiberius said, and

Dirque had to fight not to shrink from the contempt in the vampire's voice. "For too long we have been following the Oracle's words. Destroying the monsters that have sought to rip apart the Alliance members. Searching out those who can create such beasts with little more than an ill-timed touch."

Dirque made no response. Most of the creatures had been located and terminated before their strength fully developed and before their minds formed enough to allow them a level of subtlety in their attack. In other words, the monsters had raged across the earth, and that made them easy to find and subdue.

But centuries ago, before the Alliance fully understood the risk, one had survived long enough to catch Thurell off guard and rip the elder troll into so many pieces that even his own mate could not identify the remains. It had been hell keeping the true nature of the attack secret, and more hellish still destroying the monster. In the end, the Alliance had lost sixscore soldiers before they had killed the monster's maker in a fit of fury and realized in doing so that her death restored the monster to a man.

It was not a scenario that Dirque cared to see repeated, and the Alliance had suffered no qualms about terminating any female they believed possessed what had come to be known as the Touch *before* she could use such power.

He saw the irony in the situation, of course. The females were human. And to a human, the shadowers themselves were monsters, and humans would hunt them down and kill them and believe themselves to be saving the world by doing so.

Humans were fools. Certainly, they did not understand that which was truly monstrous.

For more than fifty years, the Alliance members had slept soundly, believing that each of the females wielding the Touch had been swiftly and resolutely terminated. But then the Alliance had learned of one whose family line had remained hidden—and stayed hidden until the little bitch had thrust her curse upon Sergius. Sergius might be dead now—and as there was no path of destruction laid across the hills of Los Angeles, Dirque felt it was safe to accept the word of the Division 6 medical examiner, who had tested the remains and confirmed Sergius's DNA—but the death of the monster did not remove the risk.

"The girl doesn't understand the full nature of her power, Dirque, and neither does Nicholas."

"That is no defense," the jinn said.

"No," Tiberius agreed. "In fact it may even make them more dangerous. They do not fully fathom the fire with which they play."

"Then it is time to tell Nicholas exactly who and what he has taken on."

"I agree."

"And once he knows, will he surrender the girl?"

"Knowing Nicholas, I fear not."

"What interest can he possibly have in keeping her alive?"

"Nicholas's interests are varied and eclectic. It wouldn't surprise me to learn that he wishes to study the human, rather than terminate her."

"He is a fool."

Tiberius said nothing.

"If he puts himself between the Alliance and the girl," Dirque said, "you understand that your friend may die."

"I understand."

Dirque drew in a breath. "I am pleased you see the full scope of the problem, and that your actions are not stymied by either friendship or a false sense of obligation."

"My actions are motivated by survival," Tiberius said. "My own, and the Alliance's."

Dirque's smile was slow and thin. "You're wiser than I have ever given you credit for."

"Sir," Tariq began, taking a step toward his uncle's bed. "I'm not following. What about the girl? What power?" The two Alliance members exchanged glances, and Tariq felt a sharp tug of irritation. "You have tasked me to assist the Alliance, and I'm honored to do so, but I can be very little help without knowing exactly what you are concerned about."

Dirque remained silent.

"He must know," Tiberius said. "He cannot fight what he does not understand."

"Yes," Dirque said, and Tariq saw what looked like fear sparking in his uncle's deep yellow eyes.

That, however, was impossible. The master jinn feared nothing.

"Yes," Dirque repeated. "Of course." He drew in a breath and faced Tariq, all signs of fear gone. Instead, there was only the familiar strength and a cold determination. "For over two thousand years the Alliance has waited and watched, fearing the fruition of the prophecy spoken to us by the Oracle at Delphi."

"A prophecy?"

"*From the touch of Eve, destruction shall rise—a third, powerful and changed, who emerges from the earth, and who will fell the piers upon which the shadows rule, and take back that which was stolen.*"

Tariq shook his head. "I don't understand."

"An enemy comes," Tiberius said, moving closer. "Someone created from the touch of a woman, who will destroy the Alliance."

"The Alliance?"

"The piers upon which the shadows rule," Dirque said.

"The Alliance controls the shadowers," Tariq said, as the pieces fell into place. "And a pier—"

"Supports," Dirque said. "The piers of a house form its foundation. One falls, and the house cannot survive."

"And you think the girl is this enemy?"

"No," Tiberius said. "The girl is Eve. The enemy was Sergius."

Tariq frowned. "But Serge is dead."

"And as long as Petra lives, she can create another just like him."

Understanding dawned. "Shit," he whispered. "It does fit. But what does the third mean?" Tariq asked. "The third try?"

"You are not so young, nephew. How can it be that you are not familiar with the histories?"

"You mean the mythology." A whole bunch of bullshit stories about the way the shadowers came into being.

"All myths begin with a kernel of fact."

Tariq looked sideways at his uncle. "So you're telling me that vampires and werewolves and jinns and para-daemons all descend from two warring brothers? Seriously?"

"Is that so hard to believe?"

It seemed pretty damn absurd, actually. Two brothers who crossed over from another dimension and found the earth a vast paradise, with weak humans whom they could bend to their will, either enslaving or endowing with the powers of their world, changing them into creatures no longer human. A ridiculous origination myth, as silly as stories about Zeus or Thor or whatever else ancient peoples had put their faith in.

But as ridiculous as it sounded, Tariq could see in his uncle's eyes that the stories were not myth to him, but fact. And Tariq knew better than to challenge his uncle. For that matter, he wasn't so naïve as to think that Tiberius would put Montegue's head on the chopping block unless they were dealing with some truly serious shit.

Maybe the stories were real and maybe they weren't. But something was definitely going down. "Okay," he finally said. "All right. But what's the third?"

"*Who*," Tiberius said. "The proper question is, 'Who is the third?' "

"Over time, the stories have changed," Dirque said. "They speak now only of the two brothers, fathers to the therians and vampires, the para-daemons and the wraiths. Fathers to us all."

"But there was another," Tiberius added. "A third brother. The most powerful of all. And the other two killed him, stealing his power before burying him in the earth. It is the third from whom humans draw their power when they dabble in the black arts."

"You're saying witches are part of the shadow world?"

"We are saying the third brother will rise again," Dirque said. "I'm saying that the girl can draw him forth. And when she does, he will seek revenge from those who destroyed him."

"The Alliance," Tariq said, finally understanding. "Every member of the Alliance is descended from the first two brothers."

"So the stories go," Dirque said. "But have no fear, nephew. As you said, it is only mythology."

Tariq paced the room, not sure what to think about this revelation.

"For years, the Alliance has sought to prevent the Oracle's words from coming to pass," Tiberius said. "We have sought out those whose touch brings the change. We destroyed their lines, and we thought the job had been finished."

"We didn't know about the girl," Dirque said. "As long as she walks, the threat of the end of the Alliance walks with her."

Despite the absurdity, fear slid through Tariq, as insidious as a snake. But it was a fear tempered by ambition. And by the possibility of revenge as well. He lifted his head and looked the vampire straight in the eyes. "Montegue's chummy with Lucius Dragos, am I wrong?"

He knew Luke well. Actually, he'd tried to kill the bloodsucker in Munich almost six centuries ago, and that hadn't exactly gone off as planned. He'd paid the price back then at Luke's fists, and had continued to pay the price over time, bending over and taking it whenever Luke needed a favor. Frankly, he was getting damn tired of it, but Luke was not a man you wanted to cross.

"Is that relevant?" Tiberius asked.

"Might be," Tariq said. "Luke's mate works at Division. Montegue must have had help on the inside. Wouldn't surprise me a bit to find out that Sara Constantine's knee-deep in this shit. Hell, she may even know exactly where Montegue's taken the girl." He smiled, thinking that maybe, for the first time, he had Lucius Dragos by the balls.

"You do what you need to do," his uncle said, as Tiberius stood tall and silent, frustration rolling off him in waves. "Use whatever resources you need, conscript whatever personnel you want. But you find Petra Lang," Dirque continued. "You find her, and you end this."

CHAPTER 5

Her middle came back first, then her lungs, and she gasped in air, suddenly starved for oxygen. Her arms and legs came next, and although she was aware that she was being put back together, it didn't seem strange. Probably because she'd never actually felt like she was apart.

She had no idea how much time had passed, and the small, windowless room gave her no additional information.

In front of her, Nicholas pulled off his hood, wincing as the movement irritated the knife wound in his chest.

"You're bleeding. Do you need . . . you know . . . to feed?" As a private investigator in the shadow world, she'd worked with vampires for years, but that didn't mean she understood the various ins and outs of their nature. All she knew for sure was that he wouldn't try to feed off of her—wouldn't pull her close and press his lips to her neck. Not unless he wanted to become the monster.

He didn't even glance down at his wound. "I'll live. How are you doing? The mist can be disorienting for a human."

The mist. She remembered, except it wasn't a memory as much as a dream, something wispy and unreal and utterly provocative.

They'd been twined together, body to body, blood to blood. The only time her body—albeit not her flesh—had ever touched anyone other than her brother, and even with him she'd only held hands, and the pleasure of contact had been overshadowed by the torment of the blue moon.

Try as she might, she couldn't recall anything specific about the contact with Nicholas, only the hint of sensation upon a breath of memory. Her essence remembered, though, and the heat that coursed through her made her wish all the more that she'd been aware throughout the transformation.

"Petra?"

"I'm fine. A little fuzzy," she added, the lie meant to cover the burst of unfamiliar sensations.

"I apologize. It's not the ideal way for a human to travel."

"You got me out of there. I'm hardly going to question your methods."

She squinted at him, suddenly intrigued by Nicholas as a man, and not merely an advocate. For more than a month she'd met regularly with him as he'd briefed her case. She'd noticed his good looks—because how could you not? And she'd been impressed by how damn smart he was. But she'd never thought about what it would be like to touch him. What would be the point?

Her life was her life, and she'd learned to live with it. Having to go grocery shopping in the middle of the night when the crowds were thin. Avoiding opening night at the movies. The unyielding precautions, the constant awareness that even a gentle caress was impossible. All part of the parcel that made up her life.

Most of the time she didn't mind it. Didn't even think about it, really, except sometimes late at night, when she couldn't sleep, and the dark stretched out in front of her. Then she wondered what it would be like to share her life with someone else, someone other than her brother. Someone who'd chosen to be with her. Who loved her.

Someone who could touch her, and whom she could touch back.

On those nights, she'd hug her pillow tight and think about what she did have. A brother who loved her. A house with a flower garden. A job she was good at.

And a long list of sorcerers and witches to track down one by one, with the fervent hope that one could remove her curse. Fight magic with magic. Bury it. Hide it. Change it. She didn't care, as long as she was free of it.

So far, she'd found no one with magic strong enough to change her.

Until she did, she wouldn't think about men.

That had been her creed since puberty, and although she sounded like a commercial for a fish-without-a-bicycle philosophy, it really was the truth. Men weren't on her radar. She hadn't let them be on her radar.

Apparently today her radar had decided to fight back.

The mist. The twining had awakened something in her, and she didn't know how to shut down what was now churning inside her. Honestly, she wasn't sure she wanted to.

"Lie down," he said, his brow knit with concern as

he examined her face. "You're still disoriented from the poison and the transformation."

She shook her head, determined to find her center. "No. I'm good." She lifted her eyes to meet his, felt a small shift in her gut, and pushed past it. "Where are we?"

"Safe," he said. "Right now, that's all you need to know."

"Excuse me?" Irritation bubbled inside, and she urged it on. Annoyance and anger were familiar and easily handled. "I'm happy to be alive, don't get me wrong, but how do I know I didn't just go from being their prisoner to being yours?"

"You're not my prisoner," he said.

"Fine. Then talk." There were about eight bazillion things she needed to know, not the least of which was how she was supposed to live once the entire weight of the Alliance pressed down on her. Because they *would* come after her. The shadow world did not sit idly by after it was screwed. And Nicholas Montegue and Petra Lang had just screwed them big time. "At least let me get in touch with my brother. Everything else can wait." It was a simple request, and one she expected he'd grant easily.

He didn't.

"Later." He nodded toward a cot that stood in the corner, a blanket folded neatly on top. "I need to see to things. Wait here."

"I don't think so." She moved forward, intending to get past him, to get out of this tiny little room that was only slightly less claustrophobic than the holding cell she'd so recently been occupying.

He reached for her, and she jerked away instinctively, realizing as she did that his hands were still gloved, and she was still covered head to toe in the prison-issued bodysuit.

"Dammit," she said, that stupid, knee-jerk reaction twisting her up inside more than it should. But it wasn't just the fact that she'd flinched. It had been one long, horrible, emotionally trying day, which even though it ended up pretty damn awesome in that she was still alive, was still freaky enough to mess with her head.

Yes, she was beyond thrilled to have been rescued, but she wasn't a woman who hid in dark rooms, and she sure as hell didn't want to be someone else's burden. She'd played *that* role her whole life, too. And although she knew that Kiril loved her, the fact that their grandmother had bound her twin to her—made him her protector until the curse was lifted—troubled her more than she had ever confessed to him.

She drew a breath, steadied herself, and decided to try the fly-and-honey approach. "You could have told me, you know. Doesn't seem fair I spent all of last night thinking that I'd be pushing up daisies right about now." She meant the words, but she said them with a smile and a lilt to her voice. No accusation there. Just friendly and chatty. She knew how to charm. It was one of the reasons she was good at her job.

"If I'd told you, they would have changed execution theaters at the very least. Worst-case scenario they would have pumped poison into your holding cell. As soon as the Truth Teller latched onto even a hint of trouble, you'd be dead, and this would be all over."

"And what is this exactly?"

"Sergius."

She frowned, thinking of the vampire she'd destroyed. "What about him?"

"He's alive."

The hair on the back of her neck prickled, and she sat gingerly on the edge of the cot. "Oh dear God." She drew in a breath, her thoughts a wild rush. "But how? There was a fire. I heard all about it. The ME confirmed that Serge died in a warehouse fire."

"Staged," Nicholas said. "Luke and I took some of his flesh and we burned the place. He's here, Petra. But he's not really Serge anymore."

She swallowed. "You saved me because you're looking for a cure."

"A rose for the lady."

She drew her fingers through her hair and concentrated on the floor. "But I already told you during the hearing prep that I don't know how to lift the curse. Hell, I told him the same thing before I touched him."

Her words were absolutely, 100 percent true. But what she didn't say was equally true. She might not know how to lift the curse and free herself to touch without harm, but she did know how to cure Sergius.

Sergius would be free the moment she was dead.

But no way in hell was she telling Nicholas that. He might have the face of an angel, but at the core he was a vampire. And a vampire wouldn't think twice about killing to get what he wanted.

She stifled a shiver, then looked up to meet his eyes. "There's no way, Nicholas. I'm sorry, but there's just no way."

"I refuse to believe that," he said. "As should you."

He took a step toward her, and she forced herself not to recede. "Think about it. I was born more than seven centuries ago. You escaped death after your body dissipated into mist. And once upon a time, men without so much as a compass climbed into small wooden boats and sailed across oceans. We'll find the answer, Petra."

We. Nice thought in theory, a little bit harder in practice. She didn't really do "we" all that well. She hadn't had much practice in that department. Not unless you counted Kiril, but he was her brother, her twin, half of herself if you believed some of that mystical nonsense about twins and magic and curses. "I need to call Kiril," she said. "Not later. Now. He's got to be going out of his mind wondering what the hell has happened to me."

"Most likely he believes you're dead."

"What? Why?"

"Because the Alliance damn sure isn't going to tell him otherwise. Do you think they're going to announce an escape? No. They're going to look quietly for you. They'll use a small team so that word doesn't leak. And if they find you they won't be dragging your ass back to prison. They'll execute you on site and all the paperwork will show it happened today in a small theater in front of the Tribunal witnesses. You want to get the target off your back, you help me lift your curse."

"Turn me into a woman who's not a dangerous entity as defined by the Fifth International Covenant?"

"Exactly. Take away their reason for executing you."

"I'm all for that," she said. "And Kiril can help us. He's powerful." She glanced at Nicholas, and saw the power in him, too. The power, and the determination to see this mission of his through.

And that was another reason she wanted Kiril with her. She wanted her brother watching her back if Nicholas ever found out the truth.

"He is. And that kind of power can be tracked." His stern expression softened just a little. "I'm sorry, Petra. But if you think about it, you know that I'm right."

"No. No, I don't."

He looked at her hard, so hard he seemed to be looking right through her. "Petra," he said, his voice coming from far away. "You know I'm right."

"You're right," she said, although she didn't know why she was saying it.

Or, yes she did. She was saying it because it was true. He was right. It made sense, and he'd put the plan together and thought it through—had days and days to plan and think, and she was only now getting sucked in. Of course her reactions were knee-jerk. But if she would just step back, she'd see how much sense he made. "Right," she repeated even though she didn't really want to say that at all, and deep down inside she was calling herself a fool and an idiot and a weak-minded liar.

"I'm going to go out now, but I'll be back."

"I'll wait," she said placidly, then sat on the cot and smiled up at him, all the while wondering what the hell she was smiling about.

She watched as he left the room. Then the sharp click of the lock snapped her back to herself and she launched herself across the room and pounded on the thick steel door, furious that the low-down, cheating vampire had actually resorted to getting into her head and poking around in her mind simply to win an argument. "Dammit, Nicholas Montegue! You let me out of here!"

He wasn't going to, though, and she didn't bother pounding for long. Instead, she went back to the cot and stared at the door, just waiting for him to return.

Just waiting to show him that getting inside her head was the very last thing he wanted to do.

CHAPTER 6

Sara Constantine looked up as Tariq paused in her doorway, but there was no fear in her eyes. Not even the slightest flicker. And that annoyed Tariq even more than the fact—unproven, but damn near certain—that she'd aided a prisoner's escape.

In front of her, a poltergeist rose from one of the guest chairs, then turned his attention to the doorway as well.

"Tariq, right?" Sara said. "With RAC? How can I help you?"

So she hadn't heard. That would explain the lack of a reaction. He stepped into the office. "I'm no longer with RAC," he said. "I'm on assignment to the Alliance."

"Oh?" Still no fear, but there was a wariness in her voice that made him happy. He stepped farther into the room, signaled for the creature at his left to step into the doorway—and into Sara's line of sight. "Morain here is a Truth Teller," Tariq said. "I'm not sure if you've made his acquaintance before."

"What do you want, Tariq?" She gestured to the piles of papers spread out over her desk. "I don't have much time."

"No," he said. "You don't." He crossed to her desk. "Step aside, Constantine. I need to review your keystroke log."

Her already pale skin turned a shade paler, but she stood, her attention not on him, but on the poltergeist. "J'ared, would you ask Martella to contact Mr. Bosch? I'm not sure what's going on here, but I think he'd like to know about the way Alliance agents are treating Division's prosecutors."

The fear that Tariq had hoped to see in Sara's face flared in the eyes of the poltergeist, who sped from the room like a spectral cloud.

He turned his attention back to Sara. "Move."

"I don't report to you, Tariq. And until Mr. Bosch tells me to quit working on this brief, that is what I'm focusing on." She put her hands on her keyboard and continued typing, her demeanor suggesting he was nothing more than the custodial staff, come to mop the floors.

Goddamned little *bitch*.

He pressed his hands to her desk and got in her face. "By the power vested in me by the chairman of the Shadow Alliance and the high examiner of the convened shadow Tribunal presiding over the matter of *In re Petra Lang,* I order you to step away from your computer. Now."

Slowly, she lifted her hands from her keyboard. Even more slowly, she nodded. Then she pushed her chair back and rose to her feet.

Tariq circled the desk and slid into the chair. Behind him, Sara stood stock-still. She'd fucked up, but good, and he was going to nail her ass to the wall. He was going to goddamn smell the fear on her. He was going to see it, he was going to taste it. And he was going to rub fucking Lucius Dragos's face in it.

"Morain," Tariq said, as he navigated into the security profile and patched through to the relevant logs. "No sense you standing around twiddling your thumbs. While I'm taking a peek at Ms. Constantine's computer, you take a peek into her head."

"You have no cause—no cause at all—to get into my head," Sara said, taking a step backward, and eyeing Morain, who had aimed a toothy smile her direction.

"Don't I?" Tariq asked as he punched in the final digits of the Alliance security code that allowed him to access the keystroke log that the Alliance had planted in all Division computers across the globe. He pushed away from the desk, the wheels of the chair sending him a good two feet back. With one hand, he indicated the monitor with a flourish. "On the contrary," he said, reviewing the binder release code she'd entered earlier that day. "I think I have all the reason in the world."

And there it was—*fear*. Bitter and sharp. It seeped from her pores and hid in the lines of her face. And as Morain stepped closer to her—his hand outstretched for the touch that would take him as deep into Sara's mind as Tariq had gotten into her computer—that fear filled the room like a wave of cold air.

The girl was fucking terrified.

And considering what she'd done, she damn well should be.

"*Stop.*" The voice from the doorway was firm and hard and held authority rather than fear. Tariq turned and found himself looking at the lined face and salt-and-pepper hair of Nostramo Bosch, the subdirector of the violent crimes unit, and Sara's immediate boss. Beside him, two uniformed security trolls stood waiting, arms crossed, faces flat and angry.

The subtle scent of cinnamon wafted into the room as Bosch took a step inside.

"I've got the Alliance backing me," Tariq said. "And I've got some interesting shit on Ms. Constantine's computer."

"Whatever you may think you have," Bosch said, "I assure you it does not justify the use of invasive measures. Not without a ruling of cause. And whether you're working for Division or working for the Alliance, Agent Tariq, you are not authorized to make that call."

"Is that right?" Tariq said, edging up close to the old man.

"Cross me," Bosch said, his voice low and harsh and deadly, "and I assure you that you will regret it."

Tariq hesitated, debating. On the one hand, if he backed down now, his authority would be compromised. On the other hand, he didn't know a single person who had ever seen Bosch put his powers into action. And according to the rumor mill, that was because no one ever survived an encounter with the man, a shadower who refused to make his allegiance known. A crossbreed of any number of species, possibly with the blood of all seven major groups flowing through his veins.

Well, *fuck*.

His phone chirped, and Tariq was never more glad for an interruption than he was right then. He flipped it open, shooting Bosch a contemptuous look and then giving the elder his back. "Go."

"The brother's approaching Division." It was Elric,

one of the members of the team Tariq had assigned to watch Kiril Lang, just in case Petra tried to make contact.

"Any sign of the girl?"

"None. He's heading in the main entrance now. Probably going to the ninth-floor reception area."

"Got it." Tariq flipped his phone closed as Bosch signaled for the trolls to flank Sara. "Lang just got here. Go deal with him, old man. You're the face of the Alliance here at Division, right?"

"Take her to holding on Alliance Representative Tariq's authority," Bosch said to the trolls. He turned to face Tariq. "No Truth Teller. No interrogation. She gets her phone call and she's held until she retains an advocate." He cocked his head, sending the trolls toward the door, Sara Constantine scared but proud between them.

"Constantine," Bosch said, and touched her sleeve as she passed. For the briefest of moments, something soft crossed his expression, but by the time he turned back to Tariq, his expression was hard.

"She fucked up, Bosch."

Nostramo Bosch looked him straight in the eye, and Tariq saw nothing there except ice. Then Bosch turned and walked out of the room, leaving only silence in his wake.

♦

"She is my sister," Kiril snarled, his body frenzied with the power coursing through him. He was in the Division 6 reception area, and he wanted to lash out, to set the world to spinning, to bring down the damn PEC from the inside out, and it was taking every ounce of self-control to not do exactly that.

Why he was bothering, though . . . well, that was the real question, wasn't it? Because if Petra was dead . . . if he'd lost her . . .

Around him, the wind began to whip, ripping at his clothes, making the papers on the receptionist's desk fly. "Uh, sir? You really shouldn't do that in here."

He didn't answer, and she licked pretty pink lips and refrained from saying another word. Good decision.

Still, he wanted answers and satisfaction—not to be hauled off to a cell himself.

Slowly, methodically, he clenched his hands at his sides, willing himself to calm and the storm to fade.

To his left, a set of doors opened, and an elegant-looking gentleman stepped into the reception area. Not a vamp, not a para-daemon; Kiril couldn't get a bead on him. But he was a shadower, that much was for certain.

And that meant Kiril didn't trust him. Didn't matter, though. Kiril could hold his own with pretty much any creature that walked this green earth. And they'd fucked with his sister. And that meant that today, the shadowers should be afraid of him.

"Mr. Lang," the man said, extending his hand. "I'm Nostramo Bosch."

Kiril ignored the hand. "I want to see my sister."

Bosch slipped his hand into a pocket. "I realize you're upset, but nothing could be served by seeing her now—"

"I have a right to see her body."

"No. Actually, you don't."

"Screw that." It was bad enough she had to die alone,

no way these sons of bitches were keeping him from her. He looked at Bosch, imploring. "I've always been there for her. *Always.* And you people have no right to steal that from me."

For a moment, he thought he saw sympathy flash in the elder man's eyes. But it was gone as fast as it had appeared. "The Alliance has executed her, Mr. Lang. Nothing will be gained by viewing her body."

"Goddammit, I need to see her." He could still feel her, and until he saw her body, he knew that he'd never get through his head that she was really and truly dead. "You had no right," he said. "No right. She was human."

"She was condemned by an Alliance Tribunal," Bosch said, his voice flat. "Its jurisdiction is clear."

"Its jurisdiction is shit," he spat, and around him the wind began to rage.

Bosch didn't appear the least bit rattled. "Mr. Lang, you have my condolences, but it's time for you to vacate the premises. Please, let me have one of Division's agents give you a lift home."

"Fuck your lift and fuck you. I'm not going anywhere. I'm not—" He stopped, pain and failure overwhelming him. Their grandmother had bound the two of them, charging Kiril with the responsibility of watching over Petra—of protecting her from the world and the world from her.

He'd failed. Epic fail, actually. And he was paying the price now.

But maybe not as deeply as he'd first thought.

He could still feel her.

"Mr. Lang?"

"I'll go," he said, because there could be only one explanation. "You fuckers won't help me, so I might as well go." He needed to get out of there. Needed to leave fast, get home, and meditate.

It made sense now. It all made sense. And he hoped to hell he was right. Please, God, let him be right.

They wouldn't show him Petra's body, because Petra wasn't dead.

CHAPTER 7

Nick stood in the dark and stared into the dimly lit cell at the thing that slept inside, surrounded by the gnawed and bloody bones of animals that had been dropped down from the trapdoor to feed it. A thing that looked like Sergius, but was Sergius no more.

One touch from Petra, and Nick's friend had vanished, all possibility of battling down the daemon that had risen within Serge destroyed. Ironic that so recently it had been that very daemon they sought to subdue and control—a house cat compared to the beast that now raged within. Pure evil, conjured with dark magic, no longer gaining life from blood, but from death and pain. Old magic, Nick assumed, drawn from the earth itself, and that wasn't the kind of thing that Nick knew how to fight.

He would learn, though. Nick had spent much of his life dabbling with alchemy, looking for the cure to death itself. He hadn't found it—not the way he'd expected, anyway—but he had never abandoned the love of science. Chemistry and biology had been his particular favorites, and he knew one thing for certain: Even with all their differences, humans and shadowers were nothing more spectacular than a pattern of molecules.

The girl's touch had manipulated those molecules, creating a chemical reaction in Serge that had changed him at the most basic level. But if those molecules could be manipulated to form a monster, they could be manipulated to restore the man. And even if Nick had to take the girl to the very end of creation to find the answer, he would learn how to restore his friend.

Part of Nick wanted to hate Petra for turning Serge into a monster; the other part pitied the woman whose torment surely rivaled his own. He had battled back his daemon; Petra lived with her curse every moment of every day.

The thing in the cell shifted, eyes slitting open to reveal blood-red irises. Then a slow grin spread across the creature's face. It loped to the glass, arms hanging down so that fingers dragged on the floor as it moved, apelike, toward Nick.

Once it reached the glass, though, it stood, rising to its full height, its body wide and hard, every old scar healed, every old injury gone. Days earlier, the creature had been in constant motion. It had done nothing but rage and rip, its actions hinting at madness. Lately, there were long moments of calm, during which the creature would sit motionless, its head tilted, as if it were thinking. Or, perhaps, listening.

Then, the body had been twisted, much like a shapeshifter midchange or a para-daemon in a violent fit of temper. Now, though, the body had settled into its old form. Serge's familiar shape, his familiar stance.

Even the chunk of flesh that Nick and Luke had cut out of its thigh was healed, the skin now perfect and smooth. Somehow, that made the creature that much more terrifying.

It stared at Nick, dark eyes locking onto Nick's, holding them in an eerie, unblinking gaze. Nick stared back, refusing to show fear or disgust. Refusing to lose faith in his friend now, even though he knew damn well that the thing in that cage was his friend no more.

The creature's eyes narrowed, and Nick had the impression the thing was sizing him up, trying to remember.

"Serge," he said, frustrated by the hope in his voice.

The mouth split wide in a horrible mockery of a smile, then the creature lifted its palm to its mouth and sank its fangs deep into its own flesh. Nick shuddered, but didn't turn away, and when the creature slammed its bloody palm against the thirty-six-inch-thick reinforced hematite-and-glass barrier, Nick winced and stood frozen, awed by what he saw: The creature dragged its hand over the glass, forming lines and curves on the thick barrier. Behind it, on the cement wall, Nick saw similar shapes, and as he looked more carefully, he realized what he was seeing. Mixed in among the streaks and splotches of blood were letters—A's and V's and K's and L's. Other lines swirled around those, as if Serge wanted to get a thought out, but couldn't quite remember how. The only thing that was perfectly clear, in fact, was a single figure. The numeral three, scrawled on the wall over and over and over.

Three, thought Nick. *Three?*

There was a mind in there, in that creature that had once been Serge. A mind fighting to get out. Fighting hard, but not quite making it.

With regret weighing down his steps, Nick turned away, then stopped short as a long, loud growl filled the room. He turned in time to see the Serge-creature explode in a frenzy of rage and fury, tossing itself at the thick glass, pounding and battering it. The transparent wall held, but the power of the creature's blows shook the walls, and the seams and joints trembled.

The thing was getting stronger. The cell wouldn't hold it for long.

He glanced at the eight-inch-square opening twenty feet above, now covered by a steel plate firmly bolted in place. It was opened once each day and small animals were dropped through, food for the monster. There were no other openings in the cell, none even the size of a pin, and as soon as the trapdoor closed, the seal was rendered airtight.

So far, there was no evidence that Serge had regained the ability to shift into mist, but Nick had a feeling it was coming. His mind was returning along with a level of control; soon his powers would follow.

A mind, Nick corrected, because that wasn't Serge. The thing in that cell would rip Nick's head off the instant it had the chance. No, the bond of friendship went only one way now. Nick hoped that he was strong enough to see this through.

He turned, giving the beast his back, the echoes of fists hammering against the cell walls seeming to pound inside his own body.

One step, then another.

He reached the first door, keyed in the access code, and waited for the thick steel to open.

The second room was small, existing only as an antechamber, a fail-safe if Serge escaped the cell. The door closed behind him, but even through the twelve-inch-thick walls, he could still hear the beast rage.

Again, he entered a code. Again, a door slid open. He stepped through, and the door snapped shut behind him, finally blocking out the sound. The tightness in Nick's chest lifted a little, and he leaned back against the door.

The room he was in now was completely dark, not that it mattered to him. He could still see the door to Petra's room along with the door to the exit tunnel and the slightly open door to the sleeping quarters. Between him and Luke and the werewolf Rand, someone was always in the chamber. Always ensuring that Serge remained confined, and ready to sound the alarm if the beast got free.

He closed his eyes. Right then, he didn't want to see any of it. Didn't want to remember, didn't even want to think, and yet he couldn't stop thinking. Of his friend. Of the girl.

He opened his eyes and looked at the closed door, and thought of the woman behind it. He was bound to her now, both of them responsible in different ways for what had happened to Serge. Both of them fugitives.

She was the puzzle piece that he believed he needed in order to save his friend, yet now that he had her, there was no magic formula, no easy answer. Their work had barely begun . . . and if the changes in the creature he'd just left were any indication, they needed to work fast. Soon, Serge might regain the ability to transform. Soon, Serge might have the strength to beat his way through the walls.

Soon Serge might run free, and then Nick could add

the deaths of thousands to the butcher's bill, and that was a price he didn't know how to pay.

He closed his eyes again, then opened them as he felt the cold steel of a blade press hard against his throat. *Luke.*

"Give me one reason not to kill you now," Luke said, his voice rough and dangerous.

"Because I need to fix this. I need to see it through."

"They've arrested Sara. She's in some goddamned holding cell deep inside Division."

Nick closed his eyes. "I didn't expect them to find her so quickly."

"Damn you, Nicholas," Luke said, and Nick felt the blade break his skin. "Goddamn you all to hell."

The scent of Nick's blood rose up between them, and Nick forced himself not to move. If Luke wanted Nick dead, his head would have already hit the ground. Besides, Nick had no stomach for fighting back. He'd known what might happen when he'd dialed Sara's number. Now he was facing the consequences.

"Take my life," Nick said. "If it pays the debt, then take it now, and take it fast."

A trickle of blood made its way down Nick's neck, and though he didn't move, he could imagine it staining the collar, then easing beneath the material to pool at his collarbone. The coppery scent filled the air, all the more pungent now that it was mixed with the scent of Luke's wrath.

A moment . . . then another . . .

And then, suddenly, the pressure lifted.

"She made me swear not to harm you," Luke said.

"One phone call, and she used it to tell me that she'd have my head if I took yours."

Nick closed his eyes, grateful not so much for his life, but for the chance to finish what he had started. "Then that's another debt I owe your wife." He turned to face the man he counted among his closest friends. The man he'd betrayed by pulling his wife into a goddamn hornets' nest. "I didn't want this, Luke. I had no choice. But believe me, I never wanted her involved."

"I'd say you failed miserably in that regard." He still held the knife in his hand. Now he wiped Nick's blood on the thigh of his jeans, then sheathed the blade at his side. "Let's hope the rest of the mission goes better."

"At this point, I think there's nowhere to go but up."

"Don't be too sure of that," Luke said, something in his voice grabbing Nick's attention.

"What's happened?"

"Tiberius contacted me. He wanted to give his condolences for what happened to Sara. He will do what he can."

Some of the tension drained from Nick. "Good. And Petra? Did he speak of her?" Luke said nothing, and Nick clenched his fists in anger. "Dammit, Tiberius should have argued in favor of a stay. He owes his place at the fucking Alliance table to the girl, and he damn well knows it. He should be bending over backward with gratitude."

"He says he has no choice."

"What? Because if he doesn't support Petra's termination order, Dirque will rally the troops and vote him off?"

"Is that so hard to understand?" Luke asked.

Nick frowned, because it wasn't hard at all. Tiberius was a politician, and right now he was playing political games. As an advocate for the Alliance, Nick knew all about the machinations of politics. But as a friend, he'd hoped for more.

"It's more than his seat at the Alliance," Luke said. "He said the girl's touch can bring about the end of the Alliance. He says it's been foreseen. A prophecy."

"And you believe that bullshit?"

Luke almost smiled. "The Alliance just locked up my wife. Right now, the prospect of someone bringing it down sounds pretty damn good."

Nick matched his friend's smile, and for a moment, he felt like things were right between them. They weren't, though. Things wouldn't be right again until Sara was free and Serge was himself, and both of them damn well knew it.

"It's dangerous for you to remain here," Luke said. "You and Petra need to leave tonight."

"Understood."

"Are you sure about this? Turn her in now, and we can end this. Sara can walk free tonight."

"It's Serge, Luke. The only way you can stop me now is to use that blade at your thigh."

Luke's hand closed over the hilt, and Nick held his breath. But the knife stayed sheathed. "The girl has no idea how to reverse the curse," Luke said. He dropped his hand. "Hell, she doesn't even know if it can be done."

"But it *is* a curse, Luke. That means it has a source. If we can trace it back . . ."

"*If,*" Luke said. "And in the meantime, he grows stronger. If he gets free—"

"He won't."

"No," Luke said, "because if I fear we are close to that, I will terminate him. Make no mistake. Poison, fire, I will find a way."

"You would do that to a friend?"

Luke closed his eyes. "My friend Sergius is dead."

"I intend to bring him back."

"Even if you do, his daemon is still unbound."

"Under the circumstances, I'd say that was a minor problem."

Luke nodded, then opened his eyes and examined Nick with a cold, calculating look. "Even if you succeed, the Alliance has a long memory and a swift temper. You may find yourself strapped to a slab in the execution chamber."

"I've done my homework, and this is a risk worth taking. If we can pull it off—if we can rid Petra of the curse and transform Serge back into himself—I'm confident that my superior advocacy skills will woo the Tribunal to my side."

"And if you're wrong?"

"Then I shall be forced to acquire a taste for the fugitive lifestyle." He brushed a speck of lint off the cuff of the neatly pressed shirt he'd changed into, then looked up at Luke with an ironic grin. "Fortunately, I'm not a man who sets much store by creature comforts."

CHAPTER 8

"Nick, wait."

Nick paused outside Petra's door, entrapped by Lissa's entreaty. He didn't want to turn and face her. Didn't want to be distracted by the flood of memories that would surely rise when he saw her.

He didn't love her anymore—of that, he was finally certain. But their love hadn't slipped away slowly until it was nothing more than a soft memory. Instead, it had been torn from his very flesh, and like any wound, the scab bled when picked.

There was, however, no avoiding it.

"Hang on a sec," she said, hurrying up to him and holding out a small canvas backpack.

"What is it, Lissa?"

The smile froze on her face, and she took a step back, her arm still extended with the pack. "I brought these for Petra."

He took the bag. "Thanks."

Her brow furrowed with confusion, and he felt like a shit.

"It's a good thing you did," she said. "Taking the risk. Saving Petra. I'm glad you did it."

"I'm not doing it for you," he said. "Or for her." He reached for the doorknob.

"Right. For Serge. I get it." Her cheeks flushed, and

he understood why. At the time, she hadn't known, of course. But after she'd betrayed Nick, it had been Serge who'd pulled him back from the precipice. Serge who had helped Nick battle the rising daemon.

"I have to go."

"Nick— Never mind."

He knew he should leave it at that and walk away. Instead, he released the knob. "What?"

"It's just that . . . I thought we'd made progress. I thought—"

"I've forgiven what you did to me, Lissa. Hell, I even like Rand."

"Then—"

"That doesn't mean it's easy." He met her Caribbean blue eyes, now dark like water before a storm, and wondered why she couldn't see how deeply she'd cut his pride. How much she'd made him play the fool. And that wasn't a role Nicholas played well.

"Oh." He could see she wanted to say something else. Wanted to somehow apologize and make it all better. A female's instinct to kiss the hurt and make it go away.

He didn't want the sympathy.

He lifted the pack. "What's this?"

"Clothes," she said. "I took a guess at Petra's size."

"Good. Thanks."

She turned to leave, and he started to do the same, then stopped.

"Lissa?"

Her shoulders stiffened, and there was a pause before she faced him.

"We're not going to be friends. Colleagues, maybe. But not friends."

Her face was as hard as glass and just as fragile. "Of course," she said stiffly.

He didn't watch her go. Instead, he turned back to Petra's door and slipped the key into the lock.

◆

"You got into my head, you mind-fucking blood-sucker." Petra was up and off the cot before Nicholas had even stepped through the door of her cell. Her *new* cell. Which, despite the fact that she wasn't sitting in this one waiting to be executed, still constituted one more damn prison. One more set of four walls and nothing to occupy her but her thoughts.

Right now, her thoughts were firmly of the pissed-off variety.

She held the still-folded blanket in her hands, and now she shoved it against his chest, pushing him back, hard, toward the door. "You got in my head," she repeated, "and you pushed my mind, and if you think I'm going to forgive you because you saved my ass, then let me tell you right now that you are seriously— *seriously*—misguided on that subject."

He looked at her, his blue eyes both commanding attention and conveying regret. "I'm sorry."

She still held the blanket and started to push toward him again. Started to tell him she didn't want to hear his excuses or explanations. And then his words shoved through the storm clouds in her head.

She eyed him suspiciously. "What did you say?"

"I said I was sorry."

He looked sorry, she thought, and yet this was not a moment she'd anticipated. She didn't know Nicholas well, but she knew him enough. He was arrogant, usually with good reason, and she sincerely doubted that apologies came easily.

"Well, okay, then. But you do anything like that again—you even think about poking around inside there—and you'll have one very uncooperative woman on your hands." She crossed her arms over her chest. "Are we perfectly clear?"

He took a step toward her. Too close, considering that his hands were bare. She stepped back, but he matched her, his proximity making her fidgety. Nervous. She stood still—very still—and forced herself to meet his eyes, trying to ignore the way her heart was beating now, tripping in time with both fear and something else. Something new and just as dangerous as the curse she lived with every day of her life.

"I think you're missing the bigger picture," he said, so close she could feel his breath on her skin, the sensation as warm and gentle as an imagined caress. She shivered, definitely not out of fear, and focused on something just over his shoulder. Right then, she didn't want to meet his eyes. "You want this curse lifted even more than I do. And to get that done, we're going to have to work together."

She opened her mouth, ready to lash out with a snippy comment about his definition of working together, but he got there first.

"I apologized for getting into your head, and I meant it," he said, taking a step back, and then shifting position so that she was looking straight at him. "But don't think you can dangle idle threats. We're a team now, Petra. Which means you tell me everything you know about this curse and how to lift it." He looked hard at her, and she shrank under his look. "Everything."

Not exactly an option. If he knew her death would free Serge, he'd kill her in a heartbeat, and that really didn't sit well. She wanted to live too damn much. Wanted to cling desperately to the hope that somehow, someday she really would be a part of the world instead of an outsider.

So no, she'd never tell Nicholas the truth, but there was no way she could remain silent, either. Not completely.

"Petra?"

"Deal." She glanced down, eyeing his hands. "I'd say we could shake on it, but . . ."

"Probably for the best." He tossed the backpack at her feet. "Clothes. You should change."

He already had, having abandoned the ninja look for something more L.A. casual, dark jeans, a white button-down, and a black leather jacket. Simple. Basic. Yet on him it looked like runway attire for a male model. At the very least, it looked like he should be in line for a screen test at one of the studios.

She'd seen him innumerable times in fancy silk suits that probably came from custom tailors in exotic locations, and she could remember thinking that he looked nice. Well put together. Now, though . . .

Now he looked like sin personified. Smooth and slick and completely in control.

She frowned, fighting the memory—if *memory* was

the right word—of his essence twining with hers. He'd made a mark on her, that much was for sure.

And the fact that she couldn't do a damn thing about it was one of the bigger regrets in her life. Fortunately, she was a woman used to sweeping regrets aside.

She bent down and unzipped the bag, then pulled out a pair of jeans, a long-sleeved T-shirt, and a pair of long, thin opera gloves.

"Lissa," Nicholas said, his voice oddly tight. "Hopefully they'll fit."

"Is she here?" Lissa was the werewolf Rand's mate, and she and Petra had spent many long visiting hours together, with Lissa doing her best to convince Petra that everything would turn out all right, and neither one of them really believing it.

As if in answer, there was a tap at the door, and then Lissa stepped in, Rand right behind her. The weren's eyes shifted to Nicholas. Lissa looked only at Petra. "Oh, you haven't tried them on yet. I wanted to make sure everything fit."

"I'll do it now," Petra said, then glanced at Nicholas and felt her cheeks burn. "Well, as soon as Nicholas leaves." Smooth. They were about to be existing in very close quarters, and she was wondering what it would be like to know that he was watching her. To feel his eyes looking at her *that* way, and know that even though he couldn't, he desperately wanted to touch her, almost as much as she longed to feel his touch.

Except he *wasn't* looking at her that way. For that matter, he wasn't looking at her at all. Wasn't looking anywhere, in fact. But she had the odd sensation that he was staring into nothing so that he wouldn't stare at

Lissa. There was a tension between them, something harsh and uncomfortable. And although it wasn't any of her business, she couldn't help but wonder at the thickness in the air, and the way Nicholas held himself, as if he was holding back a secret.

Lissa, too. The way her attention stayed solely with Petra. And the way Rand watched Nicholas like a hawk.

Interesting.

But what was even more interesting—and more than a little disturbing—was the way that watching them made her feel. Sort of twisted up inside, and although she liked Lissa—a lot, actually—right then she couldn't wait for the beautiful succubus to vacate the premises and let her and Nicholas get back to their conversation.

"You picked out great stuff," Petra said. "It looks like it's all going to fit."

"I'm so glad." She took a step back. "I'll let you guys finish up, but Luke wanted us to give you a nudge." She said the last to Nicholas as she hooked her arm through Rand's. "Everybody's anxious to get moving."

"Everybody?" Petra asked, wondering just how many people had helped break her out.

"It takes a village," Nicholas said wryly.

Petra frowned as Lissa retreated, shutting the door behind her. The thought that there might be more than just Nicholas both panicked and thrilled her. She wasn't used to being beholden to anyone but Kiril, and he never considered his protection a burden. She was his sister, after all. But owing someone something . . . that was intimate and scary.

"Who exactly is everyone," she asked, "and how did they help you get me out?"

"They didn't," Nicholas said. "That I managed on my own. Mostly." Some of the pressure on her chest lifted. Whoever was out there hadn't helped in her rescue. She was still beholden only to Nicholas.

"They're here because of Serge. Keeping guard."

"And no one else knows he's alive?"

"Only five people. Rand and Lissa, Luke and Sara. Me. Six now, with you." He studied her. "Do you want to see him?" Nicholas asked, as if the possibility had just occurred to him.

She shook her head. "The only reason to see him would be to remind me of what my curse can do. Trust me, I don't need the reminder. I've lived with it every day of my life."

She turned away, frustrated by the rising memory of the horrible night when she was born.

As remarkable as that was, somehow she did remember it. The blood-spattered walls. The screams of her mother. The terrifying howls of her father.

She clenched her fists, not wanting to go there, shoving hard to lock the memory away.

"Petra? Tell me what you're thinking."

She shifted so she was facing him. "It's not just me, you know. It's handed down. A family curse." The words just spilled out, and as she looked up at him, at the compassion on his face, she was struck by the sudden realization that he was such a damn good advocate because he knew how to watch and when to question. And because there was something about that face that inspired trust.

That made people believe that they could speak honestly without harsh consequences. Even people as wary as she.

She supposed it made sense to tell him what little she knew, though she had her doubts that removing the curse was possible; but he'd be no help at all without understanding how the damn thing came about.

She recalled the soft way he'd looked at Lissa, and had to admit that this was about more than freeing herself from a curse. Right then she wanted to see the sympathy that would surely blossom in his eyes. Needed to see it.

Needed the comfort of knowing that he wasn't doing this just to save Serge, but that in some small way, he could save her, too.

CHAPTER 9

"A *family* curse." Nick stared at her, a bubble of irritation rising inside him. "I was your advocate. Why the hell didn't you tell me?"

"Would it have mattered? They condemned me because of *what* I am, not *why* I am."

"It matters." He'd assumed the source of the curse could be tracked down. Now he had to consider the possibility that whoever or whatever placed the curse on the Lang family was long gone, dead and buried. Not good. Not good at all.

But a family curse meant family stories and heirlooms. Hopefully they'd find a clue there.

He started to say more, but was interrupted by a pounding on the door. "Forget fashionably late," Luke said. "Just get yourselves out here. I want everyone briefed before it's time to feed him."

"Five minutes," Nick answered, then turned back to Petra.

"Go on. I'll change and be right there."

"You'll change," he agreed. "And we can talk."

She glanced down at the bag at her feet, at the man standing in front of her. "I'm not—"

"I'll turn around," he said, then did, facing the doorway instead of the woman.

He heard the rustle of cloth as she peeled herself out

of the PEC-issued outfit, and he'd been with far too many women not to imagine how she looked, the dim light of the room making her skin glow, the shadows accentuating every curve. So help him, this woman wasn't even on his radar and yet his body tightened. Like Pavlov's bloody dog, he thought, with a combination of amusement and irritation.

"You didn't answer me," Petra said, interrupting his thoughts. "Would it have mattered?"

Without thinking, he turned to answer her, and saw that the image he'd had in his head was right. She stood naked now, all soft curves and sleek lines, her petite body athletic, but with enough flesh that no one would ever mistake her for an adolescent boy.

Her head was inside the hooded shirt, and he knew he should turn back, but he couldn't. He liked the way she looked, fresh and innocent.

She was a rare creature, he thought. One he couldn't seduce, couldn't use, couldn't touch despite the temptation to reach out and stroke her skin, to see if her body was as soft as it looked, and to experience the unique pleasure of knowing he was the first man to caress her that way.

That pleasure, however, carried a heavy price.

Her head slipped through the hole in the shirt, her dark mass of curls emerging first, then her face, eyes closed. She opened them, saw him watching her, and jerked the shirt the rest of the way down. "What the hell are you doing?"

"Admiring the view," he said, amused by the way her hands crossed down, hiding her crotch.

"Dammit, Nick! Turn around."

"I apologize. I assure you I didn't mean to look," he said, but he did turn.

"That's complete and total bullshit."

He chuckled. "No, it's true. I didn't mean to look, but once I turned around, I couldn't turn back. You're beautiful, Petra." He fought the urge to take one last look at the body of a woman he couldn't have. "Has no one ever told you that?"

She didn't answer, and he regretted his words. Of course no one had. No man had ever seen her like that; how could one have, when to see her was to want to touch her?

"I'm sorry," he said.

"It doesn't matter, and we need to go."

He could hear her yanking on the jeans, her movements abrupt and jerky. He'd upset her. Dammit, he was usually better at saying the right thing to a woman.

"One more time—would telling you that my family's cursed really have helped?"

He turned around to face her, certain now that she was dressed. "No," he said, watching the way she held her face, so bland and expressionless. "You're right. They would have looked at you, seen a long line of cursed humans, and wanted all the more to end it, right then, right there."

For a moment, silence hung between them.

"I destroyed my father," she finally said, her face and her voice hard and steady, but he could hear the vulnerability underneath. He wished he could reach out to her, but at the same time he was glad that was impossible. He could tell by looking that she wanted to appear strong, and accepting his touch would be like acknowledging weakness. Petra, he knew, didn't like to be weak.

"I was only a baby, but I know what happened. I guess it's part of the curse, but I remember it all."

"It wasn't your fault," he said gently.

"No," she said with that same steely dispassion. "It wasn't my fault. But that doesn't change the fact that he changed because of me, and because he changed, he killed my mother." He heard the hitch in her breath and saw the softness beneath the steel, the guilt so quickly masked.

"I see it every night in my dreams. I'm in the dark, warm and safe with my brother, and then there's pain. So much pain. That part's a blur until I'm blinded by light and cold and scared and alone. I'm screaming, too, because I want my brother, but he's not there with me." She met his eyes. "I'm being born, you see."

He nodded, but didn't interrupt. She drew a breath, then continued, stating facts like a soldier would give a report.

"After that, the dream shifts. I'm not inside me anymore, but it's like I'm watching a movie. There's an old woman, and she wraps me in a cloth. She knows she can't touch me. And even though my mother's still in pain—because Kiril's on his way—she's happy because she's free, but she feels guilty—so guilty—because her happiness comes at a heavy price to me."

"She's passed it on."

Petra nodded. "Firstborn. Birth both cures and curses."

"And this cycle? How long had it been going on?"

"Since the 1800s for sure. Possibly before that, but that's as far back as our family Bible goes."

"And your father?"

"My dreams don't get into his head, so I don't know why he did it. My aunt told me that he'd always been impulsive—never thought clearly—and that when he was allowed into the room, he was so overjoyed that my mother was cured, and so amazed that he had both a daughter and a son, that he didn't think to ask who was firstborn. He assumed it was Kiril, since he was bigger, and I was a puny, runty little thing." Her wry smile cut right through him. "I guess he didn't realize that power can come in very small packages."

"He touched you."

"Barely. Just the slightest brush of a fingertip against my little thumb. He was counting them, the way parents do, to prove that their children are perfect."

He watched as she drew in air, saw her shift slightly as if centering herself. He imagined this was what she did in her work, when she had to report bad facts to her clients. Deliver the news fast and flat. Nothing more than a story, a recitation of facts.

"My mother realized, and tried to stop him. But she was weak and didn't move fast enough. He changed. I can still hear him in my head as he howled, first in agony, and then it changed and sounded like joy. Like he was going to have fun destroying us all.

"Kiril and I were side by side, and she threw herself on top of us. He—" Her voice broke, and a single tear trickled down her cheek, but she wiped it away with the back of her hand, as if the tears were nothing more than annoyance.

He took a step forward, then stopped. He knew how to comfort women, knew how to draw them into his arms and let them cry it out. But how did he comfort a woman he couldn't touch? A woman who didn't want to cry?

Aware of the impotence of the gesture, he held out a handkerchief. She glanced at it, but didn't reach for it.

Slowly, he returned it to his pocket. "You don't need to tell me the rest."

She met his eyes defiantly. "You said you wanted to know everything."

"All right."

"He destroyed her," she continued. "It was brutal and bloody and horrible, but it was fast. And then he came for us. I didn't feel anything. I didn't understand fear, not really. Didn't know what was normal in this new world, but I felt fear in the room, and realized that my grandmother was still there, in the corner, watching in horror as her daughter was destroyed. She stopped him. My grandmother's the one who destroyed him, but at the same time, she destroyed herself."

"How?"

"Magic. It runs in our family, too, though it runs stronger in some than in others. In my grandmother it was pretty weak, actually, but she drew up everything she knew and did . . . something . . . to him."

"What?"

She shook her head. "I don't really know. He was there, and then he seemed to implode. There was a shimmer in the air, and then suddenly he was gone. And that was the end of that."

"You never asked her?"

"She died. She had just enough power to save Kiril and me, then to do one more spell. And then she sagged to the floor and died." She drew in a breath, a quick shake of her head the only sign that the story was getting to her. "Our aunt raised us—my mother's sister—and she wasn't happy about it. Didn't want us. Blamed us—blamed *me*—for destroying her life. The curse . . . she hated it. Thought my mother and me were evil. It was horrible."

"It sounds horrible."

"She died when we were fifteen," Petra continued. "But we didn't tell anyone. We were afraid California social services would get involved, and they couldn't separate us. There was no way I could live without Kiril, or he could live without me."

For a moment, he didn't speak, thinking instead about the strength of this woman who'd become attached to him by circumstance. Then his thoughts cleared, and he got back to business. "We'll need to look through your things. Any family heirlooms. Diaries. That Bible. Who knows where we'll find a clue."

"There's nothing."

"You don't have anything of your mother's?"

"Sure. A bracelet."

"Then I want to see it."

"Fine. Whatever. It's not going to lead anywhere."

"It may."

She rolled her eyes. "Whatever floats your boat. But I've been that route, and there's nothing there. That's why I've been looking for ways to cast a counter curse. It's not like I'm surrounded by piles of cryptic clues that just need to be translated."

He pondered her for a moment, thinking about the ins and outs of her story.

She narrowed her eyes. "What? You think I'm bull-shitting you? That I have some treatise on how to break curses hidden behind the toilet?"

"No," he said. "That's not what I was thinking. It's just—Petra, your story doesn't make sense."

She stiffened. "Excuse me?"

"It's the Touch that transforms someone else into a monster, and it's childbirth that cures the cursed?"

"Yeah." She tilted her head to the side. "Well, not the act of childbirth, but the birth of a child. I mean, if Kiril were the firstborn, then his curse would lift when his child is born. When the cord is cut, if you want to get all technical about it."

"Ah . . ." He hesitated, sounding both amused and uncomfortable. "Sweetheart, I know you're not experienced in these things, but it's supremely difficult to get a girl pregnant without actually touching her."

She blinked, then looked him dead in the eye. "Turkey baster," she said, then burst out laughing at his horrified expression. "I'm sorry, I'm sorry, it's just . . . you were approaching the subject so delicately. *You.* I think you were even blushing."

"*Me?* What's that supposed to mean?"

"Just that considering your reputation, I wouldn't have expected you to get all shy about sex."

He leaned casually against the wall. "Reputation?"

She stared him down. "Don't even," she said, then grinned. "But thanks for the laugh."

"Happy to be of service, but I still think I'm missing the big picture here."

"Right. Well, there's kind of an escape clause. Probably because whoever cursed us in the first place saw the very same problem you did, and wanted to make sure our line kept going on and on."

"What kind of an escape clause?"

"The night of a blue moon," she said. "That's when there's an extra full moon. They don't happen very often. Years can go by."

"I know what a blue moon is," he said.

"Oh. Good." She felt her cheeks burn, but forced herself not to look away. To keep this conversation strictly businesslike. "Well, during that night, from sunset to sunrise, I can touch without doing harm." She felt her insides jolt as she remembered the way she felt when a blue moon filled the sky.

She'd never been with a man—not like that—and not because she hadn't wanted to. Not that she'd ever wanted a specific man—she'd never let herself fall in love—but on that night . . . dear heaven, on that night her body longed to be taken, to be held, to be ravaged.

So far, she hadn't managed it.

The first time it had hit after puberty, she hadn't realized what was going on until it was too late. The next time, she'd been twenty and visiting Joshua Tree with Kiril—which meant no matter how freaking horny she was, there wasn't a man around to satisfy that urge.

Kiril had sat with her, though, letting her lean against him and hold his hand, so that at least for once she could feel the sensation of skin against skin, and he'd made the time pass by spinning wild stories for her. Tales that he later wrote in his notebooks and then slid into a drawer despite her constant urgings that he should send them to magazines and try to have them published.

The next time, she'd told Kiril that she was going to spend the night doing the L.A. club scene. She'd ordered clothes online, practiced her makeup for days, and fantasized about the men she'd press against on the dance floor.

But an hour before sunset, she'd begun throwing her guts up, her stomach so wrenched with a virus or food poisoning that she could only stay inside and let Kiril cater to her and tell her that there was always the next blue moon to look forward to. It had sucked, but she'd been grateful she had a brother who stuck it out with her.

While her stomach had roiled, Kiril held her hand and stroked her hair, letting her have the sensation of touch as he talked her through the night, keeping her grounded and centered. Once or twice she'd gotten so frustrated with being sick that she'd actually been disloyal enough to wonder if he'd done something to her food to make her ill, but then she'd mentally kicked herself for thinking such mean thoughts. Kiril was her rock. He loved her. And because of him she'd been able to keep her sanity on those rare, mystical nights, and for that, she'd always be grateful.

Now, though . . .

Now, she remembered the way she'd come out of the mist, full of the sensation of being twined with Nick.

She looked at him now, and reveled in the heat that seemed to flood her as she opened herself to the memory, delicious and sweetly erotic and maddeningly ephemeral.

They'd merged like a cloud with a cloud. How much more sweet would it be to feel flesh against flesh?

She didn't know, but the blue moon was coming, and this time it wasn't going to be Kiril with her.

This time, it would be Nicholas.

CHAPTER 10

"No, I'm safe. Really." Petra pressed the handset more firmly against her ear and shifted her position, giving the room—and the group within it—her back. On the other end of the line, Kiril was demanding an explanation, a location, *something,* and she felt like a complete shit because she couldn't give it to him. They wouldn't let her give it to him.

Nicholas eased up beside her, sliding into her field of vision, and a knot of irritation twisted in her gut. She knew what she had to do, but there he was, hovering as if he didn't trust her to do it.

He tapped his wrist, and even though he wore no watch, she knew he was telling her to hurry up.

"Kiril—Kiril, just let me get a word in, okay? I'm fine, but I need help. Meet me in the El Capitan theater, okay? One hour. And Kiril? Make sure you're not followed."

She hung up before he could protest anymore, then faced Nicholas straight on. "I don't like lying to him."

"It's necessary. They'll be watching him. Sending him away from where we need to be is going to buy us time."

"Maybe."

"Definitely," Nicholas countered.

She shrugged. She was being contrary, and she knew it, but she'd told him so much—exposed so much of herself to him. It had felt right in the dim light of the little room they'd stuck her in. But now, under the harsh glare of the fluorescent tubes, she wished she'd kept her mouth shut. Like he really needed to know about her birth memory. Like she really wanted him to see her cry.

"He's my brother," she said. "*He* should be helping me. Protecting me. That's what he does."

"And now it's what I do." Nicholas's voice was hard—no nonsense—and Petra closed her eyes, wishing things were different. Wishing Kiril were there. Wishing that the life she woke up to every day wasn't her own.

But at the same time so damn thankful that she was alive. And it wasn't Kiril to whom she owed her life. In a way it wasn't even Nicholas.

He'd only saved her in the hopes of saving Serge.

Which meant she owed her continuing heartbeat to the very monster she created.

Pretty damned ironic when you thought about it.

A huge conference table filled most of the room, and she left Nicholas standing by the wall, then took the seat at the far end of the table, the farthest away from the other men, Rand and Luke. From two chairs down, Lissa smiled at her, and the expression was so warm and genuine that Petra couldn't help but smile back. Then again, Lissa was a succubus, so who knew what kind of happy juice the girl was filling the room with.

"He's not being fair," Lissa said, sliding into the empty chair beside her.

"Nicholas? He damn sure isn't. If we're going to go on a scavenger hunt to end this curse, Kiril should be with me. Hell, he's lived with it as long as I have."

"I guess he has," Lissa said. "But what I meant was

that he didn't tell you why. He's not the kind of guy who does things by committee, you know? He says what he wants, and it happens. No explanation, no worries." She shot a quick glance toward Rand. "You've been living in the shadow world long enough to know that's not an uncommon male trait."

"So what didn't he tell me?"

"Your brother's a sorcerer, and pretty powerful. That kind of magic can be tracked. You travel with him, they'd find you before the day is out."

"But if it's magic they track, won't they find me now?"

"This place is protected," Nicholas said. "You don't have enough magic to push past the barriers."

She leaned back in her chair. "Well, then. I guess I'm lucky I'm so inadequate at—*oh, shit.* I didn't even think—"

"What?" Luke demanded.

"The binding spell." She looked between Nicholas and Rand. "I told you both about it before. Kiril's bound to protect me, and to do that, he has to be able to find me. That's part of our grandmother's spell. He can feel me. Can search me out."

The others exchanged glances. "Can you feel him? Is he on his way here?"

"No. It's a one-way thing. *Shit.*" She levered herself up out of the chair, then started pacing, suddenly afraid. "What if he's just playing me? What if he's not going to the theater, but he's on the way here, and they're following him?"

"We have protections, Petra," Nicholas said. "We told you."

"Not against my grandmother's spell." She could see they didn't believe her. But she knew. *She knew.* Kiril would find her.

"Even if you're right," Lissa said, "you told him you were safe. He's got to know searching you out could be a risk."

"As far as he knows, you folks are a risk, too." And they were. If they knew the truth, they really were. "Besides, you don't get it. It's a binding *spell.* He'll come for me. He has to."

There wasn't a doubt in her mind. Her brother looked after her with a fierceness that was more than just a family bond, or even the bond of twins. No, their grandmother's last spell had done the job, and done it well. Maybe too well, if by looking for her, he'd also be leading the Alliance to her.

"It will be fine," Rand said. "This warehouse is fortified with all sorts of protections, not just ones that shield magic. You're safe enough in here."

She frowned, not believing it for a minute.

"And when they leave?" Lissa asked. "Kiril will be all over Petra, and the Alliance will be all over him."

"Let me call him back. Tell him not to follow me."

"How sensitive is this binding spell?" Nicholas stood calmly against the wall, watching no one but her.

"It's—what do you mean?"

"Pinpoint accuracy?"

She shook her head, understanding what he was thinking. "No. No, just the general area. A city block, maybe. And even less accurate the farther away I am from him."

"So right now you're golden," Nicholas said. "Even

if he can sense where you are, it's too broad an area, and the signal will be even more fuzzy with our protections. Besides, he has no reason to come. Right now, he thinks you're coming to him."

"And soon you won't even blip on his radar," Luke added.

"Why?" She glanced at Nicholas, but it was Rand who answered.

"Gunnolf's prepared to help," he said, referring to the Paris-based therian—or shape-shifter—liaison to the Alliance. "Under the table, of course."

Petra bristled. "Maybe he should have thought of that before they stuck me in an execution cell."

"Maybe he should have," Rand said. "But if he had, then they'd be watching him now. This way, he can actually help you. And he wants to, Petra. He told me how grateful he is for the role you played in keeping his Alliance seat secure."

"That's me," Petra said. "The Alliance's go-to girl." She crossed her arms over her chest and scowled, but truthfully, she was pleased. Because of what she and Serge had done, the Alliance had to publicly acknowledge that the therian leader had played no role in a spate of human murders that had rocked Los Angeles. Without those charges hanging over his head, Gunnolf was able to maintain his seat at the Alliance table.

In other words, he was just as indebted to Petra as Tiberius was. Gunnolf, though, was actually doing something about it.

"Look," she said grudgingly. "That's nice but if he's not going to buck up against the Alliance, what exactly can he do for us?"

"He can lend you his plane and his pilot," Rand said. "It's here, hangared in Burbank. Same plane I flew in on a few months ago."

"And the pilot?"

"He's solid," Rand said. "He'll do whatever Gunnolf says, no questions asked."

"Then that's how we get to Paris," Nicholas said.

"Paris?" Petra asked.

"Don't expect Gunnolf to meet with you in person," Rand said. "He's offered the plane. I don't think he'd agree to a face-to-face."

"And I wouldn't ask for one," Nicholas continued. Something like regret shadowed Nicholas's face, and he looked away, focusing his attention only on Luke. "I need to find Ferrante."

Whatever Luke might have been expecting Nicholas to say, it wasn't that, and surprise registered on those stoic features. "Do you think that's wise?"

"We need a cure," Nicholas said. "And if anyone can find one, I think it's Marco." He straightened his shoulders. "It has been a very long time. He will not turn me away."

She couldn't hold her questions in any longer. "Wait a sec," Petra said, moving to stand in Nicholas's line of sight. "Who is Ferrante?"

Nicholas hesitated, but she shook her head. "Oh no. *Everything*, remember? What's good for the goose is good for the vampire, and all that shit."

"He's an alchemist," Nicholas said after a hesitation so brief she wouldn't have noticed had she not been looking for him to dodge the question. "Once, he was a friend."

She heard the edge in his voice. "Once?"

"Later," he said. "We need to move."

"Wait. How long ago did you know him?"

He met her eyes. "I haven't seen him for more than seven hundred years."

"Oh." She took a small step back. She'd lived in this world long enough not to be surprised, but still . . . "I guess he's an alchemist who knows his stuff."

Nicholas turned to Rand. "The hangar number?"

"Fifteen."

"I'm glad you're going to Paris," Lissa said. "I've remembered something from there."

Petra turned toward Lissa, her heart pounding. "Wait. What? You've remembered something?" As a succubus, Lissa had lived multiple lives. And although she didn't remember many of those lives in detail, she'd once told Petra that she did remember something about a monster like Serge. A monster created by touch. A clue, maybe, to Petra's background. At the time, though, she couldn't recall any of the details.

"Not much, but, yeah. A glimpse, a name. Rumors that her touch destroyed. And Paris." She closed her eyes as if trying to draw the memory closer to her, then shook her head, frustrated. "But that's all."

"What name?" Petra asked, hoping it was someone new, and not someone in her family tree.

"Vivian Chastain," Lissa said, and from the far side of the room, Luke swore under his breath.

"Chastain?" Nicholas repeated. "You're certain?"

Lissa reached out, finding Rand's hand, as her eyes darted between the two vampires. "As sure as I can be about a hazy memory. Why?"

Luke looked hard at Nicholas, who nodded.

"Dammit," Petra said. "What's going on? Who is she?"

"I don't know," Luke said. "Not really. But in 1714, I was ordered to kill her. More specifically, I was ordered to use a sniper's bullet. No contact." His smile was thin. "Not my usual style."

Petra's throat thickened, and she had to try twice to get the words out. "Oh. At least I got a trial. For what it's worth, anyway."

"Were you told anything about her?" Lissa asked. "Anything about her background? Her family? Anything that might help Petra?"

Nicholas shook his head. "I was Luke's second. They told us nothing."

"A second?" Petra asked. "Is that usual?"

"No," Luke said.

"Apparently the Alliance was taking no chances."

The fact that Petra's heart still beat suddenly seemed like even more of a miracle than it had a few hours ago. She turned to Lissa. "Do you remember anything else?"

"Nothing. I'm sorry."

"It's okay," Petra said, though she wanted to scream with frustration. "We know I'm not the only one. And we know the Alliance has killed to stop the Touch before." She drew in a breath. "Killed instead of cured. Maybe there isn't a way."

"We'll find one. We'll go to Ferrante."

The sharp chirp of a phone startled them all, with the exception of Luke, who pulled out his phone and eagerly opened it, then listened to the caller before ending the call and facing the group. "I can see Sara now," he said, his voice choked with emotion. And before anyone had the chance to say good-bye, he'd transformed into sentient mist and was racing toward the exit.

"We need to go, too," Nicholas said to Petra. "Your house first, then straightaway to Paris."

He held out his arms, and she took an automatic step backward.

"Only for a moment," he said. "Two layers of cloth and it will only be an instant before we're mist."

She didn't argue, realizing as she moved toward him that there was more anticipation than fear associated with the action. *Not good.* She couldn't become lax about touch. Not now, not ever.

"Why do we need a plane?" she asked. "If we can travel like this, what's the point?"

"Your body wouldn't take it," he said matter-of-factly. "Are you ready?"

But before she could say that she most certainly was *not* ready—not after hearing that traveling by mist lacked the National Transportation Safety Board seal of approval—he dissolved. And Petra, of course, dissolved with him.

CHAPTER 11

As soon as he gave himself up to the mist, with Petra twined safely around him, Nick allowed himself to relax and his mind to return to the past, to Ferrante and his studies and the hopes and dreams he'd nurtured before the change. For years, he had pondered the mysteries of the universe, exploring and studying the elements not because he sought gold or wealth, but because he wanted to unlock the key to existence.

His studies had grounded him to the earth, and pushed him to the stars, contemplating the length and breadth of infinity. Once upon a time, such activities had been the focus of his life. Searching the heavens with his mentors. Charting the movement of the stars across the sky. Looking for something bigger than the ephemeral shell of man, a shell that began to return to dust at the very moment of birth.

He hadn't found the answer as much as it had found him. And the dark kiss had made him not only immortal but like a god. Who else could live for millennia? Could move through the world as mist or animal? Could turn the will of lesser beings to their own?

Even in a shadow world filled with creatures who existed only in the nightmares of humans, vampires reigned supreme. And yet the universe still sought balance—yin and yang. For every benefit, there was a price.

Nick had paid dearly. And so, to his deep regret, had his friends.

So many years had passed, and now he must seek out Ferrante again.

He felt a stirring within, a combination of anticipation and fear. Ferrante would have every justification to put a stake through Nicholas's heart. But there was no other choice: They needed answers. They needed a cure. And Marco Ferrante was their first, best option.

The girl was soft in Nick's arms as they materialized in her kitchen, the beat of her heart against his chest bringing him back to life, back to the world, and firing the familiar desire to touch, to lose himself in a woman's embrace.

In front of him, she pushed away. Understandable, but definitely not the response Nick was used to.

"Contact," she said.

"Of course."

She looked around at the room. "How did we get inside?"

"Mist," he said. "I can't travel through walls, but stove vents work nicely."

"So all that bullshit about vampires needing an invitation . . . ?"

"Bedtime stories to keep humans feeling safe. But you've been walking in this world long enough. You didn't know that?"

"Kiril put protections on all the doors and windows." She glanced ruefully at the polished hood above the old-fashioned stove. "Never even occurred to me."

"Only need a crack," he said, looking around as well. No frills, but cozy and well stocked. A well-used room, with the aroma of garlic and basil lingering in the air along with the soft, sweet scent of the girl herself. "You spend a great deal of time here."

She glanced at him. "So?"

"Merely an observation."

"I don't like restaurants," she said, then pushed through the room toward a darkened hallway. He caught the scent of magic, then glimpsed the interior of a dark room filled with books and crystals. "The magic office," she said, following his gaze. "For our shadow clients."

"So this room is only for show?"

"Kiril practices magic in there, and he likes to write at the desk. I don't spend a lot of time in it, though."

"Don't you practice?"

She shook her head. "No."

"Why? You have power. You just told us about it at the warehouse. Hell, I saw it when we were at Division. The wall of flame. The way you almost burned through that guard's uniform."

She lifted a brow. "And you're still willing to get close to me?"

He took a step toward her, knowing damn well she was avoiding the question. "I am," he said, then traced his fingertip just below the neckline of her shirt, the cotton soft against his skin.

"Oh." She swallowed, and he bit back a curse. He was flirting, and he damn well knew it. It was so easy to fall into the pattern with women. So easy to turn it on. And so damned unfair to turn it on with her, when there could be no follow-through.

God, he was an ass.

He turned to look around the room, wanting to shift the subject and take her mind off what she didn't and couldn't have. Feeling damned protective, but that was the role he'd thrust himself into. She was his responsibility now, and he took care of what was his.

"What?" She was following the direction of his gaze, looking amused.

"I was just wondering if this is where you bring the human clients."

She laughed, the sound relieving some of the pressure on his chest. "No, we converted the entire front of the house to a reception area for the human clients. I spent a month decorating. It's all flowers and pastels. Not a deck of tarot cards or one ceremonial candle to be found."

"Sounds charming."

"It's an explosion of floral insanity," she said, cricking her finger and leading him toward the front. She opened the door, then stepped aside so he had a view that made the term *floral insanity* seem like an understatement.

"You did this?" he asked, looking at the vases of silk flowers, the huge prints on the walls, the chair and loveseat upholstered in floral material. There was a warmth to it—a vulnerability that seemed in contrast to the strong woman he knew Petra to be. "Just for the humans?"

She shrugged. "Maybe I like it a little, too. I have a thing for flowers." She pulled the door shut, then headed for the stairs. "You want jewelry and the Bible, right?"

"Anything left to you from your mother," he said,

following. "Anything and everything that might reflect your family history."

Everything . . .

She kept her face forward so that he couldn't see it, then led him up the stairs. She'd share her mom's bracelet—why not?—but the story about how she got it? That, she couldn't share. Not the whole story, anyway.

"Petra?"

She realized she'd stopped on the stairs. "Sorry. I was thinking."

"About your mother?"

"No."

"The jewelry?"

"No," she snapped. She didn't want to talk about it.

"Dammit, Petra. We agreed to everything."

"Fine. Shit. Whatever." She glared at him. "I was thinking about the first time I turned somebody. Satisfied?"

She saw him cringe. "Your father, you mean?"

"No. You're right. That was the first." She met his eyes, determined to just tell it straight out. He wanted the story, he'd get the story. "I was thinking about the second time."

"What happened?"

"There was this guy, and he snuck up on me."

"Tell me."

"I was fifteen," she said. "And I didn't get out much."

"I can't imagine why," he said. She laughed, appreciating the way he was deliberately trying to lighten the moment.

"Yeah, well, even so I managed to catch the eye of this man. No," she corrected. "Not a man. This bastard was a monster even before I touched him."

"What did he do?" Nicholas asked, his voice as tight as his face. "Did he harm you?"

She raised a brow. "That's not an easy thing for a man to do to a girl like me."

"But he tried."

"I'd been sunbathing in our backyard. Could you see it? Through the mist?"

"I saw. The garden. The fence."

"A high fence," she agreed. "We always kept it locked. And I was out there. You know, in a bathing suit." She felt her cheeks warm. "A bikini." She'd been all alone, her teenage body longing for a boy's caress, and yet forced to make do with nothing more substantial than the play of the sun's warmth over her skin, on her breasts, on the thin piece of material that covered her sex.

"I fell asleep in the sun, and when I woke up—"

She cut herself off, hating the way the memory could still make her tremble.

"He was there," Nicholas said, his voice so close that she drew in a breath, knowing that he wanted to touch her and comfort her. Knowing he couldn't, but so desperately wishing he could.

Slowly, she opened her eyes. "As close as you are now," she whispered. "Then he reached for me, and—and I screamed for Kiril." Kiril, who was always nearby—but that had been the wrong thing to do. "The man grabbed me. One hand on my arm, one over my mouth. Except he never actually got the hand to my mouth."

"He changed."

"The instant he touched me."

Nicholas lifted his hand toward her face. She flinched, backing up, then realizing he was holding out a handkerchief.

Carefully, she took it, then wiped her eyes. "I didn't even realize I was crying."

"Not for that bastard, I hope. Attack a woman— a child—and a man must suffer the consequences."

"No. Not for him. Never for him." But the tears had come, and she hated them. Crying meant weakness, and that was the last thing she wanted to show in front of Nicholas. At the same time, though, she longed to sag into his arms and sob.

Dear God, it had truly been one hell of a day.

"What happened to him?"

"Kiril," she said softly. "He came—good God, he came like a plague upon the earth, all wind and storm, and they fought, and . . ." She trailed off, not wanting to remember. "Kiril almost died. The monster was barely even formed, so he was still comparatively weak—but he beat Kiril up so badly. I think it was his pain and anger, but I've never seen Kiril conjure such a storm. He brought down a tornado to rip up a tree. The monster practically broke it up into toothpicks, but it kept the creature occupied, and—and that gave Kiril time to use the sword."

"What sword?"

"My aunt had come running with this old Civil War

sword that had belonged to her husband. And Kiril took it, and he sliced the monster in half."

"Thank God."

Her smile was halfhearted. "No. There's not much I thank God for."

"Petra . . ."

"I was so glad he was dead. I felt so guilty, because I'd made him something horrible, but I was so glad he was dead." She met his eyes. "I was young, then. When I think back now, I only hate the memory. The bastard attacked me. I'm sure I wasn't the only girl he'd done that to. There's no guilt. No guilt at all."

"Good. What changed?"

"I might have become the well-adjusted person you see standing before you, but it was through no help from my aunt."

"What did she do?"

"She'd never been kind to me, not really. But after that day, she wouldn't even look at me." Petra realized she was clenching her teeth and forced herself to relax.

He didn't speak, as if he knew she needed time. She turned, and headed the rest of the way into her bedroom, with Nicholas following. Once inside, she peeled back the rug, then pulled up the loose floorboard. A box was inside, and she opened it, revealing the platinum and emerald bracelet that she cherished above all else. "My aunt gave it to Kiril right before she died. Cancer. He gave it to me."

"It was your mother's?"

She nodded, her throat full of tears. "There's a saying carved on the back. Latin. *Manus fati.*"

"The hand of fate," Nicholas said, his voice barely a whisper.

"My aunt had kept it away from me all those years." She fell silent, remembering how pathetic she'd been, trying throughout her childhood to entice a smile or a kind word from her aunt. No luck there. The closest she'd gotten was the Christmas she'd been fourteen, when her brother had given her a small bound book, and in it he'd written a story featuring the three of them—Petra, Kiril, and their aunt. It had been one of those alternate-history things, and in the story the aunt missed her sister, but loved the twins with a sweetness that had brought Petra to tears.

"Petra?"

She managed a thin smile. "Sorry. My aunt never even tried with me. I had the curse, and she hated what I was, and me along with it."

"There are a lot of monsters on this earth," Nicholas said. "Some of the worst don't even live in the shadows."

"Isn't that the truth."

"So what happened to the monster? You and your brother were only fifteen. What did you do with the body?"

Petra forced back a shiver, trying to sound matter-of-fact. "Kiril burned it."

"Your brother really does take care of you."

"Yes," she said. "He does."

Kiril. They were away from the protections of the warehouse now. Soon he'd sense her. Soon he'd come.

"Do you think they're watching the house?" she asked. "The Alliance, I mean?"

"I'd be shocked if they weren't. But the windows are covered and the night hides the mist."

"But if Kiril comes racing back—"

"They'll figure out we're here."

"We need to go." She put the bracelet on her wrist, then grabbed the Bible and her journal off her dresser and shoved them into her backpack. "My notes. All my leads on sorcerers who could do a counter curse."

"How long have you been looking?"

"Almost a decade."

She could see him doing math in his head. "You were just a kid."

"Yup. That's how I ended up working in the shadow and human worlds, too. When I started looking, I didn't even know your world existed. But I found it. Hints and pieces, I mean, when I started looking for someone who could remove the curse. After a while, I realized that's where I belong. After all, as far as humans are concerned, I'm as much of a freak as werewolves and vampires are." Her mouth quirked ironically. "Considering the warm reception from the Alliance, though, I probably should have continued living like a human. Bought a cabin and lived by myself in the woods."

"Eventually, they would have found out about you," Nicholas said.

"I know," she said. "I'm cursed, remember? Bad luck is in my blood."

CHAPTER 12

Disney's ornate El Capitan theater was a bustle of activity, and Kiril frowned, wondering why the hell his sister would want to meet him in a crowd. Crowds and Petra did not go together, although he supposed that if she was hiding, a crowd was the best place to do it. As long as she was adequately covered, it was probably smart.

His fingers itched to pull out his notebook and scribble a few thoughts. He was working on a spy story, and the idea of hiding in a crowd was a good one. But now wasn't the time. Now he needed to find Petra.

She'd said that she would be seated, and if he knew his sister, she would have filled the seats on either side of her with packages and bags, pretending to save them for someone. That should make her easier to find, as he could look for gaps in the rows.

Except he'd already peered into the auditorium, and she wasn't anywhere to be found.

He could feel her, though. When he reached out with his mind, he could find her in the blanket of magic and mysticism that surrounded and bound the earth, much as an aura surrounded a human.

He closed his eyes, oblivious to the dirty glances of moviegoers trying to balance their popcorn and tug their children into the theater. They weren't his problem.

Only Petra mattered. Finding her, helping her, saving her.

Fear rose within him, and he clenched his fists, forcing it back down. He couldn't let himself think about losing her. Had to concentrate on finding her. Thinking positive. That was the ticket. Thinking . . . and feeling.

He kept his eyes closed and tried to relax, only to be jostled by a rush of people.

"Get the hell out of the way, dipshit," a gawky teenager snarled.

Kiril just smiled. Didn't even pull up the magic. Just looked him in the eye and smiled.

The kid hurried away, fear in his eyes.

Yeah, smart kid.

He started to relax, trying to find the zone again, when, *bam*, there she was. *Petra*. Not in the theater, but in him. Gloriously, totally, completely in him.

Nearby?

He tilted his head, trying to pinpoint the location. Not close, and yet he could feel her so clearly. Which was odd, because usually she had to be near for it to feel so sharp and crisp. Right then it felt as if they were—

Home.

Goddamn his sister! She'd sent him here while she went home.

He had no idea what the hell was going on, but he was certain that whoever had spirited her out of the execution chamber was pulling some sort of shit. Maybe they thought they could keep her alive, but he knew better. *He* was the one who looked after her. *He* was the one who protected her. She was *his*, goddammit. His responsibility. His sister. His whole life and purpose.

And he was the one who was going to get her back right that very moment.

Around him, loose papers began to flutter as his temper rose. He didn't even try to tamp it down, despite the humans looking around in confusion, grabbing on to counters and kids. In the crowd, he saw a dark face standing unperturbed.

A jinn.

Kiril could feel the magic, and he knew damn well that a jinn hadn't just wandered into the Disney theater that day. He was being followed. He was being used as a goddamn magnet for his sister.

Well, let them try to follow him now . . .

With a growl of understanding, he began to spin. Humans stared, backing away in terror as a wind whipped up around him, moving him like a cyclone through the shattering glass doors, then down Hollywood Boulevard, as people grabbed for signposts so as to not end up like Dorothy in his twister.

Some even pulled out video cameras, but he didn't care. They'd explain it away. Weather phenom. The devil. Who knows.

Right then he didn't give a fuck.

Right then, he could think only of getting his sister back with him where she belonged.

◊

Nick glanced around Petra's room as she shoved a few personal things into her backpack—underwear, toothbrush, dental floss. Typical fare for a woman on the run.

Her room was as tidy as the kitchen—lived in, yes,

but also uncluttered in a way that was almost sad. A room in stark contrast to his own apartments in Los Angeles, New York, and Florence. Apartments filled with antiques bought during an age when the pieces were considered modern, the polished surfaces of tables and desks now covered with evidence of his various passions. Pages from Leonardo's notebooks, the journals of his friend Galileo, the brilliant scribblings of Roger Bacon, and Nick's own transcriptions of his long conversations with Marco Ferrante.

Over the years, philosophy and art had come to fascinate him as much as science, and his walls were covered with the works of both the masters and aspiring artists he had discovered over the years, many of whom had never found fame but had true talent in the way they wielded a brush.

Petra's shelves were crammed full of books, but they did not lie open and scattered about as Nick's always did. Nick had the impression of being in a cell rather than in a home, and when he looked at Petra again, he saw a girl who moved through the world but did not in fact live in it.

"Are we leaving or not?" she demanded.

He realized he was standing in the doorway, his hands clenched as if in protest of something he didn't understand. A problem he didn't know how to tackle, yet he wasn't certain what troubled him.

He shook off the feeling and stepped from the room into the hall. "We'll transform in the kitchen, closer to the vent. Less time for you to be forced into that form."

Her brows lifted. "Less time by about four seconds. Is it really that dangerous? I mean, I do have a car."

"Mist is safer."

"You're sure?"

"Absolutely," he said, with more surety than he felt. At some point, her human constitution would rebel against the repeated transformations. For that matter, at some point he would have to feed, as the strain of transforming her along with himself would soon take its toll. Now, though, it was most important to get out of there. And for that, mist was best.

"Guess I'm ready then—oh, wait." She paused in front of her dresser, grabbed a lipstick, and scribbled *I love you—I'm safe* on the mirror. "Okay?"

He only half nodded, his interest captured instead by the calendar taped to the upper corner of that same mirror. Interesting primarily because there was nothing written on it. No engagements. No birthdays. Nothing except one date circled in red. The fifteenth. Only one night away.

Petra followed his gaze to the calendar.

"A blue moon is coming," he said.

"Yeah. I know. It's my calendar."

He grinned, that charming lady-killer grin. "How interesting."

She felt her cheeks heat, but held his eyes, willing her face to remain bland, to not reveal anything to this man. This vampire who had a reputation of bringing women to his bed, of using them for his own pleasure. And for theirs.

She'd known a bit about his reputation, of course, simply from working within the shadows. She'd learned more once he stepped in to represent her, asking discreet questions within the confines of her cell, and sending Kiril out to do the necessary legwork.

He used women, but he didn't hurt them. The women who entered his bed did so willingly, presumably with no illusions. Nicholas Montegue wasn't known as a man who would bind himself to one woman. Not ever. His encounters were about physical pleasure, not romance. Not love.

All of which was perfectly fine with Petra. More than fine, actually, since she could never bind herself to a man, either.

Her life was lonely by necessity, and she couldn't help but wonder why Nicholas's was lonely by design.

The answer didn't matter, though. His simple "how interesting" was an invitation—she was certain of it. And although she was nervous as hell, a man's touch had been at the forefront of her fantasies for all her past blue moons. Fantasies only, though, since fate always intervened.

This time, it wouldn't.

This time, she would know a man's touch. When the sun set again, she would take what he so willingly offered to so many other women, and she would hold on to it forever, cherishing the erotic memory of skin against skin.

There was more he could offer, too. The idea had been buzzing around in the back of her head since she told him about her birth memory. *Her birth.* The event that cured her mother, and her grandmother before that.

And if she were to have a child . . .

She pushed the thought away. A cursed child. Damned. Like her.

Yet she couldn't get the thought out of her head. The fabulous, amazing, joyful possibility that after nine short months she would, finally and forever, be free.

But the cost—dear God, how could she live with herself if she did that to a child? How had her mother and her grandmother and all her ancestors before them?

They had, but Petra couldn't. She'd figure out another way to free herself of this curse, or she would die childless. And the curse would die with her.

He was looking at her, his expression so intense she feared he could read her mind.

She hurried past him and began down the stairs, moving so quickly she could feel the stairs shaking beneath her step.

Except she wasn't the one making them shake.

"*Petra.*" From behind, Nicholas grabbed the hood of her shirt. Then yanked her up against him.

"Careful!"

"We need to go now," he said, as everything within the room below began to swirl, as if a tornado were filling the room.

"*It's Kiril,*" she cried. "Nicholas, please, just wait here!" She wrenched her shirt out of his grasp as Kiril appeared in the midst of the whirlwind.

"Petra!" he called.

"Dammit, Petra." Nicholas grabbed the hood again, this time not gently, and she gagged as he jerked her backward toward him.

"Keep your fucking hands off my sister." Around them, the objects swirling through the room picked up speed, and Kiril himself seemed surrounded by white wisps, the air that he was manipulating turning so cold under his power that all the moisture in the room had crystalized into tiny ice pellets.

"Don't interfere," Nicholas said. "I'm the one who saved her life."

Kiril didn't answer, and Petra knew damn well that any gratitude he might feel for Nicholas was buried under a fierce determination to protect her at all costs. Nicholas may have gotten her out of prison, but as far as Kiril was concerned, it was his job to take over now. How could he believe anything else?

Kiril held out his hand, his clothes and hair whipping around him. "Petra," he said. "Now."

She jerked free, terrified that if she didn't, Kiril would surely kill Nicholas. Under normal circumstances, a human was no match for a vampire. But a pissed-off tornado could rip even Count Dracula apart.

It wasn't the right move.

Faster than she could see, her brother whipped across the room, the whirlwind tightening around him, pulling everything in toward him. Everything, including Nicholas.

A chair drew close to Kiril, who stood at the eye of the storm, then shattered into a million splinters before finally reaching him.

Inside the swirling wind, Nicholas was being drawn closer and closer to her brother, his planted feet and firm grip on the banister no match for the force of her brother's power.

With his free hand he reached for her. "You can't stay with him. You know it, Petra. I'm your last, best chance."

"And I'm Serge's," she whispered, her hair fluttering

in the wind. Otherwise, though, she stood in a pocket of safety, her brother's whirlwind both avoiding her and shielding her.

"Serge?" Kiril repeated. "The monster lives?" It didn't take her brother long to do the math. "This vampire wishes only to use you," Kiril said, his voice raw and his skin red from the strain of conducting so much power through himself. "Petra, you know what will happen if you go with him. You cannot go with him."

"Now, Petra," Nicholas said, his composure never faltering.

She faltered, and hated herself for it. Kiril was safety and comfort and familiarity. He was her brother. A hand to hold during a blue moon.

Nicholas was danger. He didn't care about her, only about Serge. And, yeah, he'd kill her if he knew that was the cure. But he *didn't* know. And until he did, Nicholas represented hope and the possibility of freedom.

Her heart pounded. Freedom. And if not freedom, maybe one night. One single night to feel the beat of a heart and a finger stroke on her skin. Just one.

She had to try.

With one thick cry of anguish, she ripped herself away from her brother's protection, then launched herself into the whirlwind—and into Nicholas's arms.

He changed almost instantly, her body disintegrating painfully as they shifted into mist. Something was wrong. Something was horribly, awfully wrong.

She had no voice with which to cry out, no way to give release to the wrenching agony of this transformation. Terror ripped through her—the fear that the transformations had damaged her. That as Nicholas had said, her body couldn't take it.

But it wasn't her body—it was Kiril. And with sudden understanding, she knew what was happening. Knew that the wind that was her brother was whipping through the room, its violent motion dissipating the mist, lashing out in anger and—unknowingly—destroying her in the process.

Stop! Stop!

In her mind, she cried out to him, fighting against his anger, mentally trying to cling to Nicholas, whose energy was surrounding and protecting her, his essence whole despite the winds, protected by his vampiric nature.

And through it all the pain kept growing, turning her thoughts red, blurring her mind, ripping through limbs that didn't exist and spilling blood that flowed only in her mind. But the pain was real—dear God, the pain was real—and she cried out for her brother to stop, to stop, to stop before he killed her.

As quickly as it began, it ended, and in her mind she breathed deep in relief, grateful for the reprieve. Short lived, though, because even as the thought entered her head, pain seared through every molecule of her body, and relief came only with the sweet breath of nothingness.

◆

"Hold back! Hold back!" Tariq called out to his team, his voice low, but his words forceful enough that his men responded instantly.

Beside him, Elric crouched, pointing up at the sentient mist rising into the night. "We got here too late."

"No shit," Tariq said, rocking back on his heels. "That's what happens when you follow a fucking tornado through Hollywood."

A rustle in the bushes, and then Vale appeared, his pale skin almost iridescent in the waxing moon. "The target's alone, and he's looking pretty ripped. I think we can take him."

"I bet he's fucking destroyed," Elric said. "Magic has a price, and our bad boy used a butt load of it."

"No."

They both turned to Tariq, who considered his options. He'd left Division to join Elric and Vale in the field while at the same time giving orders to five other teams to watch the airports, infiltrate vampire hangouts, monitor magic-power surges, and basically do the legwork that went with trying to find a person who didn't want to be found.

"The brother's not our target," Tariq said to the others. "His sister is."

"And you know damn well he's in touch with the bitch," Elric said. "She called him or something. That's why he raced back home."

But Tariq just shook his head, his eyes on the house and the shadow he could see inside, pacing—*stumbling*—back and forth in front of a gauzy white curtain. "I don't think so. I think Sis is pulling this one on her own."

"Or Montegue is calling the shots," Vale said.

"A likely scenario," Tariq agreed. "Whatever the reason, our boy here doesn't know where his sister is."

"But he rushed back."

"He can sense her," Tariq said, thinking out loud. "It makes perfect sense. He can feel her. He's trying to find her, just like we are. And you can damn well bet he's going to follow her." He looked at his buddies, his team. "And we'll be only a few steps behind."

CHAPTER 13

The cell was small, uncomfortable, and too damn familiar. Sara had been in the detention block dozens upon dozens of times to interview prisoners or negotiate pleas. Always, though, she'd had the power to call the guards back. To have one of the cadre of security trolls disengage the locks on the glass-and-hematite-walled cells and see her safely back into the hall, and freedom.

Today, she was the prisoner, and no matter how loud or long she called, no one was coming with a key.

She didn't much like it.

At the same time, she didn't regret what she'd done. The hearing against Petra Lang was a crock, the execution order even more so.

Still, it would have been nice not to have been caught . . .

She got up from the small stone bench and began pacing again, telling herself not to worry. That Luke had powerful friends. That no matter what, she wouldn't be stuck in this cell. She wouldn't serve a life sentence or be staked for aiding a prisoner's escape, no matter how much she deserved it. She'd broken the law, after all. But she wasn't sorry. In Petra's case, the law deserved to be broken.

She sighed, knowing that Luke would get her out even if he had to break her out, and if they were on the run . . . well, at least they'd be together.

She closed her eyes and pressed her forehead against the cool glass, the comfort of knowing Luke would always be at her side warring with the horrible loss of her job as a prosecutor. It was all she knew—it was what she was. And if she was convicted of helping Nicholas and Petra—and, really, why wouldn't she be?—she could kiss that job good-bye.

Frustrated, she slammed her palm against the glass, then jumped when she heard not only the thump of her palm but the sharp *clank* of the security door being opened at the end of the hall. At first she thought nothing of it—she wasn't the only prisoner on the block, after all. Then she heard the familiar cadence of Luke's footfalls, and she looked up to see his worried face as he hurried toward her.

He pressed his hand to the glass, and she lifted hers to match his, blinking back the tears that were welling in her eyes, not from fear as much as from the relief of seeing him again.

The ogre escort moved as if slogging through Jell-O, and she wanted to scream before he finally managed to disengage the series of locks, then pull the door open for Luke to enter.

"Ten minutes got you," the ogre said.

Sara looked at him, this ogre who had escorted her down this very hall any number of times. "Only ten?"

The massive shoulders sagged. "Twenty you gots." He drew in a noisy breath, then gave a sharp nod of his head. "Twenty-five."

He left before she even had time to thank him.

Without a word, Luke pulled her into his arms. He pressed a kiss to the top of her head, and she felt as if she would melt right then. The tears she'd been holding back—that she promised she wouldn't show to her husband—began to flow. "Sorry," she said. "I'm okay. Really. It's just the stress."

"Cry all you want," he said. "I've got you."

"I know," she said through a throat clogged with tears. She took a deep breath, then another, then pushed back from him. "No. No, I promised myself I wasn't going to melt down. I can handle this." She took his hand, then tugged him to the bench. She glanced up toward the corner of the cell where they both knew microphones and cameras were hidden.

"It's okay," he said. "I've made arrangements."

She nodded, absurdly grateful for the skills and connections that used to vex her. "You talked to Tiberius?"

She didn't need to hear his words to know his answer. The anger was rolling off him in waves.

"Tiberius is too concerned about his seat on the Alliance to think about anyone but himself." He closed his eyes, visibly composing himself, pushing back the daemon that wanted to erupt with the anger. He didn't touch her until he was calm, then he gently stroked her face.

She reached up to catch his hand, then pressed her cheek into his palm. "Who would have thought that between the two of us it would be me that forced us to live like fugitives?"

"We won't," he whispered. "I will find a way. I will see you free, Sara. I won't rest until I do."

And though she couldn't imagine how, this was Luke talking—her husband—and she believed him.

◆

"Petra!" Nick knelt in the narrow airplane aisle, his attention on the unmoving girl. "Dammit, Petra, wake up!"

Her clothes were in tatters, her body covered with scratches, long red welts, as if claws had ripped through the mist and torn her open. But the external injuries were nothing compared with the battering she'd taken inside. He was certain of it. Already the scent of approaching death clung to her.

What the hell had her brother done, whipping his wind around a human traveling as mist? Her essence hadn't been able to withstand being shaken like that. Hadn't been able to re-form properly after the battering.

But this wasn't her brother's guilt to shoulder alone. Holy Christ, Nick had insisted she travel as mist, knowing that she was weakened. Knowing that he was as well.

Dear God in heaven, he'd done this to her.

Something cold and heavy penetrated his chest. Regret. And something more, too. *Fear.*

He had to keep her safe. Had to tend her injuries. Had to ensure that she survived.

He needed her.

He needed her to save Serge.

Dammit. He lashed out, hard, his fist pounding against and hopelessly bending the armrest of a nearby seat.

Damn him, damn her, and damn her goddamned meddlesome brother.

He leaned close, listening for the beat of her heart, and now he heard nothing.

Goddammit!

Frantic, he took his jacket off, then tossed it over her chest. He positioned his hands on the jacket over her heart, and he pressed down, fast and firm, but careful not to put his full strength behind the thrusts. He wanted to revive her, not puncture a lung, but the truth was that he'd never actually delivered chest compressions before. And when he'd been human, the technique had not been known.

Press, again . . . again . . .

Press, again . . . again . . .

Were it not for the curse, his lips would close over hers, and he would use his functioning but unnecessary lungs to breathe sweet life into her. With Petra, he could only manipulate her heart and try to start it beating once again.

Press, again . . . again . . .

Press, again . . . again . . .

Nothing, and the fingers of fear that had been clinging to him tightened their grip. He couldn't lose her—not now. Not before their quest had even truly begun.

"Dammit, Petra, come back!"

"Holy fuck!" The voice came from the cabin, and Nick spared a look. A werewolf stood there, concern on his face.

"You're Gunnolf's pilot?"

"Yeah. Name's Pyre. What happened?"

"Get me a pitcher of water," he said. "And then get us in the air."

Pyre did, and Nick doused her with it, the action equal parts instinct and anger. "Dammit, Petra. Goddammit, don't you fucking do this."

Another compression . . . and another . . .

And then a sound.

So soft he almost didn't hear it over the roar of the engine. Wouldn't have heard it were it not for the preternatural hearing inherent in his nature.

He stilled, listening again, every muscle in his body tense with anticipation. He needed her, and until he knew that he had not lost her, he couldn't relax, couldn't let down his guard or—

She moved.

"Petra!" He tossed the jacket back over her and gave a gentle shake as the plane broke contact with the ground and rose into the air. Beneath his hand, she shifted, and the surge of relief that flooded through him was so palpable he had to sit back, press the heels of his hands to his forehead, and say a silent thank-you to whatever power had decided to look out for him.

Her eyelids fluttered, then closed again. *Fuck.*

"Petra." He leaned close. "Petra, can you hear me?"

She made a low moaning sound, and Nick frowned, terrified that the damage within would drag her back toward death.

"Petra," he said softly. "Open your mouth."

She didn't answer, but her lips parted slightly. It was enough. He lifted his wrist to his mouth, closed his eyes, and sank his fangs deep into his wrist. He couldn't press the wound to her lips, but he let the drops of blood fall onto her lips, into her mouth. And slowly, ever so slowly, the color returned to her skin and her eyes fluttered open.

"Nicholas?" She blinked, then turned her head from side to side, taking in her surroundings. "We're on the plane? What happened?"

"Your goddamn brother killed you. Your heart stopped and everything."

"What?" Her forehead crinkled in confusion and shock, and he forced himself to rein in his anger. Now wasn't the time to rag on Kiril, especially when Nick was to blame as well. And now that the danger appeared past, he could afford to be generous to both of them.

"It's okay," he said gently. "You're okay now."

"Kiril?"

"He didn't realize, but that damn wind of his— I thought it was going to pull you apart."

She shifted, then propped herself up on her elbows with enough energy that he relaxed, realizing the blood had done its trick. "I did, too," she said. "He would have, I think, if I hadn't told him to stop."

Nick rocked back on his heels, her words not making sense. "If you hadn't what?"

"Told him." She sat completely up, then lifted her fingers to massage her temples. He shifted, realized he was about to put his arm around her in a gesture of support, and pulled back.

She licked her lips, her forehead crinkling as she frowned. "That's blood. My blood? Or . . ."

"Mine," he said, then eased closer as she scooted backward, shaking her head in protest.

"Wait a minute," she said. "Wait just a minute. What the hell did you do to me?"

"I told you. For a few seconds, you died. I did CPR— heart compressions. But it wasn't enough. I—"

She stopped, her body stiff, her eyes right on his. "Died?"

"If I hadn't given you some of my blood, you would

have slipped back into death. What?" he asked, looking at her face. "What is it?"

"Nothing," she said, but she didn't look at him as she spoke, and her forehead puckered slightly as if in question.

"Doesn't look like nothing."

"Just . . . I feel strange. Shivery." As if in illustration, she trembled. "Probably just shock or something. I'm okay. Really."

He considered arguing, because he was certain she wasn't being completely honest. It wasn't something he had the chance to pursue, though, because her questions continued.

"Am I going to change? Your blood, I mean. It doesn't make me a vamp or anything, does it?"

"No. It only helps you to heal, might possibly make you a bit stronger. Give you more energy." That wasn't entirely true, but considering how pissed she'd been when he got into her head, he didn't think this was the time to tell her that he was now attuned to her. That he could find her in his thoughts. That he could lose himself in her emotions.

"Nicholas?" This time she met his eyes dead on. A stray hair curled against her cheek, and he had to clasp his thumb inside his fist to fight the urge to brush it away, to feel the silk of her skin under his touch.

"Yes?"

She hesitated, and he wondered what she intended to say. When she finally uttered a soft, "Thank you," he was certain that wasn't what she had first planned to say.

He chose not to call her on it. "Anytime."

She reached up and grabbed an armrest. "I think it's

standard to actually sit in the seats when on an air-plane."

"Standard, but not nearly as interesting."

The plane had only eight seats, two sets of four, each set surrounding a table. They both took window seats facing each other, and as soon as they were seated, Petra pressed her hand to the shade. She didn't move to lift it, though. The sun was dipping toward the horizon, but hadn't sunk yet, and he realized that she understood what that meant for him as well as he did.

Her mouth curved into a quick frown as she pulled back from the window. "Gotta admit, I've never been crazy about flying. It seems . . . unnatural," she added, then grinned at him. "Kind of a crazy thing to say considering what I am and the world we live in."

"More crazy when you consider it's one of the most natural things in the world."

She raised her brows. "Several tons of steel soaring through the sky is natural?"

"The forces that make flight possible have been present since the dawn of time. Weight, lift, drag, and thrust. Just because it took men a while to recognize them and learn how to manipulate them doesn't make the action itself unnatural."

"Point taken," she said. "But that doesn't change the fact that we're thirty thousand feet in the air, and it's a long way to the ground." She leaned back in her seat and sighed. "Then again, it's better than the alternative."

"The alternative?"

"Duh. Mist. What do you think? That was the freakiest thing ever."

He recalled what she'd said about telling Kiril to stop, the import of her words suddenly hitting him. "Are you telling me you were aware?"

She grimaced as she flexed her arms, then looked at him with a curious expression. As if he was either joking or an idiot. "Well, yeah."

"This time. But what about before? When we left the prison? When we traveled to your house?"

"I'm getting the distinct impression that I'm freaking you out."

"You're human. You shouldn't feel anything when you're mist."

"No? Well, that doesn't seem fair. Although this last time I would have been happy to have been blissfully unaware."

He leaned back, his mind whirring with the possibilities. "You *are* human?"

"Well, yeah. I mean, I'd know if I wasn't, wouldn't I?"

"You felt me," he said, thoughtfully. "Back at the warehouse. You realized that I'd gotten into your head. Most mortals can't feel that, either."

She laughed. "And that makes you wonder if I'm mortal? Or are you just frustrated that you got caught?"

He surprised himself by grinning in return. "A little of both."

"Not used to things not going your way, are you?"

"I'm not."

"Stick with me," she said. "I've got it down to a science."

She sat there, still unsteady, and yet self-assured as well. A woman who could take care of herself, who'd had no choice but to do exactly that. A woman with secrets, who was so much more than met the eyes. "What did you mean when you said you told Kiril to stop?"

"Is this a trick question? I told him to stop. Screamed it. I couldn't take it—he was ripping me apart. It was like all the bits and pieces of me were supposed to stay together, but he was messing that all up, and it hurt. Oh God, it hurt so bad."

"He was," Nick said. "And somehow you told him so."

"And that bugs you?"

"It may be a clue."

"To the curse?"

"I don't know," Nick admitted. "But the more information I have about you—about what makes you and your family tick—the better." He cocked his head, looking at her thoughtfully.

"What?"

"What's the source of your power, Petra Lang? You say you're human—that your family is—but if that's so, then where does your power flow from?"

"Are you saying I'm more like you than my next-door neighbor? Believe it if that makes you feel better, but I'm human. I can get sick, I can die, and whatever power I have is channeled through me. It's not part of me." She looked him up and down. "I haven't changed into something else entirely."

"Interesting," he said, more to himself than to her. He'd often pondered the nature of humanity. He'd started out human, and yet vampires were decidedly not. Still, though, he had retained his passions, his interests and fascinations. He was still capable of love, and an opera could make his heart swell to the stars.

So wherein exactly did humanity lie?

It was not a question to which he had an answer, and as his years on this earth ticked by, Nick had become acutely aware that he still had more questions than answers. What was the point of immortality if the most basic of mysteries were left unresolved?

With Petra, perhaps he could explore at least some of those questions. "From where do you channel the power?"

"First of all," she said, "I don't. I already told you. I pretty much suck."

"And yet you almost burned through that guard's uniform and conjured a wall of fire."

"Score one for the man in the tight denim. I can manage a little. But not much."

"I'm not asking about volume," he said. "I'm inquiring about the source."

"Mother Earth. Same as all witches. The earth. The universe. Power of nature." She lifted a shoulder. "Whatever."

"Power of the earth," he repeated. "Maybe we're not as different as you think. Perhaps we have the same point of origin."

"God?" She spoke the word as if she'd just blurted out the most amusing of jokes.

"Do you believe in God?" he asked, curious despite himself about the way this female thought.

She exhaled, managing to make the simple puff of air sound like *hell no*. "Not in a benevolent god, that's for sure. Look what he's done to me." She crossed her arms and looked at him. "You?"

"I remain undecided."

"Yeah? I would have thought after all these years, you would have picked a side. Or maybe it's not that interesting a question to you anymore?"

"What do you mean?"

"Well, does it really matter?" she asked. "For someone who's going to live forever, I mean."

"That's the same as saying that simply because one won't experience something that it holds no value. I would argue that your premise is unsound."

"You would, huh? I have a feeling you'd argue about a lot of things."

At that, he had to laugh. "Yes, well, you would be right about that."

"Bring it on."

He was tempted. It had been a long time—too long—since he'd gotten lost in the joy of arguing the nature of the world simply for the sake of arguing, but now was not the time.

He stood.

"Hey, wait a sec. You were going to tell me how we're the same. Obviously the God guess was wrong."

He knew he should go. That he should let her sleep. That he shouldn't get too used to losing himself in conversation with this woman.

He sat anyway. "I wasn't speaking of God. Not like you meant, anyway."

Her eyes narrowed, and she cocked her head. "What? That shadow mythology? The bit about the two brothers?"

"There were three, actually," he said. "Three brothers from another dimension who crossed over, and then did battle among themselves. The third was the strongest, and the other two coveted his power."

"They killed him," Petra said. "Yeah, I remember this now. I heard some of those stories when I was doing a job a few years ago." She pulled her feet up onto the seat and hugged her knees. "You believe all that?"

"Not word for word, but is it any less possible than vampires or werewolves?" He conjured a smile. "Or soaring thirty thousand feet above the ground?"

"Okay, you win. For the sake of argument we'll say it's all true. Family feud among the big guys, just like Zeus getting all gnarly with the Titans. But what does it have to do with me?"

"Legend says that the brothers buried the third in the earth after draining his power. But they didn't destroy his body, and the corpse housed its own raw power."

"Black magic," she said. "Voodoo and all that stuff. It's supposedly from the earth."

"White magic, too. Power is power; all that changes is the way it's used."

She was nodding, her expression suggesting that she understood what he was saying. Believed it, even. "So all this Mother Earth stuff. It's really Father Earth? Or Big Brother Badass Earth?"

He cupped his chin to help suppress a laugh. "Something like that."

"It does make some sense. Kiril's gifts focus the air, mine focus fire." She rolled her eyes. "When I can make them work, that is. And my curse . . ." She trailed off, her forehead creasing in thought. "If it comes from the earth, too, then that would mean—"

"That would mean that you turned Serge into nothing less than a force of nature. And a pretty damn pissed-off one at that." He frowned as he spoke, realizing he'd just put voice to a theory that had been growing quietly in his mind.

Petra's eyes were wide. "Wow. You really think so?"

"I don't know," Nick admitted. "I'm just articulating a hypothesis."

"If it's right, though, then we really are going to the right place," she said.

"What do you mean?"

"To find an alchemist. Because isn't alchemy all about the earth and elements and stuff?"

Nick grinned. "At its most basic, yes."

"Well, that's what I'm saying. If my curse is earth magic and Serge is some earth monster, then getting help from an alchemist really does make sense. Maybe he can do with science what no sorcerer has been able to do with a spell."

"You doubted my plan?" He added a tone of mock shock to his voice.

"Actually, no," she said. She tapped her temple. "Considering what you've got going on up here, I'm not inclined to doubt you. Not about alchemy being the way to go, anyway."

"Then what?"

"Is Ferrante going to help us? Back in Los Angeles, I had the impression you two had a falling out, and—"

"He'll help us." He spoke firmly, intending to stop the conversation in its tracks. Petra, however, didn't take the hint.

"How can you be so sure?"

He wanted to drop it. To smother her with platitudes

and end the conversation right there. But she deserved to know whom they were searching for—and why their one, best hope might tell them to take a flying leap. "I'm not sure," he finally said. "But as far as I know—as far as anyone knows—Ferrante is the only one who ever achieved one of alchemy's ultimate goals."

"Immortality."

Nick nodded. "And with immortality comes the concept of the universal panacea."

"A cure for anything. So either he's got a formula that will cure me—"

"Or he has the expertise to find a way."

"And you worked with him?" she asked.

"He was my mentor for many years."

"And then something bad happened," she said, leaning forward, obviously interested in his story. "And you haven't talked to him in hundreds of years."

"That is a very accurate summation."

"So what happened?"

Nick closed his eyes, fighting the pain of those memories, the horrors of the past rising up to taunt him. He'd never spoken of it to anyone, not even to Lissa.

"It's okay, you know," she said, sounding both reassuring and matter-of-fact. "We're in this together, right? And think about who you're talking to. As bad shit goes, I'm a walking worst-case scenario."

"I betrayed him," Nick said, surprising himself with the words. "I betrayed him in the most horrible of ways."

She looked at him, and he was certain she was looking at the vampire, not the man, and at the daemon inside. "How?"

"It doesn't matter."

"If this guy's going to blow us away with a shotgun if we even get near him, then, yeah, I think it matters. You said 'everything,' and 'everything' isn't just me, me, me. It matters."

"The why of it doesn't," Nick insisted. "But yes, it's quite likely that he will be less than thrilled to see me. He should have no reason, however, to harm you."

She pressed her lips together, and he braced himself for an argument. "Why Paris?" she asked, the question taking him by surprise.

"I'm sorry?"

"You betrayed the guy, and then you two parted ways. How do you know he's in Paris? Alliance connections? Have you been keeping tabs?"

"He stays under the radar, actually, though I'm sure the Alliance could find him if need be."

"Then how?"

"He remains human, and he lives in the human world. But he's immortal, and so must reinvent himself every generation or so."

"Right. Fake death. New name. What of it?"

"A few centuries ago, I sought him out."

"Yeah? Why?"

"I wanted to apologize for the past, and to see if we could make amends." He realized how stiffly he was sitting, and forced himself to relax.

"Why then?" she asked, and he was struck once again by how perceptive she was. Because that was the crux of the matter, wasn't it? Why then, indeed.

"Nicholas?"

"Because I understood then how it felt to be betrayed." To have someone he trusted turn on him. To have someone he loved destroy so much that was sacred to him. He'd understood . . . and he'd hated himself all the more for the deep loss that must have accompanied the horror he'd brought upon Ferrante.

"Someone betrayed you," she said, her voice low. "So you found Ferrante?" she asked, and he was grateful that she didn't ask about the nature of the betrayal. "How?"

"He had traveled, remaking himself in various countries, but in every place he would make himself available for certain humans."

"Alchemists?"

"No. Once he discovered the secret, I don't believe he wanted to share."

"Who, then?"

"Sorcerers," Nick said. "Humans who practiced black magic. They would come to him seeking help with spells or concoctions. He would guide them, help them find rare ingredients, that kind of thing."

"How do you know all of this?"

"My connections are varied and broad, both in and out of the shadow world. As a PI, surely you can appreciate that."

"You keep your finger on the pulse," she said. "Got it."

"I asked the right questions, met the right people, and learned the protocol for getting in touch with him."

"Which was?"

"A chalk mark upon his tomb in le Cimetière de Passy."

"His tomb?"

"As you can imagine, he has died many times."

"So you make a mark and then come back the next day to pick up a message about where to meet him."

"Exactly."

"Very James Bond. Did it work?"

"To an extent. He saw the mark. He responded."

"He said no." Her voice lay flat and heavy.

"Essentially, yes. I went to the meeting place, and he didn't show."

"He was watching, and when he saw it was you, he blew you off."

Nick didn't bother acknowledging the truth of what she said.

"So what makes you think he won't say no again? Assuming he's even still in Paris and checking that tomb."

He considered the value of presenting himself as the optimist, and knew that she would see right through it. "To be honest, I hope that he will be intrigued by your presence with me. Either because you're a beautiful woman, or because the stories of who you are and what you've escaped from have not only reached him, but interested him."

"In other words, we're going to follow some set of instructions we pick up off a grave, and then stand stupidly around some Parisian corner while an immortal alchemist checks us out and decides if he wants to give us the keys to his clubhouse?"

"That would be a fair summation, yes."

"Dangerous," she said, eyeing him with narrowed eyes, as if daring him to disagree. "We're fugitives, remember? What if he's hooked up with the Alliance?"

"I think it's worth the risk." He hesitated, and then,

because he truly wanted her opinion, asked, "Do you agree?"

"Yeah," she said. "I guess I do. But keep your spidey sense turned on, you know. Just in case."

"I'll be wary of even the slightest tingle," he said, but his mind wasn't on his words. Instead, it was on the girl.

"Hey, did I lose you?"

He shifted, and realized that time had passed, and that he'd been watching her, thinking about her cleverness and her instinct for self-preservation. He stood abruptly, driven by the need to be alone and clear his head. "You should get some rest," he said.

Her brows lifted. "Wow. That was out of the blue."

"I intend for us to use all of the night. With your human constitution—"

"So now you're handling me? Great. I'm not that fragile, you know."

"You really don't like anyone taking care of you, do you?"

She looked at him hard. "You're not really interested in taking care of me. You just want to find a cure for your friend."

And with that she pushed her seat back and closed her eyes, leaving him to face the unexpected fact that although her words would have been true when they had started this journey, he couldn't deny that things had changed.

And that was one hell of a remarkable thing.

CHAPTER 14

"Something's going on with Serge."

Lissa snapped her head up as Rand walked into the conference room, his notebook computer open in his hands. "What? What is it?"

He lifted the computer, as if words weren't an adequate answer and he had to show her. He set the thing down in front of her, then stood behind her so that when he bent to put his hands on the keyboard, his chest pressed against her back. She closed her eyes, comforted by the feel of him against her. Everything was going to hell around them—Serge a monster, Sara arrested, Nicholas and Petra on the run—but no matter how horrible it got, she knew she could find comfort in Rand's arms, and she was grateful for that every day.

"See?" he said, tapping the screen. He'd opened the monitoring program and was running the video feed from about half an hour prior. She watched, heartsick, as Serge stormed about in the cell, clawing at the concrete wall and banging on the glass. The walls were littered now with nonsense words written in his own blood, and over and over again the number three, scrawled on the wall with no apparent context.

He loped and ran and slammed and raged throughout the small space, everything about him screaming violence.

The way he moved, the way his eyes flashed, the way he ripped into the food that was lowered into his cell, not the least bit affected by the sedatives hidden in the meat.

"What am I looking for?" Lissa asked.

"Coming up," Rand said, as they both watched Serge stand in front of the insanely thick glass wall and beat his palms upon it. The volume on the computer was turned most of the way down, but still Lissa could hear Serge's animalistic wails, and they ripped straight through her heart.

"Do we have to watch? It's so—"

"*Here.*" He pointed at the screen, and Lissa sucked in a breath. The camera had caught Serge in the middle of a horrific frenzy, beating at walls, ripping apart the carcass that was the remains of his lunch. He was wild and angry, and then, suddenly, he wasn't.

He simply went still and stood there, motionless, in the middle of the cell. A moment passed, then another, and he looked down at his body, then held his hands out in front of him.

And then, through the speakers, Lissa heard the coarse, whispered voice asking, "What the hell?"

"He's okay?" She squeezed Rand's hand. "Oh my God, Rand, he's okay."

She started to stand, wanting to run to the cell and see in person what she couldn't quite get her mind to believe, but Rand's strong hand on her shoulder held her down. "Wait," he said. "And watch."

On the screen, Serge stood for another beat, his expression baffled. And then, as quickly as it had come, the humanity disappeared. Serge tossed his head back and wailed—a gut-wrenching sound that ripped a sob from Lissa's throat as well—before he went back to battering the cell, slamming against the cement walls, pounding on the glass, and then lifting his eyes and snarling straight into the camera.

"What happened?" she asked. "Why did he change like that? He looked himself again, and then . . . oh dear God . . ."

"I don't know. Something, but—I don't know." Rand shut the laptop, cutting the sound and erasing the image, but even so, she could still see the pictures clearly in her mind. The Serge-creature thrashing wildly.

The creature with pure evil in its eyes.

Evil, and dark, raw power. *Real* power. It coursed through the creature. Filling it. Fueling it.

So potent that its touch alone left a hand-shaped imprint etched in the glass.

The glass was thinner now. Weaker.

Soon, the monster thought, with rare clarity.

Soon it would be free.

◆

"Your report?"

Tariq sat across from his uncle, Tiberius, and the para-daemon Trylag. A triumvirate of power, and he forced his chin up high and his eyes to meet each man's. This was an opportunity to prove himself, and he knew it. He wasn't going to fuck it up.

"Sara Constantine's in custody, as you know, but we

don't have any indication that she knows where Nicholas and the girl have gone." He focused his attention on Tiberius. "Division's being uncooperative about allowing us to use a Truth Teller, but if you could push on that, we might learn something new."

"I doubt Constantine knows," Tiberius said. "I know Nicholas well. He would not be so clumsy as to leave bread crumbs."

"I agree," Tariq said. "But we will still pursue the lead."

"Not our priority, I hope," Trylag said. "If Constantine is most likely a dead end, I don't care to see us wasting time arguing with Division about the appropriateness of a Truth Teller."

Tariq nodded, feeling more on the spot than was comfortable. "Right. Of course. And Constantine is not our primary concern." He cleared his throat. "I've ordered multiple teams into the field. I have agents searching Montegue's known residences, monitoring cellular communications, observing Montegue's associates, the works. I have teams in other cities ready to move at a moment's notice, as well. But none of that reflects our primary plan of attack."

"And what is that?" Tiberius asked.

"The girl's brother," Tariq said. "Our observation has led us to believe that he has the ability to locate her. Some spell most likely, though possibly related to the fact that they're twins. The reason is irrelevant at this point. What's important is that if we follow the brother, we'll find the girl."

"Then you are following him, I assume?" his uncle asked.

"We are," Tariq said, sitting up straight. "I'm personally leading that team. At the moment, the brother is asleep. Passed out, actually. The universal counterbalance. He pumped out a lot of magic getting across town to his sister's earlier location."

"Where you missed her, if I read your report correctly," Trylag said.

Tariq forced himself not to ball his hands into fists. "That is accurate. We were not aware of his ability at the time. We expected the sister would be coming to him, not the other way around. But as a result of that failed mission objective, we gained valuable intelligence. Follow the brother, we find the girl."

"When will he be on the move again?" Tiberius demanded.

"I can't be certain, but we believe it will be a while before he has the energy to go after her. In the meantime, my team members Elric and Vale continue to monitor his home. They'll contact me if anything pops."

"Good." His uncle nodded with approval, and relief surged through Tariq. "In the meantime, what else have you learned?"

They were seated at a corner booth in a bar overflowing with humans. Tiberius and Trylag passed easily, but Dirque and Tariq had tossed up glamours—the power of illusion wielded by even the youngest and weakest of the jinn—to hide their unusual eyes and the inhuman pallor of their skin. The glamours layered their conversation, too, so that to other customers, the shadowers appeared to be businessmen discussing nothing so interesting that it required even a second thought.

Dirque had dragged the group to the bar, ignoring Tariq's protests that the high examiner's temporary office at Division was a secure location. Then again, there was a reason Dirque was the Alliance chairman. The man took nothing for granted, accepted nothing as fact, and questioned every convenience or bit of good luck.

It had kept him alive for centuries, and it was an approach to life that Tariq tried to emulate. Tried, but often failed. His impetuousness had kept him tied to RAC as a team leader instead of moving up to commander or even transferring to a position with the Alliance itself.

Now, though, he had an opportunity to prove himself to his uncle. And his uncle was able to get Tariq a position pretty much anywhere he wanted.

So, yeah, if Dirque wanted to drag him to some human-infested bar, then Tariq was all over that plan.

A waitress in a white shirt and skintight black pants sidled up to the booth. "Lawyers, right?"

"How did you guess?" Dirque said, his voice as smooth as shark skin.

She grinned at him, but her focus was on Tariq, who smiled up at her, the kind of smile that he knew women liked. "You have that sharp, deadly look," she said.

"Sweetheart, you don't know the half of it." Just for fun, Tariq let the illusion drop from his face. No more than a split second, but it was enough for her to see his yellow eyes and diamond-shaped pupils. Enough for her mind to register that these men weren't lawyers. For that matter, they weren't human.

Or maybe her eyes were just playing tricks on her.

She took a step backward, looking at the four of them as she fumbled for her notepad. "Sorry. I—it's been a long shift."

"We understand," Trylag said. "Scotch," he said. "Neat is fine. He'll have the same."

She nodded, then turned as if she couldn't get out of there fast enough. Tariq hid a smile . . . which faded as he met his uncle's eyes.

Dirque leaned back his huge body, putting a strain on the booth's bench that only Tariq could see. "Well?"

Tariq cleared his throat and looked at the three men. "I've been thinking about why Montegue would risk rescuing that human, and I can't come up with a damn thing. Not unless we alter our premises."

"What premises are those?"

"What if Sergius isn't dead?" Tariq asked.

Tiberius cocked his head and Dirque leaned forward. "Go on."

"I'm just wondering if the fire was faked. There was never a body, just DNA. Granted, Sergius is a vamp, but I'm still dubious."

"We've seen this type of monster before," Trylag said. "It tears a path across the earth. If Sergius were alive, we would have heard of it. Hell, the destruction would be the lead story on every human news channel."

"Unless he was captured. Unless he's being held. Montegue was with him right after the change, isn't that so? And Lucius Dragos was there, too. I think it is reasonable to assume the two of them would do whatever is necessary to protect their friend."

"You think they somehow subdued the monster, and now they hold him captive as they search for a cure?"

"No," Tiberius said. "Dragos is my closest confidant. Montegue is my personal advocate. I would know."

Dirque looked at him. "Would you? Then perhaps you do."

The vampire's face grew hard and his eyes darkened. Otherwise, he didn't move, but nonetheless Tariq could sense the daemon rising. "Do you accuse me?"

"I say nothing," Dirque said. "I'm merely playing with the hypothesis my nephew has raised, as I assumed you were doing." He smiled, so cold and menacing that even Tariq, who couldn't give a shit about Tiberius, had to stifle a shiver. "If Sergius is alive, and you speak the truth that you were not told, that says something itself, don't you think? Either you're lying to us, or the bond between you and those highest among your ranks is fraying. More's the pity."

Trylag looked at the other two. "*Enough*. Now is not the time. Our goal is to terminate the girl. Once we do that, it will not matter if Sergius is alive. Upon her death, he will be restored."

"Trylag speaks the truth," Dirque said. He turned to Tariq. "Go back to your team. Continue your surveillance. Direct your subordinates as you have been doing. With luck, you will be on the move soon. With even more luck, your efforts will not even be necessary."

Something sharp like fear cut through Tariq. "What do you mean?"

"Things have been set in motion," Dirque said. "High-level things."

Tariq sat up straighter. "Sir, it is my job to—"

Dirque cut him off with a hard swipe of his hand. "We are after the same result, nephew. You search for the girl in your own way," he said, and a thin, smug smile stretched across his face. "And I'll seek to destroy her in mine."

CHAPTER 15

"What's going on?" Petra asked, as Nicholas came back from the cockpit where he'd answered a radio call from Rand.

He didn't answer right away, but nodded to Pyre, silently signaling for the weren to return to the front and take the controls off autopilot.

"Rand thinks our injured friend might be recovering," Nicholas said once Pyre was gone.

"Why?"

"Apparently there was a moment when our boy was himself again. Said he could see it in his eyes, his posture, everything. Rand said it was as plain as day."

Ripples of cold understanding flooded her. "But?"

Nicholas cocked his head as he looked at her, as if wondering why she was so damn certain that there was a "but" coming. "But then it passed," he said. "The moment passed and he was . . . ill again." He studied her. "But you already knew that."

She nodded, miserable. Of course she knew it. She'd died—sort of—and Serge had been cured, at least for a moment. But then she'd come alive again, and that meant he'd been cursed again, too.

But there was more than just that; something bubbling inside her. An insidious awareness that she'd been avoiding, but now had to examine. "I think he's getting worse," she said. "Not better."

He took a step toward her. "How the hell do you know that?"

She had to push the words out past the fear. "I'm not sure, but I think I can feel him."

"You *think* you can feel him?"

"That shivery feeling I told you about. It's . . . I don't know . . . *dark*. But it's so subtle. I'm not even certain that's what I'm feeling. I mean, how can I know for sure? It's not like one of them has ever stayed alive this long. It's not like I've got experience in empathizing with monsters. And you know what? I don't like it. Not one little bit," she added, and took some relief from the compassion she saw on Nicholas's face.

"No," he said. "I don't like it, either." He rubbed his temples. "Perhaps this can work to our benefit."

"How?"

"I don't know. But it's something new in the mix. A new variable. And no matter what that means, the game has changed slightly. We'll have to wait and see."

She licked her lips. Dear God, she'd created this thing. This monster that was going to burst out and destroy. And, yeah, he was definitely going to burst out. The only real question was when. As Nicholas said, they'd have to wait and see.

She sat still, lost in her thoughts, and as she did, Nicholas stretched his hand out and laid it on the table. Slowly, deliberately, he took a napkin from the table service and spread it over his hand. *Comfort*. He was offering her comfort.

Did he really think she needed it? Did he not understand that she'd taken care of herself her entire life?

She glanced down, and the hand was still there, as if beckoning her. As if tempting her to just try a little and see if she liked the taste of it.

She wasn't going to. Wasn't going to give in. But then her hand was moving, and before she could talk herself out of it, she put her gloved hand on his. More than that, she kept it there.

One beat. Then another.

Then she couldn't take it anymore and she yanked her hand back. She knew he'd write her actions off to fear of the touch, but that wasn't it. Not really.

No, what scared her was the way his touch made her feel. The way want built up inside her when she thought about him.

She'd taste it during a blue moon, that much she promised herself. Anytime else, though? That was thoroughly off limits. Nicholas belonged in a blue moon bubble, and outside of that bubble she simply didn't care.

Right? Right.

She pressed her fingertips to her temple. And she was a goddamned liar.

"Petra?"

She looked up, searching his eyes for something she didn't find, then stood up. His glance skimmed over her, and she turned her head away, not wanting to be the subject of scrutiny. Suddenly just wanting to be left alone.

"Your clothes," he said.

She pulled at her shirt, realizing that one of the rips

revealed the swell of her breast. She tugged the cotton closed, then bent over to grab her backpack. She didn't mean to, but she glanced at him, and saw then what she'd fantasized about only moments earlier. A flash of desire. A hint of heat.

Her cheeks warmed, and she swallowed. "I should change."

"You should."

"And sleep. My head's all muddled."

"Understandable."

"Right." She hugged the pack close to her, covering most of the rips and tears. "I'll just do that."

When she came back—now in a long-sleeved T-shirt, gloves, and fresh jeans—he wasn't in his seat. Probably up front talking to the pilot, but she couldn't ignore the niggle of disappointment. She was so exhausted, though, that she didn't think about it. Just closed her eyes and let herself drift.

She heard him come back, and she waited for him to take the seat opposite her. He didn't, though, and she had to force herself to keep her eyes closed when she heard him sit down across the aisle. She was being absurd. Foolish. And it had to be because she was tired. So tired.

So exhausted from running, from hiding. But she had to keep going.

The monster was chasing her, chasing her, and she couldn't get away.

Soon it would touch her. Would change her.

Soon it would kill. Destroy. Tear.

Blood. Limbs. Walls dripping with blood.

Screams echoing through the air.

And the stench of fresh death, so sweet, so sweet, so unbearably sweet—

"Petra!"

She stirred, the dream pulling her back in, not wanting to let go.

"Petra, dammit!" This time the voice was accompanied by a hard jolt to her chair, and she jerked forward, thrust out of sleep, and found herself looking in Nicholas's concerned face. And she found herself holding Nicholas's hands.

Not completely. Not really. The blanket and her gloves were seeing to that. "Petra?" He was right there, his eyes meeting hers. "Are you okay?" His hand squeezed tight.

She wanted to scream that she wasn't. That this nightmare had been different. Like she'd been in Serge's head. Like she'd been seeing what he craved.

She wanted to pull him close and let him comfort her, but she couldn't. She had to stay alone, and he just didn't seem to get that. Him, with all his science and studies, just didn't get that if she wasn't careful, people ended up dead. Or worse.

"Petra, dammit, talk to me. Is it Serge? Do you feel him again?"

"I don't know. Maybe. It was . . . brutal. Blood. Images of killing. Nothing specific. Just horrible." She looked up and met his eyes. "But maybe it was just a regular, old-fashioned nightmare. I have them all the time." All her life. Almost every night. And every night there was no one to hold her or comfort her.

She'd be a fool to think she could start finding comfort now. She wasn't a fool, though, and no matter how much she might want his soft words, she knew better than to open that door any wider than the crack they'd already managed.

She took a breath, then pushed the words out, speech coming harder than it ever had before. "Please. I just want to be alone."

She probably wouldn't have noticed the way he flinched if she hadn't been watching him so closely. But he did, and he pulled his hand off hers, the blanket remaining warm from his touch. "Of course," he said, then stood up. "No problem."

He didn't look at her as he walked across the aisle and took his seat again.

She shifted, moving automatically to stand and follow, then stopped herself. She'd meant to push him away, and it had worked.

Slowly, deliberately, she tugged the blanket up around her shoulders and turned to look out the window and into the night. It was better this way. She didn't need anyone else. Didn't need his hollow comfort. She'd always taken care of herself. Even with Kiril at her side, that was the way it had always been. There was no other way it could be. There were no hands to hold, no hugs to steal, no shoulders to cry on.

In the end, she had no one to rely on but herself.

◆

With precise, calculated movements, Nick moved away from Petra's chair. He stopped by the bar on his way back to his seat, helping himself to two small bottles of scotch and a glass. He didn't bother with the ice. He sat, unscrewed the first, then poured.

He downed it easily, frustrated when the burn in his throat did nothing to soothe the wounds her coldness had inflicted.

He shouldn't care. Goddamn it all, he shouldn't care at all.

He closed his eyes and gripped the edge of the table, as if the physical act could force control into his limbs. He didn't need to like the girl. Didn't need to talk with her or do a damn thing with her.

All he needed to do was use her, save Serge, and then be on his fucking way.

He poured the second bottle, then shook his head as a deep loneliness overcame him.

Shit.

He wasn't even thinking his own goddamn thoughts.

All this anger and loneliness . . . well, he had to own up to some of it, but most of it was her. And because he'd given her his blood, the pain in her heart now coursed through his veins.

Loneliness, anger, fear.

And not fear of Nick, or of Serge, or even of being on the run.

No, what Petra feared was exposure. She wanted the world to see a woman who needed no one other than herself, and anyone who got even a peek at the truth deserved a slap across the face.

He sighed, his irritation fading slowly, as her emotions bubbled inside him. Not just exposure, he realized. No, she'd pushed him away for another reason, too. *Desire.*

He closed his eyes, letting the warmth of that emotion flow over him, knowing she would be mortified if she realized he could feel her desire, and yet also realizing that had he simply opened his eyes he could have seen it as plain as day, no blood connection necessary. The flush on her cheeks. Her arousal in the mist. Emotions that were new and overwhelming, heady and exciting.

New.

He turned the word over in his mind, realizing the ramifications. She was untouched. Despite the blue moons that must have filled the sky in her adult years, she had not yet been with a man. He was certain of it, and that certainty both intrigued and saddened him. Twenty-six years she'd walked this earth, her body wanting, and yet remaining untouched.

How many years had it been since he'd lain with such a woman? Too many to count, and he imagined what it would be like to pull her close and stroke skin that had never been stroked. Kiss flesh that had never been kissed.

He wanted to take away the pain of that loneliness, and the depth of that want troubled him. He didn't usually empathize with his clients quite so much, but he had to admit that her situation was unique. Not to mention they were stuck together for the duration.

And, of course, he hadn't gotten laid in a very long time.

So was it any wonder he was thinking about touching that smooth skin he'd only glimpsed, so provocative beneath the rips in her shirt?

No, no wonder at all.

But there wasn't a damn thing he could do about it.

He lifted the glass, but the liquid was gone; he'd drunk it without even realizing. Fuck. He stood, and though he didn't intend to turn around, he found himself glancing backward at Petra. She was snuggled deep into her blanket, breathing softly.

The nightmares, at least, had abated.

He took a step toward the front of the plane. Damn, but he needed another drink.

At the service area, he paused. Through the closed door, he could hear Pyre talking into the radio. He didn't know the weren, but right then company sounded better than a drink.

He turned the knob and pushed the door open, then stepped in, facing the pilot's back.

"We'll be over the Atlantic in less than ten. A few hundred miles should dump us straight in the middle of nowhere."

He frowned, now on alert—but it was too damn late.

In the split second it took for him to realize something was wrong, Pyre had pulled a gun and nailed him with a bullet.

And not just any bullet, Nick realized, as he staggered backward, strength flowing out of him like water.

Hematite.

CHAPTER 16

Petra burst awake as the plane banked sharply to the left as a gunshot rang out in the small cabin.

She dove sideways into the aisle, and when she looked up, she saw Pyre holding a gun in one hand and a parachute in the other, pushing himself unsteadily from where he'd apparently fallen against the wall.

Behind him, Nicholas stumbled, his face contorted in anger, his fangs bared and chest bloody. But he managed to catch the guy around the legs and jerk him down hard.

The parachute was knocked out of his hands with a thump, and the gun went skittering, but Pyre didn't slow down at all. He kicked back, catching Nicholas in the face, then scrabbled forward, rising from the floor even as he grabbed the chute again and moved with exceptional speed—not toward her, but toward the emergency exit door only a few feet from Nicholas.

Holy shit. *He'd tried to kill her. He'd done a number on Nicholas. And now he was going to leap to freedom and leave her and Nicholas in an out-of-control plane.*

Fuck that.

She stumbled to her knees, trying to get to her feet as the plane pitched wildly.

She wasn't fast enough. In one quick movement, Pyre

yanked the handle. The door popped off, flying away as it was caught by the wind—the resulting vacuum sucking Nicholas out into the black night as well.

She heard a scream, and realized it came from her.

Terrified, she grabbed on to the metal legs of the table, the pitch-black sky looming like a void of terror.

Except she couldn't hold on. The werewolf slammed his shoes against her fingers, and before she knew what was happening, she was drawn through the air toward the dark maw that opened onto nothing but the air at thirty thousand dizzying feet.

"Noooo!" Her scream ripped from her throat, and she reached out, grappling for the werewolf, catching him with her gloved hand.

He jerked, trying to free himself, but she held on.

She wasn't going down alone.

They'd made her a victim, but she wasn't. Not really.

No, she was a weapon, and she would damn well— *damn well*—defend herself.

And with a final burst of strength, she tightened her grip and forced herself closer, her lips aiming for his cheek.

That was all it took.

One brush of flesh against flesh, and the curse shot through him, making his body tremble and the parachute fall from his hands. And the raw energy of the werewolf's change was so powerful that it knocked her free—and sent her tumbling out into the night, and into the arms of death.

◆

Even as he was sucked from the plane, Nick was grappling at the wound in his chest, his slick fingers trying desperately to obtain purchase on the hematite slug now jammed between two ribs, lodged so firmly that he couldn't get a sufficient grip to pull it out.

A freefall to the earth from a plane took about three minutes, which was too close for comfort, especially considering that his slippery fingers weren't giving him much cooperation.

Above him, he saw Petra burst out from the plane, her scream ripping through the sky.

Fuck it. As long as he could avoid sunlight, he'd survive a fall to the earth. Petra would not.

He grabbed the flesh of his chest and pulled, gritting his teeth from the pain of flaying his own skin and muscle until he had revealed the very white of his bones.

Using his fingers as a lever, he pried his ribs apart, his fingers straining to keep the gap open as he hooked his index finger into the cavity, probing and then—*yes*—pulling out the slug, now smashed almost flat from the impact with his flesh and bones.

He dropped it into the night, then focused his attention on getting to the girl.

Weak from loss of blood, the transformation wasn't easy. But with effort, he managed, shifting his body into the form of an eagle. He spread his wings, and with keen eyes, he searched the sky, finding her above him, her body spread wide to slow her fall.

Clever girl, he thought, but his pleasure was short-lived as he saw what was above her—the plane itself, turning sharply, the steel hull so overwhelmed by veloc-

ity and gravity that it would soon spin out of control—
with a trajectory that would surely intersect Petra.

With a mighty flap of wings, he burst forward as the
inevitable roll began and the plane started to tumble
from the sky. The engines whined in protest, and he
could see that Petra heard, even through the rush of air
past her ears. She shifted, turning her head so that she
could look up.

Nick heard her sharp intake of breath, and expected
to immediately sense her panic.

It didn't come.

Instead, she knifed her body, increasing her angle
toward the earth, her speed increasing as she sliced
through the air.

It was a gutsy, brilliant maneuver, and one with
which he wouldn't have credited many humans.

Too bad it wasn't going to work.

The plane's descent was too rapid and her trajectory
too steep with no time for correction.

Nick was her only hope, and he still had distance to
cover.

Faster he moved, his avian body cutting through air
now disturbed by the mass of the falling plane.

He fought the wind it generated, frantically cutting a
path to Petra, the steel beast getting closer and closer
until he had only seconds to maneuver. But she was right
there, so close, and he reached out, gripping the back of
her shirt tight with his eagle's claws. And then, with her
squeak of surprise muffled by the whoosh of air from
the plane, he forced his wings to give one final, mighty
flap before dropping them both into a controlled, angled
dive.

Behind them—missing them by only inches—the plane fell through the sky. He extended his wings wide, flapping hard to fight the wake that was trying so desperately to pull them to the ground as well.

And then, so quickly that the horror seemed like a bad dream, the air was calm again, and thousands of feet below them the plane continued to fall, faster and faster until it impacted the earth and the fuel tanks ignited into a fiery ball, the heat waves from which once again rippled the air around them.

He couldn't continue to hold her like this, but shifting into mist was dangerous, too. She was weak from multiple transformations into mist, and he was weak from the hematite and from giving her his blood. He would need to feed soon—hell, just being near a human was making his fangs tingle with need. But feeding off Petra was not an option, not even were she willing.

Nourishment was a problem for later, though. Right now, he had to try to hope for the best.

He pushed through, urging his cells to transform. The change didn't come easy, and he could feel her molecules protesting—but it did come, and right then, that was all that mattered.

She was mist now, as he was. He let his consciousness twine close around her, telling himself he wished to keep her tight against him, fearful that in their weakened state they could become separated even as sentient mist. But even as he told himself that, he knew it was a lie.

In truth, he wanted a moment of intimacy with this remarkable human. This woman who kept her head when she was thrown from a plane. This woman who now twined her consciousness with his, who was generating a heat and a longing that matched his own. He'd given her his blood and now, even more than before, he could feel her essence in the mist, her consciousness aware despite her humanity. An unexpected reality that stemmed from either her curse or her magical bloodline. But right then he didn't care, because right then it was desire that was rippling through her, rising and filling as he moved with purpose through and around her, his mind touching her, stroking her, imagining hot flesh and warm blood and soft lips upon skin.

The need for contact throbbed inside him even as he sensed it growing in her. A wondrous awareness and longing for more. So much more, and he wished he could give it to her. Wished he could transform into himself and strip her naked in the air. Wished he could take her in freefall, the chill of rushing air cooling the heat they generated until they both exploded in a fiery climax that would leave them both desperately satisfied and yet aching for more.

It was not to be—in the mist there could be only passion, but not satisfaction. And, dammit, right then he needed to focus on getting them safely on the ground, not making the journey there as explosive as possible.

With regret, he shifted his energy, feeling her essence protest as he mentally pulled back. They were closer now, the earth rising up to meet them, and he put on the brakes, slowing as the high-rises of Manhattan filled his mind's eyes.

Around them, the air shimmered as the night began to dissipate, the eastern sun poised to slip above the horizon. He'd not experienced a sunrise or sunset for hundreds of years, and he would not enjoy this one, either. Not and survive. But somehow, what had never troubled him before bothered him now. For he would have liked to have stood with Petra in his arms and felt the sun warm their faces.

The streets of the city were wide now, so close that the vision of his mind could read the street signs. He found a set of stairs leading to a subway tunnel and slid in, taking refuge from the sun in the darkness of the realm of the underworld.

Even at this early hour, the station was crowded, and they twined around and among the throng of humans, some of whom moved, almost as if aware that he and Petra were there. Some saw the mist, some wondered, their question "What is that?" following as he sped toward the tracks and finally down deep into the tunnels themselves.

Safe in the dark, he shifted back, pushing Petra away with reluctance as they changed back, taking care not to touch.

Her skin was pale, her eyes cloudy, and he feared that he had done her harm.

"Are you okay?"

She nodded. "I knew you'd catch me."

He couldn't help his smile. "Did you?"

She grinned in return, but he saw a hardness in her eyes. "I changed him," she said, her expression defiant, as if she anticipated his protests. "I did it on purpose and I don't regret it."

"Good."

Her eyes widened slightly, and then, slowly, she smiled. "So who arranged this? Gunnolf?"

"Most likely." He forced his daemon down as anger

swelled. "Pyre could have been acting on his own, but I doubt it."

"Rand?"

He could see from her face that the possibility that Rand had been in on the treachery disturbed her as much as it did him.

"I hope the hell not." He drew in a breath. "Forget it. I'll call Luke and leave the matter to him."

"Call? Do you think a cell phone is a good idea?"

"As soon as we hid Serge away, we started using disposables. It's safe."

"Okay."

"Don't worry," he said, looking at her face. "We'll find the truth about who betrayed us, but right now we have bigger problems."

"Right. Of course." She frowned. "Where are we?"

"Manhattan. The subway tunnels. It's almost sunrise."

"Oh."

"You're weak. You need to rest."

She glanced around at the tunnels in which so many of the city's homeless lived, at the filthy ground littered with everything from plastic wrappers to dead rats to human excrement. "Great."

"I have someplace else in mind. It's not far. Can you walk?"

"I think so. Where are we going?"

He met her eyes, knowing that she would appreciate the irony. "Serge's apartment," he said, then turned to lead the way.

CHAPTER 17

◊ "Holy shit," Petra said as they stepped into the glass-walled penthouse. "Are you trying to kill yourself?"

In front of them, the sun was rising over Manhattan, a city that Petra had never seen but had always wanted to visit. Considering the millions of people crammed onto a tiny island, however, it was also a place that had long ago been checked off her list. Too crowded. Too many possibilities for accidental touching.

Now that she was here, the thrill of seeing the vibrant metropolis spread out like a picture postcard in front of her was tempered by the fact that Nicholas was standing in front of a wall of windows, and any second now a ray of sunshine was going to hit him dead on. The *dead* part being literal, considering he'd dissolve into a pile of ash immediately.

A prospect that troubled her on a number of levels, none of which she wanted to examine closely.

She hurried to the window and grabbed the cord to close the curtain, then groaned in frustration when the cord had no effect.

"Nicholas!" she repeated. "Dammit, move!"

The terror in her voice must have finally gotten through to him, because he turned to her, his expression so satisfied she feared he'd lost his mind and really was suicidal. "Come stand by me."

"Dammit, you are not doing this." Even as she spoke, she knew she should keep her mouth shut. He wanted to cure Serge, after all. And that meant her death.

Sooner or later, she was going to have to slip away from Nicholas. She was going to have to strike out on her own, with only her wits and, perhaps, her brother to help her avoid the wrath of the Alliance. It would be one hell of a lot easier to get away from the vampire if he were dust.

But she couldn't wish that on him. Even had he not saved her life multiple times, she couldn't bear the thought of knowing that Nicholas Montegue was no longer of this earth.

No, letting him turn to dust was unacceptable. When she left, she'd do so with him still alive—and undoubtedly pissed off—behind her.

He'd called her over, and now she was standing in front of him, her back to the window, her body trying to shield his. She was even on tiptoes, wishing she were a few inches taller so that her shadow could better protect his head.

She was swaying a bit, like an awkward dancer trying to follow a lead, when she realized he was fighting an amused grin.

She glared at him, and he lost the fight, chuckling as he asked her what the hell she thought she was doing.

"Saving your ass," she said curtly. "Though I'm not entirely sure why I'm bothering."

"Nor I." He nodded to the windows. "Serge invented the glass. And although I have always been dubious, fearing that someday I would come to this apartment and find nothing more of my friend than a pile of dust on the floor, I confess that for years I've been jealous of his ability to watch the sunrise."

"I thought you were Mr. Scientist. Why didn't you invent the Wonder Glass?"

"I'm certain I could have."

"This is your first time? How long have you and Serge been friends?"

"A long, long time."

"Son of a bitch," she said, cocking her head to study him. "You didn't invent it—you didn't even come visit Serge for a sunrise breakfast—because vampires aren't supposed to see the sun. Somehow you didn't strike me as a guy who put that much stock in convention."

"Maybe that's why I'm going to watch today," he said. "Turn around and enjoy Mother Nature's show with me."

She stood beside him, their bodies close but not touching, and she tried to watch the sun with a vampire's eyes. In a way, she supposed she understood how he felt. He couldn't bask in the sun. She couldn't touch another human. Of course, she wasn't trapped in the darkness, wasn't bound by the need for blood. And although these thoughts didn't lessen her certainty that she definitely had the crappier end of the deal, she did feel a tug of camaraderie with him. Something she'd never felt before, not even with Kiril, who had always set himself up as her superior—her protector and salvation—even more than as her brother or her twin.

She remembered the way she'd felt in the sky—not while they were falling, but once he'd caught her and changed her and twined his essence with her. *Desire.* At her side, her fingers twitched, and she clenched her hand against the urge to reach for him. She couldn't, of course, but right then the barrier tossed up by the curse seemed even more monstrous than ever.

Soon.

The thought bubbled up from deep within her, confusing at first, and then shifting into something tangible—the knowledge of what was coming. The certainty that tonight had been designed for her.

A blue moon.

Something sharp and unfamiliar shot through her, a bolt of desire that left her nipples hard and her sex tingling. It had been years since she'd experienced that desperation that flowed with the moon, and never had she been able to act on it, her brother her only company on that long, lonely night.

But her brother wasn't there now. Nicholas was. And though he hadn't said so, she'd felt his desire when they were mist as surely as she had felt her own.

She would have him. Dear God, she would have this night with him.

Antsy, *horny,* she looked out through the glass and wished the sun were making its trek downward instead of up.

Patience . . . she would have to learn patience.

In front of them, the sun crested a rooftop, sending a sparkling ray straight toward Serge's windows. It hit the glass, coloring Nicholas's face in soft yellow light. He closed his eyes, and drew in a breath, and she was awed by the intensity of the pleasure reflected on his face.

For a moment she envied the sun, because she wanted to do that to him. For once in her life, she wanted to touch a man and see him melt, lost to the power of his own desire.

Tonight. The word swept through her, soft and sensual, promising delicious things to come. She didn't want to wait, but about that, she had no choice. And hadn't she been waiting her whole life? A few more hours would make no difference at all in the grand scheme. On a personal level, though, she'd be a wreck by the time the sun set and the blue moon hung full in the sky.

Beside her, Nicholas sighed, then turned to face her, his eyes taking her in, as if he knew her secrets. She smiled, content with the knowledge that what was in her head was her own.

Of course, a man like Nicholas—both experienced and with vampiric senses—could probably sense her desire. The thought startled her, but it didn't embarrass her. She wanted him. And about that she refused to be ashamed.

She nodded toward the window. "I'm glad you got to see your sunrise. How long has it been?"

"Too long," he said.

She stood beside him, trying to look at the sunrise through his eyes. For a few moments, the silence hung comfortably between them, and she wished that they could stay that way for a while. Together, easy. But nothing was easy right then.

She drew in a breath and turned from warm sunrises to cold practicality. "Are we safe here?"

He indicated the glass. "Apparently so."

"That's not what I mean, and you know it."

"We should be safe," he said. "Serge has protections

on the apartment that should shield them from being able to detect your magic, though as you say, it's minute enough that we might be safe anyway. Perhaps Kiril could find you, but we're thousands of miles away, and even if he—or the Alliance—approaches, there are security monitors planted around the building and breach detectors. We'll have advance warning if we have to run."

"Oh." Somehow that didn't make her feel better. Already she was tired of running. And with tonight's moon, she didn't want to be racing for her life.

He was watching her, his expression gentle. "I think we are safe here, at least for a bit. Try not to worry."

She swallowed, embarrassed he could read so much in her face. "Thanks." She cleared her throat. "I'm sorry about how I acted on the plane," she said. "About being a bitch after my nightmare, I mean."

"No need to apologize. After all, you were upset, and I was trying to provide some small amount of comfort. It makes perfect sense that would disturb you." He grinned, and she laughed.

"I'm a complex individual, Nicholas. Get used to it."

"Most people call me Nick."

"Am I most people?"

His grin stretched wide. "No. You most definitely are not." He tilted his head, his eyes narrowing as a scientist might examine a new specimen. She kept silent, afraid to ask what new thing he saw in her. "It's not a weakness, you know."

"What?"

"You were mad at me because I provided something you were unable to give to yourself. Comfort."

"What are you? Freud the vampire?"

"Nothing so ill conceived, I assure you. But I am observant."

"I like the way you talk, you know. Like every once in a while you forget what century you're in."

"Sometimes, I think I do forget. After so many centuries, you find that time begins to feel as though it's circling back upon itself."

"Can I ask you something?" She spoke before she could stop herself, and once the words were out, she knew she couldn't call them back, though she knew she might be treading on dangerous ground.

"That depends on the question."

"Right." She certainly knew how that went. "It's just that when we were back in Los Angeles . . . the way you were with Lissa, I mean. The way you stood. The way you looked at her. Were you in love with her once? You know. Before."

He didn't say anything for a moment, and she tensed, afraid he would ask her why she cared, and that wasn't a question she could answer because she didn't know herself. All she knew was that she wanted to ask the question.

"I was," he said.

"Are you still?"

"No." That time, the answer came quick and certain, and when he lifted his eyes to look at her there was no hesitation. "I was . . . angry. For a long time. But it's getting better."

"That must have been hard."

He cocked his head, his brow furrowing in question. "What?"

"She was the one, right? The one who betrayed you. The one that made you want to go see Ferrante again."

He took a step back, then ran his hands through his hair. "Are you really this perceptive? Or am I so transparent?"

She shrugged and tried to flash a lighthearted grin. "I have mad PI skills," she said. "Or maybe you're transparent to me."

She saw the laughter flash in his eyes and smiled in return, liking the way that talking to him made her feel. Liking it enough that it made her tongue loose, too, which wasn't good, but she couldn't seem to stop herself. "I've never been in love," she said. "I tell myself I'm lucky, because it means my heart's never been broken." Her smile was crooked. "I'm an expert at lying to myself."

"You are lucky," he said, and she caught a glimpse of the man behind the reputation. The man who went from woman to woman, never staying. Never getting close. "Love is a damn sharp sword." He looked up slowly, then met her eyes. "Desire, however . . ."

He let the thought trail off, then he moved toward the couch, leaving her to analyze his words. To wonder, and to hope. And to look at him hard and notice, for the first time, how pale he was, and how stiff his movements seemed to be. And when he sat, she got a good look at the jacket he'd buttoned quickly after they'd shifted from mist to human. A jacket that was slowly becoming stained with blood.

"Nicholas? What the hell is wrong with your chest?" She hurried to stand in front of him. "The bullet? Why hasn't it healed?"

"It will," he said.

"Open it," she demanded.

He complied, and she gasped in horror at what she saw—a section of his chest exposed to the bone, raw and bloody.

"Holy shit," she said. "What did you—"

"Hematite," he said. "The bullet was hematite."

"But—but you got it out." Her mind was spinning. Of course he got it out. He would have had to in order to transform. But then why was he still so injured? Vampires healed at a remarkable rate. Even a wound that large should have closed by now. "What do you need?" she asked. "What can I do?"

"I need to sleep," he said. "And I need to feed. There is nothing you can do."

The words were like a slap on the face, and she shook her head, then knelt before him, speaking before she'd even had time to think about it. "Yes there is," she said. "You can feed off me."

◊

Nick looked at her, so earnestly there in front of him, and even through the thick sludge of exhaustion, his body responded, tightening with need at the very thought of her offer. An offer that he couldn't accept.

"Are you trying to get rid of me, Petra?" he said with an indulgent smile.

"No, I—" She cocked her head. "Not now. Sleep now. But tonight. When the moon rises. Can I—I mean, will you feed from me tonight?"

"What are you—" And then he remembered. *The blue moon.*

He should say no. He should tell her there were homeless in the tunnels on whom he could feed. Founts he could call—humans who were aware of the existence of vampires and charged a minimal fee, their compensation coming primarily in the form of the thrill of the taking.

Hell, he could even order out for synthetic.

And yet he said none of that. Because the truth was he did want her. He'd had a taste when they'd twined together in the sky, and now he desperately wanted to finish what they'd started. What he'd started.

She was offering her blood, but he would have more than that. He would have the woman, too.

"Are you strong enough?" he asked, tempering his desire.

"I feel good," she said.

"Let me see your skin." He spoke for no prurient purpose—he needed to see the color of her flesh and listen to the pulse of life within her. But as she slowly lifted the T-shirt she wore to expose her flat belly and tanned skin, he couldn't deny the effect that the view had on him. He was tight with need, and suddenly, nightfall seemed much too far away. "We should leave when the sun goes down. We still have a long way to travel."

"No."

He lifted a brow, not used to being contradicted.

"We don't even know how we're getting across the Atlantic yet," she said. "We seem to be safe here, and you need time to think. Time to heal. And I need—"

"Yes?"

Her chin rose defiantly. "I need to do this." He held her gaze for a moment, until she seemed to sag under the weight of it. "You saved my life, Nicholas," she said, softly. "Let me feed you."

"Is that all you wish?" He wanted to hear her say it. Her body was already speaking to him, the blood connection burning between them. But he wanted the words. Hell, he would insist upon them.

"No," she said. "That's not all."

"What else do you want?"

She stayed silent.

"Petra, what else do you want?"

"I want you to touch me." She met his eyes. "I want it badly."

"Good." He could feel her desire crashing against him like waves, stirring his own, making him curse the sun that had not yet even crested in the sky.

"Do you—" She cut herself off, as if the question was too much to ask. As if she feared the answer.

"I do," he said. "But understand this, Petra. That makes it dangerous. I want you, but I need to feed. If I don't stop in time . . ."

"You will," she said, with such certainty that his doubts almost faded. Almost.

"I don't think you fully understand the danger that you acting as a fount can pose."

"I understand more than you think," she said. "And you pose no danger to me."

He almost laughed. "Is that a fact? Why?"

"Because there is something you want even more than me or my blood." She looked at him, her expression defiant. "You rescued me in order to save Serge," she said. "You won't screw all that work up by killing me tonight."

She smiled at him, as if silently begging him to argue. He didn't. "Sleep," she said. "Rest up." Then she flashed a wicked grin before turning on her heel and leaving the room, her last words trailing behind her. "I think you're going to need it."

Nick watched her leave, overwhelmed by the odd and not entirely unwelcome realization that for the first time in a long time he'd truly met his match in a female.

CHAPTER 18

Petra barely slept.

How could she when she knew what the night would bring. A blue moon. That glorious extra full moon that she used to dread so much, the unfulfilled desire to be touched too hard to endure.

Tonight, she didn't have to.

Nicholas had stayed on the sofa in front of the window when she'd gone in search of a bed in which to curl up. Now, she stretched, enjoying the luxury of soft sheets and a firm mattress.

She felt the cool brush of her mother's bracelet moving on her wrist, and reached over to run her fingertips over the smooth stones. She'd lost everything else in the plane crash, but she was grateful she'd put the bracelet on earlier. At least she still had one piece of her past, even if the Bible and her journal were gone. And, of course, she still had her life.

She had Nicholas to thank for that, and the idea that she could thank him properly tonight made her grin like a satisfied cat. She could thank him—and she could save him, too. *She could let him feed.* The thought made her tingle with anticipation, the promise of such intimate contact leaving her breathless with desire.

She'd flirted shamelessly with him that morning, surprised by how easy it was even without the pull of the blue moon. Kiril would be shocked, of course. He'd repeatedly told her that casual sex during the blue moon would not satisfy.

She no longer believed him. This was an itch she wanted scratched, and she couldn't imagine a man more appealing than Nicholas Montegue to scratch it.

And not just because he was so damn good looking. He was, of course. Hell, she could look at him for hours, examining his body like a curator would inspect a fine work of art. But that wasn't what pushed him over the top. No, it was the whole package. The way he looked in a suit coupled with the way his mind clicked. That Hollywood handsome face complemented by a scientist's intellect. And the inherent vampiric danger counterbalanced by a heart that would risk everything to save a friend.

He'd treated her like something precious, and though she had no illusions that she was with him in this condo for any reason other than to benefit Serge, she also knew that he wouldn't use her harshly or take advantage of their intimacy. He had a reputation, after all. As far as first lovers went, she doubted that she could do better than Nicholas Montegue.

She closed her eyes, imagining him touching her, filling her. Flesh upon flesh, so close they were practically one. She'd been there with him already, as mist twined together, not knowing where one ended and the other began. She wanted to finish what they'd started in the sky. She wanted to tremble in his arms. Dear God, how she wanted it.

Had wanted it, in fact, since she'd first realized that

Nicholas would be beside her when the blue moon rose. Maybe even before.

And now, as the sun finally dipped below the horizon and shadows filled the room, the want had given way to need. And that, only for Nicholas.

Slowly, she moved to the edge of the bed, then swung her feet over. She sat there a moment, relishing the change in her. The soft eroticism of air against the fine hairs on her skin. The arousing way her jeans pressed tight against her crotch. Just like every blue moon, she was horny as hell.

This time, she was going to do something about it.

With five gentle tugs, she loosened the fingers of the glove that sheathed her right hand, then followed the same procedure for the left. She toed off her shoes, then bent down to slip off her socks. Slowly, she eased her feet down onto the thick pile carpet, then squeezed the fibers with her toes. She never went without shoes and thick socks—bare feet were just too dangerous—and now the sensation of carpet against her toes was so luxurious she thought she might have to strip off her clothes and lie naked on the floor, the carpet tickling every inch of her.

No.

The clothes were staying on. And for one very particular reason—she wanted Nicholas to be the one who took them off.

And damn if she didn't want that right now.

With single-minded purpose, she left the bedroom, crossing the large condo to where Nicholas sat in the living room, still on the couch, his eyes still closed. At some point he'd gotten up, though, and moved about, because the soiled jacket was nowhere to be seen. He wore no shirt, but he'd wrapped thick gauze over the wound, his pale skin actually seeming dark against the pure white of the bandage.

His eyes were closed. She couldn't tell if he slept. Frankly, she didn't care. Her body was humming now. Her skin sensitive even to the brush of air. She was ready—so ready—and waiting was not an option.

She paused in front of him, wondering if he would open his eyes, but he made no move. She stepped closer, then eased one knee up on the couch beside him.

Still nothing.

Slowly, she grabbed the back of the couch, then swung her leg over and lowered herself until she was sitting astride him, her sex nestled up against his. And that, of course, was how she knew that he was not asleep. She felt his cock harden under the pressure of her weight, and she heard her own soft moan in response to his desire.

"It is a brave woman who sneaks up on a sleeping vampire." His eyes were still closed, but his mouth curved into a smile.

"Not sneaking," she said. "Seducing."

"Is that so?" He looked at her, his eyes dark with desire. His gaze took her in all over, then ended on her face, a question mark reflected in his picture-perfect brow. "The sun has been down for minutes now, and yet you haven't touched me, not flesh upon flesh. Are you afraid the curse still lingers?"

"Maybe a little." There was always a hesitancy during a blue moon. Every time one had come around she'd been terrified to hold Kiril's hand, afraid of losing the one person in all the world who truly belonged with her.

"I won't change," he said. "For tonight, the curse has lifted. You feel it, don't you? Pounding through your blood. In your breasts. Between your legs?" As if to make the point, he slid his hand between their joined bodies, cupping her sex through the tight denim.

"The blood," she said. "You can feel me."

The hand squeezed slightly, and she moaned with rising pleasure. "I can feel you," he confirmed.

"Please," she whispered.

"Please, what?"

"Touch me."

"Soon," he said. "There's power in anticipation."

She wasn't sure if she should laugh or smack him. "I've been anticipating this my entire life."

"Then you know how sweet it is. I've been thinking about your taste all day. Let me taste you, Petra."

"Yes," she whispered, as he lowered his lips to her neck.

She flinched as his fangs punctured her skin, then melted into his embrace as his mouth closed over her flesh and he sucked, drawing the essence of her life into him. She was floating—giving—her body raw with need and desperate for a touch even more intimate than this.

He drank deep, more and more, until reason began to leave her. Until life, too, started to ebb away. She was floating. Gliding. And it felt glorious to be so close to being free—to no longer be trapped in a body that could only harm.

Except tonight there would be no harm. If her life

didn't slip away, this could be a night of touches and sweet caresses.

"Nicholas . . ." Her voice was soft and weak, barely audible even to her own ears.

He pulled her closer, and she gasped with the pleasure of it, the pure, dangerous, erotic pleasure of being taken to the brink.

"Nicholas." Too much, she thought. *Too much.* But the words couldn't come. She couldn't form them. Couldn't force them out past weakened lips.

She could only languish in his arms until suddenly—finally—he thrust her away, pushing her off him as he laid her back on the couch. "Petra, Petra, by the gods, Petra, I'm sorry."

She let her eyes flutter open as his hands stroked her flesh, her body weak, but her mind spinning, overflowing with raw pleasure.

He knelt beside her, the paleness of his skin replaced with the glow of life. "I'm sorry. I should have stopped. I drank too much."

She silenced him with a finger to his lips, a first for her, and one that made her smile, the effort of using those muscles almost exhausting her. "You're healed?"

"Because of you." He began to lift his wrist toward his mouth. "You must drink."

"Not yet." She closed her fingers over his wrist. "Show me." Her fingers fumbled for the bandage. He reached up, helped her to remove it. The skin beneath the bandage had knitted back together, healthy and strong, with not even the slightest of imperfections. With awe, she traced her fingertip over his chest. "I did this?"

"You did."

"I saved you," she said, then stretched lazily, feeling a power within her despite the weakness.

His grin was intoxicating. "So you did."

She propped herself up on her elbows. "It was only fair, you know. You've saved me countless times."

"Actually only three. So far."

"So far," she agreed, then matched his grin.

His fingers stroked her hair, then brushed her cheek. "You're weak, Petra. Will you drink from me? Just like before. Not enough to change you. Only enough to make you strong. Tonight, I would have you strong."

She met his eyes, saw the tenderness there, along with a desire so sharp she feared it would cut her to ribbons. "Yes," she said, the word little more than a breath. "I'll drink."

CHAPTER 19

Tariq stood outside Lucius Dragos's Beverly Hills mansion, feeling smug. For the first time, he had Luke's balls in a vise, and he intended to milk this particular situation for all it was worth.

He'd been allowed entrance through the security gate, and now he waited impatiently on the front porch. He rang the bell again, then gave the door a slap with the heel of his hand for good measure. Half a second later, the door swung open, and he found himself staring up at Lucius Dragos's massive form. "We need to talk."

For a moment, Luke simply stood in the doorway, as if taking Tariq's measure. Then Tariq saw the vampire smile, thin and dangerous and dripping with malice. "You imprisoned my wife."

Tariq lifted his chin, forced himself to be calm. "With cause."

"Of course. With cause. Much like the cause I now have to rip your fucking head off."

"Do not threaten me," Tariq said, anger mixing with enough fear to give a hard edge to his voice. "She helped a prisoner escape, and now she's paying the price."

For a long moment, Luke only looked at him, hate hard in those amber eyes. Then, finally, he spoke. "Why are you here?"

"I told you. We need to talk."

"I'm listening."

Tariq hesitated. He might have a firm grip on Luke's balls, but that didn't mean it would be wise to squeeze.

Then again, how often did someone get and keep the upper hand with Lucius Dragos? Not damn often, and Tariq wasn't one to ignore possibilities. "I've been thinking about the situation. Petra Lang's escape. The fact that Montegue helped her—no, don't bother denying it," he added, though Luke had made no move to speak. "And, of course, your mate's involvement."

"That's a lot to be thinking about. I hope you didn't hurt your head."

"Mock me all you want, Dragos, but my eyes are wide open, and what I'm seeing is pretty damn interesting."

"Is that so? What exactly are you seeing?"

"Montegue getting himself in some serious shit, for one thing. And the only reason I can think that Nicholas would go to so much trouble—the only reason I can see that he'd actually drag Sara into his mess—is if he had something huge to gain."

"Indeed?"

"Serge is alive, Luke," he said, looking hard at Luke's face. For any reaction, no matter how small. "Don't even try to tell me otherwise."

"It's an intriguing theory," Luke said, his voice calm, his expression never wavering. "Hard to prove."

"Or maybe not," Tariq said. "I've got Constantine, and we'll get Montegue and the girl soon enough."

"Interesting," Luke said, and now those eyes did change, narrowing as he peered at Tariq. He reached up and rubbed his chin, giving the impression of a man deep in thought. "Yes. Very interesting."

He didn't want to ask, yet he couldn't forestall his own words. "What? My theory?"

Luke laughed. "No, your theory is shit. But you've given me an idea. For that, old friend, I thank you." He stepped back, and without another word, shut the door in Tariq's face.

The jinn stood there, wondering how the hell this encounter could have gone so wrong. He'd come to put the fear of God—or at least the Alliance—into Dragos. But Dragos wasn't scared, not at all.

Instead, he was scheming.

And that, Tariq knew, was never a good thing.

◆

"Drink," Nicholas said, pulling her gently back onto his lap. "Drink deep." He took his fingernail and thrust it into his chest. A drop of blood rose, thick and crimson, and as she clung to him, frozen with both desire and fear, he cupped the back of her head and urged her lips to his skin.

She remembered nothing about the blood she'd taken from him on the plane, the blood that had saved her life. Now it wasn't her life she was concerned about, but the depth of her desire. As soon as she touched him, as soon as her lips brushed his skin and her tongue caught the tang of blood, she was certain that she would be lost.

"Petra . . ." His voice was raw, as if waiting for her touch was torture.

It was.

Unable to stand it any longer, she grazed the tip of her tongue upon the wound, then felt her body quiver with the first hint of blood upon her taste buds.

Nicholas moaned, his head falling back even as his arms pulled her closer, and she needed no more encouragement. She closed her mouth fully over the wound and drew in the sweet taste of him, his vampiric blood buzzing through her, bringing her senses to life and setting her already vulnerable body to tingling.

His hands slid under her T-shirt, his fingers caressing bare flesh that no one had ever touched before. She tensed, wanting it, and yet at the same time afraid of the depth of her need. She felt as if she could consume him—hell, she *was* consuming him—and while part of her never wanted this to end, the other part was overwhelmed by the wildness that his blood, that his touch, shot through her.

"No," he whispered. "Don't fear me. Don't fear this."

"I'm not afraid," she said. On the contrary, her body was on fire, aroused, and she drank and drank, taking in his blood, his essence. This was Nicholas, and dear God, how she wanted him.

"Slow," he said. "You've had enough."

She murmured a soft protest, unable to find it in herself to form words.

Gently, he nudged her lips from his skin, then tilted her head up. He wasted no time with soft kisses, but took her mouth violently in his, his fangs grazing over her lip, until the taste of their blood mingled, and she thought she would die right then from the intensity of it all.

When she finally leaned back to catch her breath, she reached out to stroke his chest, and found that the wound was completely healed. "You made me strong again," he said, then forestalled her answer with a kiss.

She'd been curled in his lap all the while, but now he moved her, laying her on the couch and sitting beside her, his fingers trailed over the material of the shirt she wore. "Don't," she whispered.

"Don't?" His voice reflected his surprise.

"Don't touch me through cloth."

He slipped his hands down in answer, palms flat against the shirt, until he reached the hem. Then his fingers crept under, finding the strip of skin above the waist of her jeans. She gasped, reflexively sucking her stomach in, as he traced gently above the denim path. Her breath came in shallow gasps, and though she wanted to beg him for more than a mere fingertip against her skin, she was afraid to speak. Afraid that if a fingertip could do this to her, then what could the press of his entire hand, his body, his lips do? She might combust beneath his touch, and while at the moment she could think of no better place to die than in his arms, she wanted this feeling to go on and on and on.

Slowly, he pressed his hands flat against her skin. Slowly, he slid them up, until the tips of his fingers brushed the curves of her breasts. She gasped, her body arching up as if it was determined to draw every ounce of pleasure from the moment. Her nipples hardened, and as she squirmed, they brushed against the cotton of her T-shirt, the sensation so intoxicating it sent shivers of pleasure through her.

She wore no bra—Lissa hadn't packed one—and she

was grateful for that. She wanted nothing between her and Nicholas's hands. Nothing to lessen the erotic caress that was sending deep purple ribbons of lust through her veins, all meeting between her legs and making her sex pulse with need.

She was wet—so much wetter than she'd ever gotten when she'd slipped her own hand between her legs, letting fantasy take her away. She'd never allowed herself to think about a specific man, or about his touch, or about anything other than the pure biological response. Because to think would be to know what she lost.

Now, though. Now she wanted to think about it. Wanted to imagine Nicholas's hands stroking her, his fingers teasing her, his cock filling her.

She moaned, then silenced it when his palms brushing her nipples made her draw her teeth into her lower lip.

"Off," he said, as he pulled her up just long enough to pull her shirt off. She was blind for a moment as it covered her eyes, and when she was free, his face was there, looking at her with an expression both hard with need and soft with desire.

She only had time to catch her breath before his lips were on hers and she was open to him, her mouth taking as much as he was giving, claiming and craving even as his fingers crept down to play with the button of her jeans.

She savored the pressure of his fingers pressed against her, the friction of her jeans sliding down her hips. Her panties were small and silk, and he cupped her triangle with his palm, the material wet with her desire.

With his fingertip, he traced the edge of the elastic, then teased the slick core of her, his finger slipping on soft skin, sliding between her folds, finding her center. "Please," she whispered, but the word was unnecessary. She could tell he had no intention of stopping, and while his mouth traced kisses down her neck and to her breast, his finger slipped inside. The sensation of being filled made her gasp, even as the thrill of his mouth on her nipple made her body tighten, as if thin wires ran through her, all connected, and he controlled the nerve center.

"Oh God." She couldn't say anything else. Couldn't form any other words. Right then, if someone had asked, she wasn't entirely sure she could remember her own name.

But she knew pleasure. Right then she knew pleasure so keen it bordered on pain.

While his mouth suckled her breast, his busy hands managed to wrangle her the rest of the way out of her panties.

She felt the air, cool against her damp sex, and sighed from the sweet sensation, so simple and yet so utterly erotic. He shed his own clothes as she watched, the removal of each item like the unwrapping of a Christmas present.

It was a lovely view, but she didn't regret it when he slid on top of her and she closed her eyes, the heady sensation of skin against skin so unfamiliar and astounding that she feared she couldn't bear it.

"You are so beautiful," he whispered. "Am I the first to see you this way?"

"How'd you guess?" she murmured, her stomach muscles tightening from his touch, her sex throbbing, and her mind screaming for more.

He laughed softly against her skin and she sighed, certain that she could lie like that forever, reveling in his touch and the lazy way he explored her body.

His lips wandered over her belly, brushing the curve of her hip bone, tracing around the hair at her pubis. He was in no hurry, as if she were a dessert to be savored, and she felt herself spinning off into heaven as he tasted her, consuming every luscious morsel, not missing a drop.

Erotic, calm, *delicious*.

And then his lips danced lower still, his tongue becoming bolder, reaching out to taste and to tease even as his fingers stroked inside her thighs, his thumbs rising up to caress the soft flesh at the triangle of her sex, and his mouth closing over her in the most intimate kiss of all.

The touch was a shock. A miraculous, astounding, mind-blowing shock, and she arched up, her body wanting more and more even as it wanted to escape from such sweet torment.

But he wasn't letting her escape.

Instead, his hands cupped her rear, and his tongue laved her, moving in rhythmic motions that seemed to grow inside her, building exponentially until it felt as though ripples of pleasure would simply burst through her body, breaking out of the confines of muscle and skin.

Until it seemed as though she was no longer flesh and bone, but simply want and need.

It felt, she realized, like it had in the mist. But this time, there was something to reach for. This time, she could find satisfaction.

She wanted it—that explosive release. She could feel

it now—could feel Nicholas delivering her so close, taking her to such intimate heights. She pumped her hips in automatic response, as if she could climb her way to the top of the precipice and send them both tumbling over.

His mouth pulled away, and she almost screamed in frustration. But then she felt the whisper of breath upon her, and the soft stroke of a finger teasing her slick folds.

"Come for me," he whispered. "I want to feel you come."

And then, as if his words held as much power over her as his touch, she felt the climax build . . . and then she cried out as her body exploded in an array of lights and colors.

She rode it, never wanting the experience to end. When she finally slid down the crest and back to reality, he held her close, stroking her skin, his soft touches silently threatening to take her back to the heights she'd just reached.

"Soon," he whispered, as if reading her mind.

"I want to touch you," she said, shifting so that she was on top of him.

Slowly, because she wanted to relish the moment, she drew her hands down his body, letting her lips follow her fingers, exploring every inch of him with touch and taste and sight.

By heaven, he was beautiful.

"What's this?" she asked, her finger tracing the geometric tattoo on his shoulder blade. A circle inside a square inside a triangle inside a circle. "Alchemy?"

"It's the symbol for the philosopher's stone," he said. "The secret to eternal life."

"One of the secrets," she said, drawing over the symbol with her fingertip.

"Yes," he agreed, as she pressed her lips to the tattoo, feeling his muscles contract under her touch, hearing him moan as she trailed kisses down his back and the soft, sensitive skin at his side.

After she'd explored every inch with her mouth, she pressed against him, full contact, wanting to feel him against every inch of skin. The sensations that ricocheted through her were beyond anything she'd ever experienced, and she never wanted it to end.

It would, though. When the sun crested the horizon, this fantasy would end, too.

In the meantime, though, she wanted more. And not even more sex—although yes, that was definitely on the agenda. She simply wanted to touch.

"You've gone away into your thoughts."

"Good thoughts," she said. "Stretch out," she demanded, ordering him to lie along the couch, his body taking up the full length of it, his head pressed against a pillow.

"Perfect," she said, then slid in beside him. She squirmed into position, until as much of her was touching him as possible.

"Keep that up, and this little break you've orchestrated is going to be over before it's begun."

"I probably wouldn't be too put out by that," she admitted. "But I do like this." She licked her lips and glanced down. "But are you, um, okay?"

His low chuckle rumbled through him. "I'm wonderful. Anticipation, Petra. It can be both powerful and pleasurable."

"Anticipation," she repeated, her fingers stroking him. "And touching. *Touching*." She sighed. "Hard to believe something so simple can be so staggering."

"There's nothing simple about it," he said. "Millions of nerve endings responding to the slightest brush. It's science and biology."

"It's amazing. And it's not science that's making me feel like this."

"Like what?"

She considered the question, wishing she could find the words. "Like I'm outside myself looking in. Like I become more myself when you touch me. Like we're melding, and yet staying apart." She shook her head, frustrated by the inadequacy of her description. "Touching you makes me feel the way I did when we were mist. As if we were connected so deeply that it wasn't a question of touching, it was a question of being."

He stroked her hair. "I understand."

"Really?"

His laugh rumbled through her. "I do. And at the same time, you baffle me."

He said it with enough seriousness that she propped herself up on an elbow. "How?"

"You're human, and yet you not only experienced the mist state, but you recall it."

"I experienced it, all right."

He followed her hairline with his fingertip. "I still want to understand why."

"Does it matter? Do you think it's relevant to the curse?"

"Probably not," he said. "But yes, it matters."

"Why?"

"Because I'm curious. It's a question, and I want an answer."

She laughed. "Can't argue with that."

"Your family," he said. "They've always been able to manipulate magic?"

"I don't know about always," she said. "But definitely as far back as anyone knows."

"Perhaps that's the reason. The power rising from the earth. Perhaps it's strong enough to keep you aware during the transformation."

"Or maybe I'm just special."

He laughed. "Yes, well, that's a reasonable hypothesis, too."

She pressed a kiss to his shoulder. "So if the tattoo is the symbol for the philosopher's stone, that must mean that your interests in alchemy lay in immortality, and not in turning metals to gold." She was teasing him, but as she spoke she realized that he'd never actually told her his particular interest in alchemy. Even so, she was certain it wasn't gold.

"Why do you say that?" he asked, when she told him as much.

"Because you're the first vampire I've met who seems . . . I don't know. Like the extra time is a gift."

His chest rumbled as he laughed. "You are more perceptive than I realized, Petra Lang."

"I spend a lot of time watching. When you don't touch, you find ways to compensate."

"Of course. And you're right. I don't regret what I have become. Not usually."

"But there have been times? The daemon?"

His face hardened and she could feel his muscles

tense, as if he was fighting to keep calm. She'd struck a nerve, and struck deep. She waited for him to tell her how, to explain what memory she'd triggered, but instead he breathed deep and slow, and when he spoke, the steel had left his body. Only his cadence gave him away. Steady, rhythmic. As if he had to concentrate to stay on task.

"The daemon is a part of me, of course, as it is in every vampire. I battle it constantly, but the battle is familiar now, and I know I'll come out on top. But there have been two times when that wasn't the case." He drew in a breath. "The first was when I was made. The second was when I was betrayed."

"Lissa," Petra said, remembering the conversation on the plane. "I shouldn't have brought up bad memories. I'm sorry."

"No. It's okay." He shifted so that he faced her more directly, then stroked her arm slowly with his fingertip. The gesture was sweet and simple and so intimate it made her want to cry, especially since he didn't even seem to be aware he was doing it, as his full attention was on her face. "It was Serge who guided me through those months, forcing me into the Holding and making me battle my daemon. More than that, giving me the strength to prevail."

"I find it hard imagining you broken."

"Do you?"

"It's just the way I see you. Strong. Competent." She lifted a shoulder in a shrug. "If I'm wrong, keep it to yourself."

"Of course," he said with a grin.

She laughed, then laughed even harder when he

pulled her close and kissed her ear, his arms tightening around her waist.

"And that's why you're doing all this now? Trying to save Serge the way he once saved you?"

"It is."

"I hope we can do it. Actually, I guess I hope Ferrante can do it."

"Yes," Nicholas said, but his face had gotten hard again.

"Nicholas? What is it?"

"I tell you this because with luck you will meet the man, and you need to know what there is between us."

"All right," she said, her voice soft, matching the solemnity of his.

"But I also tell you because I want to. Nothing more, nothing less. I simply want you to know."

"I—" She realized he was going to tell her about the way he'd betrayed Ferrante, and she wanted to say something, but "thank you" seemed strange and inadequate when placed against the urgent heat in his eyes, a heat that twisted her up inside and made her regret all the more that the sun had to eventually rise.

So she said nothing, merely nodded and gently squeezed his hand, hoping that through her touch he would understand how much it meant to her that he would let her see a bit of his heart, and shoulder a bit of his pain.

"When Marco took me in, I already had a solid education in the classics, in mathematics, in science and philosophy. I was as well educated as a young man of good family was expected to be, and my father wished me to marry and take over the management of his properties.

He was a wool merchant in Florence, and though my family never rivaled the Medicis, we were quite successful."

"I'm guessing your interest wasn't in wool."

"It was not," Nicholas said. "Ironic, perhaps, since I was so very interested in everything else."

"A Renaissance man," she said, grinning. "When was this, by the way? Was it actually during the Renaissance? Or were you ahead of your time?"

"When the light of learning ripped through Europe, I was already walking exclusively in the dark. My mortal education took place at the end of the thirteenth century, and though I was well educated by the time I reached my twenty-fourth year, I was not expected to do anything with that learning other than step into my father's role as a wool merchant." He shrugged, as if nonchalant, but she could tell his emotions were anything but. "I defied my family and apprenticed myself to Marco Ferrante."

"You had a passion," she said.

"Some would say I was irresponsible."

"Were you?"

"No. As you said, I had a passion. My younger brother took over the business, and it thrived. Had I stayed, he would have entered the priesthood, and I would certainly have run the business into the ground out of nothing more than sheer apathy."

She couldn't help her grin. "I don't believe that for a moment. You have too much pride. You would have done it. But you would have hated it."

"Apparently I really am transparent to you."

She shrugged, feeling pleased with herself. "So you

skipped out on your family and hooked up with Ferrante. Then what?"

"He was already making great strides in alchemy, and his mind . . . dear God, his mind was so sharp and his thoughts so precise. I had been arrogant enough to believe myself to have a good mind and a quick wit, but I paled next to Marco. And Marco paled next to Giotto."

"Who?"

"Giotto Marciello," Nicholas said. "When I joined his household, Marco was already working with a partner, and he was even more brilliant than Marco. Just to sit and watch Giotto think was an education, and every day I thanked God that these two had allowed me to work with them."

"What happened?" she asked, not wanting to rush him, but knowing that this story would end badly.

"For years I worked by their side—and for years we thought that we'd gotten close to finding the answer. To actually harnessing death and holding it at bay."

An iron band seemed to tighten around her chest, and she realized that she'd been holding her breath.

"I became frustrated by the delays. Angered by all the false paths leading nowhere. I stopped spending the evenings with Marco and Giotto and instead took my pleasure at a local inn, where the wine flowed and the women were eager. I had only a few friends, but they knew about my work, and would ask me about my progress, some inquiring seriously, others teasing. But we spoke of it in that inn, and I'm certain that is where she heard that I searched for immortality."

"Who?"

"A woman. A dark lady. A vampire."

Her breath hitched. "She changed you."

"I wish she had right then, because then I would have no guilt. But no, she did not change me. Instead, she offered me a gift."

She stayed silent, certain she knew where this was going.

"I went back to Marco and told him about the woman, about what she'd offered. He told me I was a fool to even consider it. That the lady was most likely a trickster who would steal my purse and leave me dead in an alley. That there were no such things as vampires, no shortcuts to immortality. And even if there were, I would be consorting with the devil."

"You didn't believe him."

"Or maybe I did, but I didn't care. He could see that he wasn't getting through to me. He urged me to wait— assured me that Giotto was close to a breakthrough. That they hadn't told me because they wanted to be sure. But I didn't believe it. How could I, when we'd thought we were close so many times before?"

"You went back to the lady."

"I did," he said, then closed his eyes. He was silent and still for a moment, and when he finally looked at her again, his expression was dark and disturbed. "I went to her willingly, having been told of the consequences, but I didn't truly understand. Or maybe I thought that I could control the daemon. I was certainly arrogant enough back then to believe that."

"You couldn't."

"Few can in those first days, and upon my change, I tore through Florence, a whirlwind of destruction aimed right for Marco's workshop. I don't remember what happened, not completely, but I know that I attacked Marco. He got away somehow, and I was angry—so angry that I ripped the place apart. I was searching for Giotto, you see. I knew that Marco couldn't complete the formula without him, and the daemon wanted to hurt, and hurt deep. That's what it does best—torment those you love the most."

"You killed Giotto."

"I did. Maimed him, tortured him, killed him. And although my daemon is now suppressed—although I am not now the man who did those things—still my guilt is as massive as my regret."

"Nicholas." She didn't know what to say, so she said nothing. Instead, she simply held him close, and hoped that silent comfort would be enough.

"And that is why I never watched the sun rise through Serge's windows before today. I chose the night with full awareness, and once I had battled the daemon down—once I learned to live with what I had done and what I had become—I swore to myself I would never regret my decision."

"Do you?"

He shook his head. "Some vampires do. They look inside themselves at the daemon and hate themselves and what they have become. I've fought down my daemon, and I look now at what I am, immortal and strong with the entire world open to me, an eternity of knowledge and inquiry." He drew in a breath. "I deeply regret what I did to Marco, to Giotto. But the choice? What I am now?" He stroked her cheek. "Most of the time I don't regret it—after all, there is something soothing about searching the heavens. But after centuries, I do miss the warmth of the sun upon my skin, and I think about Marco sometimes and am ashamed that I envy him for not being bound to the night."

She pressed a kiss to his chest and smiled at him, wanting to lift the dark mood. "Tonight, we're both bound by the night. I think maybe we should enjoy it some more."

He brushed her lips with his fingertip, the heat in his eyes a counterpoint to such a gentle touch. "You wouldn't rather sleep?" he asked, his voice teasing.

She swung a leg over him, then shifted so that she was straddling him. "No," she said, breathless as his hands reached to stroke her. "I really wouldn't."

CHAPTER 20

Nicholas was going out of his mind.

Her smooth skin, her responsive body, and her soft moans combined to take him so close to the edge that he wasn't sure he could last much longer and not bury himself deep inside her. And yet he wanted to last—wanted to draw this out. Wanted to fill the night with touches and caresses and skin against skin. It might be years before another blue moon, and he wanted her to have this night to hold on to.

Which was all true, but completely discounted the fact that the woman in his arms had set his blood to burn in ways he hadn't experienced in years. Hell, in centuries.

They were still on Serge's sofa, a huge down-filled monstrosity roughly the size of a small bed. He'd found a blanket and they were wrapped in it, loosely, though, so that he had the freedom to touch her. He'd discovered that he had to touch her after the first stroke of his finger upon her skin. It was as if that moment embodied every desire he'd felt since he'd been around her, desire he hadn't wanted to examine, much less act upon. Now, with her naked and beside him, he couldn't imagine how he had lasted this long without the feel of her.

"How often?" he asked, twining a stray curl around his finger. "How many blue moons have there been in your life?"

"My life?" she asked, with a mischievous smile. "Or since I was old enough for this?"

"This."

She lifted a shoulder in a casual shrug, but he caught the shadow in her eye. "Four," she said. "Only four."

The sadness in her voice cut straight to his heart, and he shifted so that he was balanced on top of her, his lips finding the hollow of her neck and his tongue tasting her sweetness. "We'll make sure this blue moon is particularly special," he whispered, then captured her lips with his kiss.

"Nicholas."

He trembled, his name on her lips arousing him as much as the taste of her. "I can't wait any longer, Petra," he said, his hands stroking her body, caressing every smooth inch of her. "I have to be inside you."

"Yes," she whispered, but he saw hesitation in her face.

"Petra, if you're not sure . . ."

"I am! But we need . . . I mean, I can't risk getting pregnant."

He stroked her face as he looked into her eyes, and realized that her words surprised him. From what she'd told him earlier, childbirth would release her from the curse, yet she worried about it now?

"I can't do that to a child," she said. "Not even to be free."

"No," he whispered, overwhelmed with awe and respect for this woman. "No, you couldn't."

"Do you have something?"

"I don't," he said, and was flattered by the desperate regret that flashed across her features. "But Serge is careful, and he wouldn't have wanted to sire any dhampires with the vermin he brought in as founts and other entertainment."

"Dhampires?"

"Half vampire, half human. Rare, but they're around." He pushed himself off the couch, absurdly grateful for Serge's more colorful methods of fighting his daemon. "Don't go away."

"Never."

It took him less than three minutes to find what he was looking for, and he returned with a box of condoms to find her smiling at him on the couch, her expression so joyous upon seeing him that he felt humbled by her desire. "Please," she whispered. "Don't wait."

He couldn't have waited if he wanted to. He sat beside her, his body humming with anticipation merely from the proximity, and when he touched her, electricity shot through him, as if every secret he'd ever longed to understand was right there in her touch, and the universe opened to him through this woman.

Slowly, he dipped his hands between her thighs, sliding over soft skin, making her even wetter, even more open for him, and when he was certain she was ready, he sheathed himself, then leaned over her, taking his weight on his arms, and found her inner core.

She moaned, parting her legs, and he thrust inside, groaning at the pleasure of her tight fit, relishing the fact that he was the first man to explore the woman.

"We'll go slow," he said.

"No." Her hands cupped his rear, and she pulled him toward her, lifting her hips in response. She tilted her head back and moaned, a sound of pleasure combined with pain, and she begged him not to stop, not to hold back.

He didn't. Hell, he couldn't. It was as if he was fire and she was oxygen, and he couldn't stop until he'd consumed her completely.

He wanted her, no doubt about that. But as much as he wanted to take his pleasure of her, he wanted even more to draw her up. To bring her to amazing heights. To experience everything she had so far not felt.

Hell, he wanted Petra to make up for lost time, and he wanted to be the one who brought her that gift.

Beneath him, her body bucked and her breathing became more rhythmic. Her face flushed. She clutched him tight, her fingernails digging into his skin, and she pulled him closer as if she couldn't get there without touching every part of him. Her passion spurred his own, and he thrust harder, deeper, until his climax hovered before him, hanging on a precipice as he waited—desperately—for her to go over the edge. He would follow—by the gods, he would follow—but in this, she would go first.

"Petra," he whispered, and as if her name were an incantation, she exploded beneath him, crying out his name as her body tightened around him, pumping and claiming, draining him dry with the force of her passion.

When the orgasm subsided, she lay beside him, her fingers lazily stroking him, and a sense of contentment and wonder enveloping her. He closed his eyes, basking in the scent of her pleasure, only opening them when she shifted position and gently brushed his cheek.

He opened his eyes to find her smiling down at him. "That was wonderful."

"It was," he agreed.

Her eyes danced with mischief. "Want to do it again?"

He laughed, surprised by her as always. "Desperately," he said.

"Good." She shifted, urging him onto his back, then moved to straddle him. She ran her hands over his chest, then wriggled her hips in a manner clearly calculated to drive him completely insane. "This time, I'm in charge," she said, then lifted her brows and gave him a saucy look. "Think you can handle it?"

He managed to stifle a laugh. "I look forward to the challenge," he said, but the words faded into a moan as her hands slid down and her mouth closed over his nipple.

He closed his eyes, relishing the sensations. Relishing her. *Petra.*

With sudden clarity he saw how deeply she'd affected him. Affected his heart. He told himself that he didn't want to be affected.

He told himself all of that, and yet right then, there wasn't a damn thing he could do about it. More than that, he knew that he didn't really want to.

♦

Someone was watching.

Even with its eyes closed, the monster that used to be Sergius knew that someone was watching it, and it sat for a moment longer, nostrils twitching as it judged this new enemy. *A werewolf,* who carried the stench of loss and pain, but no fear.

The weren did not fear the monster, and that would not do.

Abruptly, it opened its eyes.

The werewolf stood there—*Rand.* He had brought

no food, no comforts. He had come without purpose. And now he stood and watched, his dark skin allowing him to fade easily into the shadows that surrounded the cage of glass and concrete.

The monster didn't like that. Didn't like being on display. It growled, low in its throat, an expression of its extreme displeasure, but it had learned. It had changed. And it did not rage against the walls. It no longer had to.

Instead, it loped to the glass, then peered out at the weren. It pressed its hands against the glass, felt the substance begin to melt away. It had touched the floor, the walls, the metal of its bed with no effect. But the glass, made of sand heated and re-formed of the earth, shifted beneath its hands to do the monster's bidding.

Rand stood silent, not noticing the approaching danger.

The monster threw its arms out to the side and roared, letting the universe batter it, letting it feed the monster with the knowledge of what was out there. Of what the monster could take from this world.

Kill.

The command rang through its head, harsh and unrelenting.

Kill. Tear.

Destroy.

It tilted its head, letting the earth speak of the monster's power. This earth that had nourished the monster, that had given up her power for it to become.

It saw, and it knew that it was time to leave. Time to grow strong.

Time to revel in the glorious scent of spilled blood and the bitter taste of ripped flesh.

Once again it pressed its hand to the glass. This time, however, it didn't hold back.

The glass shifted under its touch, growing weaker, until with one massive punch shattered glass filled the room.

The weren was already through the steel door and into the antechamber, trying to trap the monster in this next ring of hell, but the monster would have none of that. It leaped, catching the weren and dragging him to the ground, the door still open.

Immediately, the weren shifted, his features elongating, transforming into the man/wolf hybrid that the monster had seen before. Memory curled around the monster, distracting it, and the weren took advantage, attacking with intense strength, trying to contain the monster in the room that would become yet another cell if that door closed and locked.

No.

It reached out—not with its hands, but with its power.

It reached out, and it took what the weren was.

And as it did, the weren collapsed, its wolven form disappearing as the monster's own hands elongated, tufts of fur rising at the wrists.

"*No!*" On the ground, the weren protested, but the cry was feeble.

The monster ignored it, then loped through the door, and closed it tight behind him.

It was in a cavernous room, and it tilted its head, testing the air, finding the scents of both power and food in the room to the left.

It raced in that direction—and the moment it crossed

the threshold, a woman scurried backward, her face contorted in terror, even as a vampire rushed forward.

The monster met the vampire head-on, knocking him back, sending him flying up against the far wall, as the woman—*Lissa*—screamed, crying out Rand's name over and over.

The monster turned, wanting to stop the sound as much as it wanted to share her gifts. The unique powers of a succubus could prove useful.

It took a step toward the girl, and fell to the ground as the vampire tackled it.

The monster roared, reaching out, reveling in its own power as the vampire's grip weakened.

It stood, sending the vampire tumbling to the floor. Its muscles tightened, ready to destroy the vampire that had dared to attack it. From the cell, the weren cried out for his mate, but she stood still, too terrified to call back.

"Serge," the vampire said. *"Sergius."*

The monster froze, confused, as it drew in the strength of the vampire, the rush of power muddling its thoughts. *Lucius.*

"Serge," the vampire said again, his voice weak, drained. But the monster was no longer listening. The command once again filled its head, an unrelenting pulse. *Kill. Kill. Kill.*

The monster listened, and understood where it was to go. Who it was to find.

Not the vampire. Not today.

Then it took one last look at the vampire before loping away, using the vampire's own power to transform into mist, and disappear from sight.

CHAPTER 21

They made love throughout the night. Wild and frenetic, softly and sweetly. Her body tingled, aware of
each touch, each caress. Aware, even, of every glance her
way. She felt alive and sensual and deliciously seductive.

It was nice, which was pretty much the world's
biggest understatement. It was amazing. Mind-blowing.
Absolutely perfect.

She could get used to it.

Except, of course, she couldn't. For her, this kind of
thing happened once in a blue moon, just as the saying
said. And that reality was neither comfortable nor easy.

She shifted, pushing the melancholy thoughts away,
then stretched out beside Nicholas on the floor, her body
twined up in the blanket that now tied her to him. "Take
me dancing," she said. "Someplace loud and crowded.
The kind of place where you can't move without jostling
into some other person."

"Dancing?" he repeated.

"Yeah." She sat up. "I've never been."

"I don't think now is the appropriate time. Out in
public. Us being fugitives. Probably best we lay low,
don't you think?"

She did, though she didn't like to admit it.

"I just want to get lost, you know? I've never felt
that—the pulse of music, the press of bodies."

"No? Well, we're not going to hit the New York nightlife, but I think I can arrange a suitable alternative."

As she watched, curiosity warring with amusement, he got up and moved naked to the far side of the room where a technical center that rivaled anything NASA boasted lined one entire wall. After a few false starts and one moment of ear-piercing feedback, Nicholas managed to make music, and the room filled with something fast and retro and oddly familiar.

After a moment, she recognized it, and started laughing so hard she couldn't stand up.

After another moment, she took his hand and started bouncing to the frenetic strains of Cyndi Lauper's "Girls Just Want to Have Fun."

"Appropriate," she said, as the song died out. She drew in a breath, winded from dancing wild and naked in front of Serge's windows. She sashayed closer. "But maybe something a little slower?"

He trailed his finger down her shoulder, over the swell of her breast, and then around her waist, before pulling her close.

As if in answer, the deep, sultry strains of "Can't Get Enough of Your Love, Babe" filled the room.

"You want slow?" Nicholas asked, pulling her tight against him. "I give you Barry White."

"Perfect," she said, laughing as she threw her arms around his neck. "Even better than a night on the town."

"I will take you out," he said. "You want to go clubbing, I'll take you there."

"When the curse is lifted," she said.

He pressed a kiss against her ear. "Or the next blue moon," he whispered, his soft breath and sensual tone making her tremble as much as the idea of being in his arms years from now when an extra moon filled the sky. It wasn't the kind of thing she usually let herself think about. But tonight . . . well, tonight she would let herself believe in miracles.

They danced for hours, their bodies moving in time with the music, in front of the windows overlooking the city, in the shower with water sluicing over them. Danced, and made love, and when her body couldn't handle it any longer, she fell asleep in his arms, feeling warm and utterly content.

At least until the dreams started.

Her mother, screaming out her name.

Her father, reaching for her.

Nicholas, stroking her skin, then changing. Shattering and shifting. Changing into something horrible. Something vile.

Except it wasn't him. It was Sergius. And suddenly he was sinking into the earth. Disappearing. And Petra was breathing a sigh of relief.

And then he was rising back out again, full of purpose, full of the need to kill. And he stormed over the earth, ripping off limbs, tearing off heads, until all Petra could do was stand in a pool of blood that grew deeper and deeper and—

"Petra!"

Nicholas. Not shattered. Not dead.

"Petra! Wake up." He shook her. Gently at first, then harder. "Wake up, dammit. Wake up!"

She blinked, realized he was holding her, then scrambled away, her heart pounding in fear even as her mind ordered her to calm down, telling her it was a blue moon, she was fine, she could touch, it was fine.

Slowly, Nicholas came to her, then gently hooked his arm around her. She closed her eyes and leaned against him. She'd pushed him away on the plane. Now she wanted him. Wanted him, and wanted the comfort he could give.

"He needs to kill," she said, realizing the truth of her words as she spoke. Somehow, she knew exactly what Serge would do. "Nicholas, oh God, it's like he's compelled to rip and tear and kill and—"

"Shhh. He's locked up. You had a dream, and it's horrible, and we're going to fix it. But right now, he's locked up tight."

She nodded. "Right. Right." But somehow she couldn't stop shivering.

"I've got you," Nicholas said, stroking her hair. "We have plenty of time before sunrise."

"Will you hold me?"

"I am holding you," he said. "And nothing's going to make me let go."

◆

"The sun's going to rise in just a few short hours," Petra said. She'd been pressed up against him, her warmth easing through him. Now she sat up, and the shock of cold air from her departure made him shiver.

He pressed a hand to her shoulder, and she covered it with her own, then stood. She went to the window and pressed her hands to the glass. He turned on a light, not because he needed it to see, but because he wanted to see her face reflected in the glass, and with the room darkened he could see only the sprawl of Manhattan.

Right then, he cared nothing for the city or the view. He cared only for her.

He flipped the switch, and she flinched, then brushed her eyes with the pad of her thumb, as if she realized what he'd done and intended to reveal nothing.

"Now I have two reasons to dread the sun," he said.

Her shoulders rose and fell as she took a breath, then she turned to him. "Are we staying here for the day?"

"No." He stood and began to pull on his clothes. "We need to get to Paris."

"Of course." She looked back out the window. "Do you really think he'll help us?"

Nick stepped up behind her and clasped his hands around her waist. "You mean will he help me."

She nodded.

"It's a fair question after what I did—what my daemon did. But Serge's rampage is a lot like that, and I think—I hope—that he will want to help us stop that kind of carnage from running loose in the world."

"If he doesn't?"

"He will," Nick said, with all the certainty he could muster. "I truly believe that. Marco has a scientist's mind, and you're something unique, Petra. Despite the history between Marco and me, I think he will want to help us, if only for the selfish reason of studying you."

"Great," she said, but she was smiling. After a minute, though, the smile faded. "It's hard not to be too hopeful."

"I know. Come here." He pulled her into his arms

and pressed a soft kiss to her forehead. He didn't want it to, but his heart twisted. He'd touched her, so intimately. And though it was unexpected, she'd touched him. Him, Nicholas Montegue, who knew how to manufacture the illusion of desire. Somehow, he'd gotten caught in the real thing, and the burden of it weighed heavy and unfamiliar upon his shoulders.

He'd desired many women for their flesh, for the sweet pleasure of their company, but to truly desire the woman? That he had not experienced since Lissa.

Until now.

Rationally, he thought that he should be pleased to know that his heart hadn't shriveled up and died. But he wasn't pleased. He had no need to pursue intimacy. The world had much to offer, and the pleasures of the intellect could fill the gaps of a thousand lifetimes.

He used to believe that utterly, and he'd gotten comfortable with his routine. One night, one woman, with repeats only when both parties fully understood the score. Nothing that would foster intimacy. Why would he want it, when the last woman he'd let close had betrayed him and then beat the shit out of his heart?

So was it any wonder that the way Petra had wormed her way into his mind troubled him? Especially since Petra was a one-night woman by definition. There would not be another blue moon this year. Perhaps not even next, or even the year after that.

He would not touch her again soon—but dammit, he wanted to.

"What's wrong with you?"

He realized he let her go, and was now jamming his arm through the sleeve of his shirt so hard that the material was at risk of tearing. "Nothing," he said. "I'm fine."

"Good to know. Of course, if this is fine, I'd hate to ever see you truly angry."

"I'm sorry. I'm . . . frustrated."

"Me, too." Her smile was both sad and sultry, and he felt guilty for speaking to her at cross-purposes.

"The way you feel beneath my fingers will be forever burned in my memory," he said. In saying the words, he hoped only to make her feel better, but as soon as he spoke, he knew the words were true.

"Get dressed," he said. "We need to beat the sun."

"How are we getting there, anyway?"

"We're flying."

"Gee, great. Another chance to get thrown out of an airplane. Lucky me."

"Serge has a plane that he has kept unknown to the Alliance. We should be able to travel undetected."

"Who's going to fly it?"

"I will."

She squinted at him. "That means you have to sit in a cockpit and look out a window." She pointed out the window. "In case you forgot, the sun's going to eventually rise."

"The windows are of the same material as these."

She nodded. "And you can really fly?"

"Hundreds of years provide ample time to advance one's education in a number of areas."

"You're talking old-fashioned again."

"Perhaps you affect me that way."

"Some women bring a man to their knees with only a glance. I make them talk all hoity-toity. It's a gift."

"Or a curse," he said, pleased to see her mouth twitch with the joke.

"I've already got one of those," she said. "Trust me when I say that I don't need another."

Her brow furrowed, then cleared as she turned to look out the window.

He knew her well enough now, though. Something was on her mind. "The nightmare?"

"Sorry. It just left me feeling antsy."

"It was just a dream."

She met his eyes in the reflection. "I would have thought a man like you would be more open to the idea that dreams have power."

"I am," he said, then pressed a kiss to the top of her head. "But not if the dreams upset you."

She moved away from him, focusing on the window instead of the man. *Making* herself focus on the window, because, dammit, all she wanted to do was cling to him. To stay in this apartment with the blue moon forever suspended in the sky. Her whole life, she'd managed to deal with what she was, but somehow with Nicholas, she'd lost the ability to cope.

She wanted him, and she couldn't have him, and she wanted to rage against the injustice. But there was no one to rage against. No one except herself, because she'd been stupid enough to open her heart, telling herself silly lies about how all she wanted was sex. All she wanted was to feel a man's touch.

She'd been a fool. She wanted more, so much more, and it pissed her off that she couldn't have it no matter how hard she wished.

"Petra?"

She turned to him and conjured a forced smile, hoping he couldn't see her pain, because he would try to soothe it, and right then she didn't think she could take the kindness. "The sun will be up soon. We need to go."

"There's something we need to do first," he said, then headed toward the kitchen. She followed, her curiosity growing when he began pulling an odd assortment of things from the cabinets. "Dump these out," he said, handing her three plastic soda bottles. "Keep the caps, but rinse them well."

She complied, knowing he had a purpose even if she couldn't see it yet, and also knowing that it was important they hurry.

"When you finish that, take the tinfoil and make a dozen or so small balls."

"Right," she said. She finished the bottles, started on the balls, and couldn't hold her questions in any longer. "What are we doing?"

He turned to her, serious. "Making bombs."

She glanced down at the crumpled balls of foil, then back up at Nicholas. "Whatever you say."

"This apartment has protections," he said, "and we had no indication of any Alliance flunkies approaching, and all of that is good. But I'm not inclined to trust our good luck to continue, and when we leave, I want us prepared to defend ourselves."

"You're a vampire," she said, because she'd seen over and over again in her work the kind of damage a vampire could do.

"So I am," he said. "But you're not. And if there are several waiting to ambush us, even my skills will be insufficient to ensure our safety. So I intend to go into the mix as well armed as possible."

"We could go as mist. Not all the way to Paris, but just to the airport."

He shook his head. "No. You were too weakened the last time."

"But I drank from you."

"To cure damage already done." He looked at her, and the heat in his eyes nearly brought her to her knees. "No. I won't risk you that way. Not if we have a choice."

"Okay." She nodded. "So we make bombs." She looked at the stuff he'd pulled out onto the counter. The foil, the soda bottles, toilet bowl cleaner, some flour, a cigarette lighter, even the box of condoms.

"Fascinating what chemistry can yield, isn't it? Refreshment," he said, pointing to the soda bottle and flour. "Pleasure," he added with a nod to the condoms. "It's all about the mixture. All about the proportion. In many ways, chemistry is a metaphor for life."

"So you know all this chemistry and science stuff, but you ended up being an advocate." She finished with the tinfoil balls and climbed up onto a stool to watch him work. "What's up with that?"

"If you're done, maybe you should concentrate on a weapon of your own."

"What?"

"Fire," he said. "You managed during our escape because of adrenaline and focus."

"I did?"

"I'm quite confident. What you want to do is practice honing the focus so that you don't need the adrenaline."

"Oh."

"Go on," he said. "I've got a few more minutes with this before we're ready to go."

Since he insisted, she tried, focusing on her hand as she tried to conjure a tiny, whirling fireball.

Nothing.

"Talk to me while I do this," she said. "Answer my question. How'd you end up being a lawyer type?"

"You're assuming they're mutually exclusive," he said. "But what is chemistry but the process of finding balance in the universe, and what is the law but the process of finding balance in society?"

"Okay," she said, her eyes on her palm, her mind on the fire. Calling. Bringing. "But?"

"But nothing. I realized after a while that although that axiom is true, there is also a fundamental difference."

"Yeah?" *The earth, the sun, the power . . .*

"Chemistry is precise. Two hydrogen and one oxygen atom always make up water. But the law fluctuates. It falls out of balance. Within the law there is room to maneuver, and after I was offered the chance by Tiberius to study the shadow law, I learned that I had a gift for those maneuvers."

"Skirt the law, walk the line," she said.

"Something like that. Now," his voice lowered. "Keep your focus. Draw it up. And push."

She tried, pulling and drawing and then— *Poof!* A tiny fireball erupted above her palm, fading just as fast as it had appeared.

"I did it! Holy shit, I did it!"

"I never doubted for a minute. Control. That's the key."

"And how do you know so much about it?"

"Some vampires' daemons live close to the surface," he said. "Trust me when I say that I understand control. And that I've mastered it." He swept his hand, indicating the countertop, now littered with homemade pyrotechnics.

"Very cool," she said. "These are bombs?"

"Explosives," he said, pointing to the soda bottles filled with toilet cleaner. "And smoke bombs," he added, this time pointing to the condoms blown up like balloons, filled with flour, and tied at the ends.

"This is the kind of thing you used when you got us out of Division, isn't it?"

"Similar," he said. "I had access to more precise ingredients and the luxury of choosing what I wanted to create. The Du Yao Yan Qiu that burned your eyes was a modification of an ancient Chinese poison bomb."

"Temporary poison," she said, unable to suppress the wish that he'd taken the Tribunal members out once and for all.

He flashed a crooked grin, obviously understanding the direction of her thoughts. "I had a few deadlier options at hand, just in case I needed more firepower."

"Really? You would have really killed Alliance members?"

His expression was hard and unyielding. "To save Serge? Of course. Without hesitation, without doubt."

Petra swallowed, but nodded, hoping he couldn't see her discomfiture. Because right then all she could think of was what she'd known back when he'd first taken her from Division: that if Nicholas knew her secret, it would be she—and not the Tribunal—who would die by his hand.

◆

Dirque paced the living room of the home he kept in Los Angeles. A fortress, really. Two acres in Beverly Hills, with an eight-foot fence surrounding the property, and armed Alliance soldiers guarding the perimeter. Possibly overkill for one with his innate power, but in light of Tariq's latest report, he felt that caution was advised.

Sergius alive. By the gods, surely that couldn't be possible.

Not that Dragos was admitting it—Tariq had made that clear in his report. But they both knew that Lucius Dragos knew how to keep his own counsel. If he didn't want a thing revealed, then it would not be revealed.

But whether Dragos admitted it or not, Tariq's theory made sense. Serge had disappeared from the crime scene after the girl had changed him, as had Montegue and Dragos. The vampires had testified that they'd subdued the monster in a warehouse, that there had been a horrific fight, that the building had burned, and that Sergius had been caught in the conflagration.

The evidence had supported the story, and after the Division 6 medical examiner tested remains from the scene and pronounced that the DNA in fact belonged to Sergius, the search for the monster had been suspended.

Dirque snorted, wishing he could be more disgusted with Division for its shortsightedness and lack of imagination. But he'd been just as guilty. Even knowing the prophecy, he still let his guard down. Allowed himself to be lulled into a false sense of security simply because of the identification of partial remains and the lack of a bloody path ripped across the city.

But there would be no bloody path if Montegue and Dragos had managed to subdue and confine the creature.

Where? That was the question. Where the hell was the monster? And what was it like now?

No monster created by the Touch had ever lived so long. Undoubtedly the beast's strength had increased, but had it developed reasoning ability? Was it still wild and uncontrolled? Or had it learned the art of stealth, such that it no longer cut a bloody swath through the land? If so, the monster had become even more terrifying than before.

He was tempted to call Tariq back and have him lead the search for the beast, but he tempered the impulse. His nephew's focus was on tracking the girl, and with regard to Petra Lang, nothing had changed. A living Sergius might be a threat to the Alliance, but at the moment all the evidence suggested that he was locked up tight. And while Montegue and Dragos might be searching for a cure, Dirque already had one—kill the girl, and Sergius would be free.

Slowly, he tilted his head to the side, replaying his own thoughts: *Kill the girl* . . .

He frowned. God, what a fool he was!

Tiberius might not be able to get in touch with Montegue, but Dragos undoubtedly could. All Dirque needed to do was get the message to Montegue. *Kill the girl, free your friend.*

Within minutes, the girl would feel Montegue's knife at her neck. She'd slump to the ground, dead and gone. The threat of the Touch would disappear, and Sergius would return to normal. He'd undoubtedly be executed as a rogue vampire, but at least he'd be himself.

He crossed the room to the phone and was reaching for the handset when he heard a loud *thump* in front of the house. He abandoned the plan to call Tiberius, and rang the guardhouse instead.

There was no answer.

Fingers of dread crawled up his spine.

Trouble.

The thought had barely formed in his mind, when a loud *crack* echoed through the room and the thick, wooden front door came flying in.

A creature stood in the gap, part man, part wolf. And yet not weren.

Serge.

Dirque swallowed, and for the first time in his very long life, he truly understood the meaning of fear.

CHAPTER 22

Kiril moved through the darkened room, pushing furniture toward the walls, making room for what he had to do. How many hours had he spent in this room? Lost in his fantasies, his stories?

He'd never done anything with them, just shoved them into a drawer, letting Petra see only the tiniest portion of what he'd crafted in his imagination.

She'd told him over and over he should submit his stories to magazines or anthologies, but he never had. He never thought he was good enough, even though his teachers had told him he had a gift, and Petra had always said the stories made her laugh and cry.

It was the rejection he feared, he knew that. He who wasn't afraid of anything. Who knew exactly what he wanted and was willing to sacrifice so much to get it.

And now he'd lost the most important thing in the world to him—Petra. She was everything to him. Sister, yes. But so much more. She was his heart, and he'd lost her, and it was killing him. How much worse could rejection be?

He would submit. As soon as he had Petra back—and he *would* get her back—he would send out all his stories, and damn the fear.

When the furniture was out of the way, he drew a chalk circle on the floor, then stood in the middle, a photograph of his sister clasped tight in his hands. The picture was one of his favorites, taken when they were both ten. He'd been on the porch, writing in his notebook, and as always keeping a close watch on his sister.

She'd been in the garden, cutting flowers to put in vases around the house. She still did that today, filling the front office with arrangements of flowers to complement the overwhelming floral theme that she thought made human clients feel more at ease.

Back then, he'd been playing with the camera his aunt had given him for his birthday, snapping random photos of the house, the garden, his sister. He'd planned to tape the pictures in his notebook, and then write a story about each. He'd been thinking about a story for Petra—something about a princess cursed by an evil witch, and only the kiss of her prince could save her—when she'd looked toward him and smiled, then thrown a handful of flower petals into the air. Magically, he'd actually caught the shot—Petra, laughing her head off, with petals dancing in the wind around her.

It was a beautiful picture, and he kept it framed beside his bed, where he could look at it every night. That was the way he liked to remember her, laughing and innocent. And safe.

Dear God, he hoped she was safe right then. Hoped she would remain safe until he could find her, until he could protect her from Montegue's inevitable discovery that he was dragging the cure to Sergius's change all over the goddamned globe.

With care, he took the candles from the polished ash box, then placed them gently on the chalk line. He burned no incense, but instead scattered fragrant herbs and essential oils outside the circle. Then he sat, his legs crossed, his elbows on his knees, and the photograph tight in both hands.

He looked into his sister's face, breathed deep of the scented air, and then closed his eyes.

The exhaustion following his power surge had left him sagging and hollow, but he'd slept and meditated, and although he wasn't 100 percent, he felt strong enough to seek.

More than that, he knew he had to. That son of a bitch advocate had Petra, and there was no way Kiril was leaving her to that vampiric fucker's mercy.

Slowly, methodically, he focused on his breathing, clearing his mind, cleansing his soul. Once his mind was empty, he began to fill it again, this time with memories of Petra. The way she looked, the way she laughed, the way she smelled.

His chest tightened, and he had to force emotion down. Now was not the time for longing or fear. Now was the time to be calm. To reach out.

To find his sister.

His mind thrust into the darkness, probing and searching, seeking her aura, her spirit.

Seeking, but not finding.

Fingers of panic traced up his spine, and Kiril gripped the picture tighter. She was far now—Montegue had taken her far away, and the bond between Kiril and his sister had stretched thin. But it hadn't broken. He could follow it. Could move in his mind along the frayed ends of the thread, soaring over mountains, over highways, over grassy plains.

He moved with unimaginable speed in his mind,

crossing the country, soaring over the ocean, and then—nothing.

He stopped.

Simply stopped.

Dear God, was she lost at sea? Needles of panic burst through him, and he almost stood, almost broke the spell. But he forced himself to stay calm. To think, and to seek.

To call out for his sister and find *her*. Not the spiritual trail she'd left, but her. Her mind. Her thoughts.

Her destination.

He closed himself off, open only to her. Reaching out only for her.

But there was nothing. Only blackness. Only silence, until the weight of loss and horror bore down on him with such intensity that it was almost too much to stand.

Then, like a pinprick of light against a pitch-black wall, he felt her. He caught her. Not where she was, but where she was going. And although he couldn't hold on tight—couldn't grasp hard enough to track her to her current location—there was no mistaking the one, single word.

Paris.

◊

"Excellent," Tariq said into his phone. "Head out on my authority, and call me when you have them in custody." He snapped the phone shut and shot Elric a smug glance.

His lieutenant shifted his attention from the brother's house to Tariq. "New York?"

"You got it."

"Good call there, man," Vale said from the backseat, where he had binoculars trained on Kiril's house. The brother had been moving around inside for a while. He'd leave soon, and when he did, the team was poised to follow.

"It was a damn good call," Elric echoed, and Tariq had to nod in agreement. "Hell yeah. The noose is tightening. Maybe my uncle's idiotic attempt did us a favor after all." He'd been furious when he'd learned—after the fact—about the in-air attempt on Petra Lang's life. He'd told his uncle categorically that not only should he have been informed of the operation, but that it was too damn risky in the first place. When the goddamned plane had fallen from the sky he'd felt absurdly vindicated. For that matter, he'd wanted to call his uncle and gloat, but reason and common sense had kept him from dialing.

The plane had crashed in a field in New York State, and there'd been no human casualties, which was fortunate, as it made the administrative bullshit easier to navigate, and Division could ease in and push the human authorities out. But that didn't matter much to Tariq. What he considered a blessing was the fact that the girl and Montegue's escape meant that he knew they were in New York. And Sergius's apartment was his best guess as to where.

"Fenrig has a mole in Division 12," Tariq said, referring to one of the Alliance operatives stationed in New York. "He just got his hands on their surveillance and investigation file on Sergius, and now we've got the address of the vampire's condo and underground fortress.

He's sending teams to both locations. It's a good bet they're at one or the other."

A damn good bet, and he was certain that soon—very soon—Fenrig would have Montegue in custody and the bitch would be dead.

He only wished he could get across the country fast enough to watch it.

But no, better to stay on the brother. His gut was certain they were in New York, but until he had solid confirmation, he was going to work the case. Stay on the brother, see where he goes, and wait for a report from New York. He had a team in place in Paris, too. The crashed plane belonged to Gunnolf, and it was a good bet that the weren leader had lured the targets to France by offering them sanctuary. They probably wouldn't continue now that they knew Gunnolf had fucked them over, but you never knew. They might have another reason for running there, and Tariq wasn't going to overlook any possibility. Not now, when his future was on the line.

He fingered his phone, considered calling his uncle and telling him about the New York situation, but he hesitated. If he got Dirque's hopes up and then the mission failed, his uncle would see it as Tariq's failure.

No, better to wait and call his uncle when he could tell him the girl was dead.

Satisfied, he closed his phone and slipped it back into his pocket. His uncle would keep.

"Hey, look," Vale said. He was watching the house, whose lights were rapidly flicking out. "We may have something."

Elric turned the key, firing the engine, but leaving the

headlights off. They all watched the front door and the car parked at the curb just in front of the house.

"Come on, big boy," Elric said. "Lead us to the little bitch."

As if the words held their own power, the front door burst open. Tariq held his breath, waiting, but the brother wasn't there. "What the fuck?"

In the front yard, the rose bushes started to sway, the movement setting off the motion-detector floodlight, which snapped on, the harsh glow of lights illuminating the area.

"Storm?" Vale said.

"Shit no," Tariq said, scanning the area, looking for the bastard. "He knows we're here."

Tariq's words were still hanging in the air when that very air began to swirl, with such violence that the Explorer began to shake and then, nauseatingly, to spin as it rose off the ground, higher and higher, spinning faster and faster until the wheels were level with the roof.

"Fuck!" Elric yelled. And then, before they could draw weapons or think how to respond, the wind stopped and the vehicle dropped like a stone to the street.

The men grunted, jolted by the impact, then looked up to find Kiril Lang smiling at them through the driver's-side window. The engine was still running, and Elric hit the control to roll down the window.

"Not polite to spy on folks." Kiril smiled, wide and white. "Just thought I'd share that tidbit with you, in case your mothers hadn't taught you well."

"Where is your sister, Lang?" Vale demanded, and

even though Tariq wanted to smack the idiot for revealing the reason for their surveillance, at the same time he damn sure wanted to hear the answer.

"You really want me to tell you?" he asked. "Where's the fun in that?" Then he winked once and walked casually to his shiny red Honda, as if he owned the whole goddamned world.

"What now?" Elric asked.

"You heard the man," Tariq said, dreading putting *this* in his report to his uncle. "We follow."

◆

"Something's wrong," Petra said, feeling the wildness rise inside her as they stood in Serge's entrance hall. It was a harsh sensation, cruel, and although it welled up inside her, she knew it wasn't her own.

"What?" Nicholas said, immediately at her side. He gripped her wrist. "Are you okay?"

She tugged her wrist free, regretting the fact that she hadn't yet slipped on her gloves. "Sunrise is soon. We can't risk getting too comfortable."

His eyes were soft but his expression was hard as he took both her hands in his. "What's wrong?"

"Something with Serge," she said, relenting to the allure of his touch and sliding close to him. He wrapped his arms around her, and she soaked up the safety he offered. "I don't know. *I don't know.*" She spat the words, frustrated by the haze that seemed to linger over these feelings or visions or whatever the hell they were. "The dreams are still totally freaky, but when I'm awake, the feeling's getting clearer. I still can't pinpoint it, though.

It's like a fog that's lifting, but you still can't see. But there's something in the fog, Nicholas. Something horrible, and it wants to do horrible things."

He eased away from her, and though she hated that he was breaking the contact, she knew it was so that they could see each other's faces.

"That's why we're doing this," he said. "Why we're looking for a cure. So that whatever horrible thing is looming, we can stop it before it happens. He's locked up tight, though. So whatever thoughts of his are filling your head, just remember that they're only thoughts. No matter how horrible it gets, it isn't real."

She drew in a breath and nodded. The Serge-sensation was fading, and she forced the lingering remnants down, focusing only on Nicholas. And on getting the hell out of there before sunrise.

"We ready?" Nicholas asked. "Got everything?"

Petra nodded. Her own backpack had been lost when the plane crashed, and while she hated losing her journal and the family Bible, there'd been nothing remarkable about either the pack or her clothes. She still wore jeans, but she'd changed into one of Serge's long-sleeved T-shirts. It was too big, but it was comfortable and clean, and right then that's what counted.

She'd shoved some of his socks into a satchel, along with the five condom smoke bombs. The satchel's side pockets held two soda bottles filled with toilet cleaner, and her pockets held tinfoil balls and a cigarette lighter.

She'd considered dumping all the gear into a back-pack—Serge's apartment rivaled a department store for all its choices—but Nicholas had insisted on the satchel.

"Wear it so that it hangs in front of you. Easy access to your weapons, and your hands are free."

He carried a similar bag filled with similar items. And once they had filled their satchels, she put her gloves on and they headed for the stairs. The apartment was on the thirty-fifth floor, but Nicholas was concerned about their safety in an elevator. "It's even more enclosed than a stairwell," he'd said, and although she agreed, her legs were less than thrilled with the plan.

"At least we're going down and not up," she said as they reached the landing for the twelfth floor.

"How close are we to sunrise?" he asked as they continued their downward trod.

She stopped to glance at her watch. "Forty minutes. We need to hurry if we're going to get to the airport without me needing a dustpan to get you on the plane."

Apparently he wasn't down with the hurry-up plan, though, because instead of continuing down, he took the two steps back up to her.

"What are you—"

He silenced her with a kiss, long and deep and lingering. "Hold on to that," he said. "Even once the sun rises, I want you to remember my kiss. I want you to remember my hands upon you." He pressed his hand to her cheek. "We are in this thing together. To the end, Petra. And beyond."

She swallowed, overwhelmed by both his words and the knowledge that she was keeping secret from him the very cure that had gotten him into "this thing" in the first place. She wanted to tell him—wanted desperately to find enough trust in her heart to believe that she could tell him the truth and know that he would stand by her and protect her.

But even as she opened her mouth to speak, the words wouldn't come. Instead, a single tear traced a path down her cheek, and he wiped it away with the back of his thumb, then pulled his hand away. "No more," he said, then quirked a smile. "But we have the next blue moon to look forward to."

She knew he was trying to make her feel better, and she returned his smile, but there was no pleasure behind it. She felt raw and empty. Her whole life she'd longed for this night, and now that she'd had it, the weight of her life pressed down on her even heavier than before. She knew now what she was missing, and while she liked to believe that she would be satisfied merely by the memory of Nicholas's touch, she knew that was a load of bullshit. Nothing would satisfy her except the real thing, and that was something fate had screwed her out of.

Goddammit.

Temper quickened her steps, and she took the lead for the next few floors, but when they reached the fourth-floor landing, Nicholas told her to stop, then hurried his pace to get in front of her.

She expected they'd leave the stairway at the lobby level, but instead, they continued down to the basement. "This way," Nicholas said, leading her through the musty hall and into a laundry room noxious with the odor of detergent and mildew. "Here."

He pulled aside a drape hanging down from a table to reveal a hole in the wall that led—well, she wasn't sure where it led.

"I'm going first," he said. "Stick close."

They entered a dark tunnel system filled with the smells of human waste and rotting food. She kept close to Nicholas, skirting over the legs of a few homeless people who slept down there, and pausing when the ground around them began to rumble.

"This connects up with the subway system," Nicholas said. "We're going to come through a service tunnel to one of the platforms and then take the train to the airport."

A good plan, she thought, especially after they'd walked for five more minutes and still saw no sign of any Alliance agents waiting to jump them. All that work making things that go boom, and they didn't even need them.

"Left here," Nicholas said as they approached an intersecting tunnel. "And then it's not much farther."

She said a silent thank-you—her nose was going numb from the stench—and rounded the corner eagerly . . .

. . . then drew up short when they were attacked by three huge guys: a jinn, a vampire, and a werewolf by the looks of them.

The three leaped upon Nicholas, obviously trying to get rid of him and leave her unprotected. But she was *so* not letting them get away with that. She snatched a soda bottle out of the satchel, opened it up, dropped three tinfoil balls in, and then tossed it near their feet.

"Nicholas!" she called, and watched as he threw himself to the side, while the other three, slower to react, got thrown backward by the force of the blast.

A *lot* of force.

She gaped at it, pretty damn impressed.

Nicholas, meanwhile, had prepared another bomb, and threw it into the group. It exploded at the vampire's feet, catching his clothes on fire.

The creature transformed to mist immediately, the action itself extinguishing the flames, and Petra took one of the smoke bomb condoms, lit it, and tossed it into the mist.

She had no idea if that would mess up the vampire's navigational power, but it made her feel better.

As she did that, though, the jinn had attacked Nicholas, knocking him to the ground. She ran toward them, planning to kick the creature off Nick, but she was pulled back by a tug on her arm. She stumbled toward the weren who'd grabbed her, and he held a hand out to stop her, his fingers brushing her cheek as he did.

She froze, and so did he.

And he didn't change.

She drew in a breath, realizing it wasn't yet sunrise. It was still a blue moon. And that meant she could touch.

With teeth clenched tight, she balled up her fist, got some power going, and slammed her knuckles right into the bastard's nose—all while he was still standing there, shell-shocked, obviously wondering why he hadn't turned into Monster Boy.

She shook out her fist. It was sore, but damn it felt good.

"Smoke bombs!" Nicholas said. While she'd sucker punched the weren, Nicholas had gotten out from under the jinn.

A huge explosion rocked the area, and she realized he'd tossed in the last of his explosive bottles. Now he wanted to cover their tracks with smoke.

She ran toward him, trying but not managing to light the things as they went. In the end, she passed them to him, and they dropped four. The bombs exploded in succession, leaving the intersecting tunnels a smoke-filled mess.

"Hurry," Nicholas urged, and as they ran, she heard the chirp of his cellphone. He didn't answer it, not until they were sure they'd lost their attackers and were settled on the train heading toward the airport.

Only then did he punch the button to retrieve voice mail. And while he listened, Petra leaned back on the molded plastic seat, breathing hard, but feeling alive. She looked at her punching hand. Alive, she thought, and kick-ass.

Nicholas slipped his phone back into his pocket, and she was about to ask if he'd seen her first-ever punch. But the expression on his face stopped her. "What's wrong?"

"Serge is out," he said, his tone flat.

"He escaped?" She couldn't get her head around it. "How the hell could he have escaped?"

Nicholas just shook his head. "Luke was there with Rand and Lissa. Somehow, he just went through the glass."

She slammed her hand down hard on the seat beside her. "Dammit! He's out there because of me, Nicholas. He's going to kill because of me."

"We're going to stop him," Nicholas said, his voice firm. No nonsense. "Luke and Rand will find him. They'll capture him. And we'll cure him."

"Yeah? Well, here's a question—why the hell are they even still alive?"

That was a damn good question, Nick thought. "I don't know," he said honestly. "Neither does Luke. Serge attacked, and he—well, apparently he stole their essence."

She stared at him. "Come again?"

He explained, and when he was done she was still staring. "But . . . but are they okay?"

"Luke says they're both fine. Although it took hours, they got back to normal."

"Thank God. And he didn't hurt them?"

Nick hesitated. "Luke thinks he would have. But he stopped. Luke isn't sure why. Said it looked like he had other plans." He stared hard at her. "Your feelings. Petra, is there anything more you can tell me?"

She shook her head. "No. I told you. It's murky. Strange. I didn't even realize he'd escaped. The connection just isn't that tight."

Nick nodded, and even though that connection could help them, he could only be glad that among all her other burdens, she didn't have to live inside the mind of a monster, too.

CHAPTER 23

Luke had seen a lot during his years on earth, but the bloodbath inside Dirque's mansion was enough to make even *his* stomach roil. One of Dirque's perimeter guards had discovered the body—or, rather, the pieces of body—less than an hour before at a shift change, and now the house was crawling with crime-scene techs and investigators, including Agent Ryan Doyle, a percipient daemon whom Luke had once called friend, and now tried not to call on at all.

It was almost three hours until sunrise, and most of Los Angeles still slept. But not in this house, now painted, literally, with blood. The walls were splattered with blood, and in the carnage a finger had traced the word *kill* over and over and over. And everywhere, the simple number three.

Amid the carnage, activity reigned, everyone as busy as possible, their minds focused on the job so they wouldn't have to focus on the question that hovered silent in the air—who the fuck could have done this?

That question wasn't on Luke's mind. He already knew the answer. *Serge.*

Beside him, Tiberius stood still and tall, his dark eyes surveying the room. As the Los Angeles area governor and a member of the Alliance, Tiberius had been notified of the murder immediately. Tiberius, in turn, had called Luke.

Across the room, the front door opened, and Tariq rushed in. He looked around, his glance stopping only briefly upon Luke, then halting on Tiberius. He stood straighter, shoulders back, and hurried to the governor. "Sir," he said, and as Luke watched, he realized there wasn't the slightest sign of mourning in the jinn. Only a desperate ambition so thick that Luke had caught its scent from halfway across the room.

"It appears that my theory was right," Tariq said. He stood facing Tiberius, but his eyes shifted sideways, taking Luke in.

"That may be so," Tiberius said, "but it has yet to be established. You are currently observing the girl's brother? Should I assume by your presence here that you have lost him?"

A deep red color began to creep up Tariq's neck, and Luke knew that Tiberius's arrow had hit home. "I was coming to report on that very subject when I got word of my uncle's death."

"You have my deepest sympathies," Tiberius said. "What of the brother?"

"We followed him to the airport, and in light of his earlier actions, we believe it is safe to assume that he is traveling to meet up with his sister."

"Where?"

Tariq cleared his throat. "He bought five tickets online before leaving his house, sir, on different airlines, all with essentially the same departure times."

Luke bit back a laugh. The brother was clever, all right.

"I've tasked five agents, each with a ticket on one of the flights. They will remain at the airport until boarding just after dawn, and we will see which flight Kiril truly takes. That being said, I believe I already know his destination."

"And why is that?"

"The tickets are for London, Zurich, Paris, Frankfurt, and Rome. Of all of those, we are already aware of a Paris connection."

"You wish to take that chance?"

"I do," Tariq said. "If I utilize a Division para-daemon as escort, my team and I can travel to Paris by wormhole and arrive prior to Kiril."

"And if he does not arrive at all? If he steps off a plane in Rome?"

"Then at least I am already in Europe."

"I can find no fault with your reasoning. Go. And report to me upon your arrival."

Tariq inclined his head. "Sir," he said, and then turned to leave, without giving Luke even a second glance.

Tiberius looked at Luke. "You didn't like him three centuries ago, and you do not like him still. Why is that?"

"He is a snake."

"He's ambitious. Is that a crime?"

"He is a snake," Luke repeated, and thought of Sara in her cell and his plan to free her. With luck, the opportunity would present itself here.

Beside him, Tiberius was once again looking around at the carnage. "Tell me true, Lucius Dragos, not under the bond of friendship, but under the bond of *kyne*," he said, referring to the secret brotherhood that served the Alliance. "Did Tariq stumble upon the truth? Does Sergius still live?"

Luke considered lying, but abandoned the notion. No matter his misjudgments, Tiberius was his friend. More than that, to the extent he controlled his daemon, Luke had Tiberius to thank. The elder vamp had forced him into the Holding, had made him *kyne,* had trusted him with his life more times than Luke could count.

He had kept the secret for Serge's sake. But the monster was out now, and Dirque's death was only the beginning. When he and Nick had captured Serge right after the change, he'd been wild and raging and strong, and that had seemed plenty bad. In the months that had passed, though, he'd grown exponentially stronger and had developed some pretty nasty new skills along with a significant level of control. Luke thought about the way Serge had pulled power from him. The way he'd taken on the appearance of a weren after stealing power from Rand.

Most of all he thought about the way Serge had stood there with awareness on his face, his expression turned inward as if he were calculating or reviewing a plan of attack.

Serge was something new and even more dangerous, that was for damn sure. Earlier, Tiberius had told Luke that Petra's touch could bring about the end of the Alliance. Now he believed he understood what the master had meant.

"Yes," Luke finally said. "He lives."

"I see." Tiberius stood tall and straight, power seeming to radiate from him, as if he was having to work hard to hold it in, as if one wrong word would make the whole world explode. "And yet we had no sign. The streets have been free of violence—of this level at any rate. It begins only now. Why?"

"He was being held," Luke said.

Tiberius's brow rose. "And you decided to simply let him go?" There was a hint of humor under his words despite the seriousness of the topic, and for that, Luke was glad. There would be retribution for him and for Nick, but perhaps the rift between them and Tiberius would not be permanent.

"Not exactly, Excellency."

"And has it been confirmed that this is Serge's handi-work?"

"I don't know," Luke said, searching the room until he found Doyle in a corner, his face pale and his muscles slack. His partner, Severin Tucker, held Doyle's arm and began to urge him toward the door. Luke moved to intercept, with Tiberius beside him.

"A word," Luke said.

"I'll give you two," Doyle said. "Fuck off."

"What did you see?" Tiberius asked, apparently unperturbed by Doyle's venom.

"Ask him," Doyle said, lifting his chin toward Luke. "Goddamn selfish bastard, going and getting his woman involved in this mess. Getting Sara tossed in a cell. You don't deserve her, you fucking bloodsucker."

Luke stepped forward, hands clenched in fists of tight rage even as the daemon rose within. Only Tiberius's hand upon Luke's shoulder saved Doyle's ugly face from becoming even uglier.

"I am asking you, *Agent* Doyle," Tiberius said.

"Fine, goddammit."

"You were able to get a clear vision from Chairman Dirque?"

"Yeah, we got lucky. The guard found him when he was still warm." Luke knew that Doyle's gift allowed him to take the last vision and emotion from a victim. To see it and process it. But once the death was cold and the aura faded, even Doyle's gifts couldn't coax out a vision. He looked between Luke and Tiberius. "I don't think I'm telling either of you anything you didn't already know, but in case you want to hear it all official-like, then yeah, our perp is Sergius."

Tiberius's nod was quick and sharp. "Thank you, Agent. That will be all."

Doyle hesitated before succumbing to Tucker's tug at his arm, and in that brief hesitation, Luke saw Doyle's contempt for vampires painted all over his face, so clear he was certain Tiberius saw it as well. The governor, however, didn't speak of it.

Instead, he railed on Luke.

"You did this for friendship?" he asked, leading Luke to a quiet corner where they would not be overheard. "Do you have any idea what horrors your friend can wreak?"

A cold rage snapped within Luke. "I saw my wife today for twenty minutes, Tiberius, in a goddamned cell. *A cell.* Tell me what you wish to tell me, and do so plainly. Or tell me nothing at all."

Tiberius studied him, then nodded. "I told you earlier that it has been prophesied that Petra's touch could bring the destruction of the Alliance."

"You did."

"It is through the monster that she creates." He drew in a breath, and began to recite. *"From the touch of Eve, destruction shall rise—a third, powerful and changed, who emerges from the earth, and who will fell the piers upon which the shadows rule, and take back that which was stolen."*

Luke listened to the words . . . and feared he understood them. He turned, looking across the room at the wall covered with violent graffiti and the shape of the number three. "The third," he said. "The third brother? You're saying the third brother is manifest within Serge, and he will destroy the Alliance?"

"The piers upon which the shadows rule, yes." Tiberius swept his arm over the room. "It has begun," he said. "And now I must call upon the obligation of friendship and upon your oath as *kyne*."

Luke tensed, listening. As *kyne*, he often undertook missions for Tiberius in his role as vampiric liaison to the Alliance, eradicating those who presented problems that the Preternatural Enforcement Coalition was unable to adequately resolve. Now he was afraid that Tiberius would send him after Serge. And even though he knew his friend existed no more, that was not an assignment he wanted.

Even so, he drew in a breath and asked, "What do you ask of me, Excellency?"

"You will serve as my bodyguard until this danger has passed."

Luke let the words—and relief—flow around him. He knew that he should accept without hesitation, but he didn't. Instead, he was examining the chance that

Tiberius's request offered. A chance that Luke had been hoping for, but one full of risk.

It was worth the risk.

"I would be honored, Excellency," he said. "Would you care to know the cost of such service?"

As he expected, Tiberius's eyes widened with both surprise and anger. "Cost? Are you not *kyne*?"

"I am," Luke said, keeping his speech formal and respectful. "And friend, too. But my wife is accused of treachery and even now sits in a prison. You can set her free."

"She assisted a prison escape."

"She was accused of such," Luke acknowledged. "She was framed."

Tiberius tilted his head to study Luke. "Was she? By whom?"

"Who can be certain?" Luke said. "But I do know that Tariq was charged with finding the person within Division who assisted Nick, a task he accomplished with remarkable swiftness considering the number of people on Division's payroll. Ironic, isn't it, that he arrests the wife of a man he despises." He smiled thinly. "As you pointed out, there is great animosity between us. A shame it had to spill over onto Sara."

Tiberius considered all of this, and Luke could see from his face that he was considering the true situation, and not simply the convenient lie that Luke was spinning. "I could insist that Sara go free. I can even urge Bosch to accept that she fell victim to a frame. I understand she has a promising career, and that should repair any damage to her reputation. But the evidence against

Tariq is all circumstantial. There would never be a sufficient case made to convict."

"A pity," Luke said, knowing that fact would ease Sara's conscience. She would not be comfortable walking free while another paid for her crime. "Perhaps knowing that his attempt to frame her failed would be punishment enough."

"And you will remain at my side until this matter with Sergius is resolved?"

"I will."

Tiberius nodded. "Then you have my bond. See me safely through this crisis, and your Sara will walk free."

Luke relaxed, careful not to let Tiberius see the depth of his relief. He had expected a more protracted battle and significantly more indignation on Tiberius's part. That the master vampire conceded so easily was testament to the weight of his fear.

Luke ran a hand through his hair, trying to organize his thoughts. That meant that the situation with the monster was worse than he'd imagined, and yet . . .

He looked at Tiberius, voicing his thoughts as they became clear. "We agree that it is not Sergius who committed this crime, but the monster. The third."

"That is so."

"Then I tell you this as a friend. Nick is on a quest. He believes he can lift the curse and restore Sergius. If he does, will our friend walk free?"

"Nick is with the girl?"

Luke hesitated, weighing his options, and decided that truth was the moment's best ploy. "He is."

"Then tell him to kill her. The moment he does, Sergius will be restored."

CHAPTER 24

Luke and Tiberius stood unmoving inside Trylag's temporary office within Division 6. The para-daemon liaison to the Alliance was pacing, his swarthy face red with frustration and anger and, Luke saw, with fear. Luke kept his position at Tiberius's side, a massive tranquilizer gun strapped over his shoulder, an automatic pistol holstered at his side, and a knife sheathed at his thigh. Not his usual contingent of weapons, but necessary if he would have any hope of defeating Sergius. Even then, he was probably not well armed.

"You suggest I run?" Trylag demanded, getting into Tiberius's face. "You suggest I hide?"

"I suggest that we do what we can to forestall this prophecy from coming to pass," Tiberius said. "You are the governor of Australia and the Far Eastern territories, are you not? Go there, then, and lock yourself in someplace impenetrable until our agents can kill this monster."

Trylag sneered. "And yet you walk free. Do you think I cannot smell a trick? Do you think I believe that the enmity that has passed between us has simply been erased?"

"You small-minded fool," snarled Tiberius. "I speak not of petty disputes among the Alliance liaisons. We are concerned now with the sanctity of the Alliance as a whole."

Luke stepped forward. "Tiberius will be concealed somewhere that Sergius cannot find him." That much was true. Rand and Lissa were preparing a hidden chamber in a warehouse recently acquired through a series of false names and companies. The concrete was thick, the locks were massive, and the security system state of the art. Even then, Luke intended to bring in Alliance guards to man the doors. He would take no chances guarding Tiberius. If the master vampire died, the deal to free Sara died with him.

Trylag ran his hand over his chin. "Narid has gone already?"

"He has." The wraith liaison had needed no extra persuasion, a fact that had chilled Luke. Wraiths were notoriously difficult to destroy, and it was not brawn that did the trick. If the wraith liaison was indeed so scared, then there was much to fear from both the prophecy and Sergius.

He thought of the bloodbath he'd witnessed inside Dirque's home, not to mention the mangled bodies of the guards found along the perimeter. *Yes. Much to fear.*

He shifted the tranquilizer gun on his shoulder, hoping that he wouldn't have to use any of his weapons, hoping that Nick could turn Serge around before Luke was forced to defend Tiberius. He had no desire to kill his friend. To save Sara, though, he wouldn't hesitate. Tiberius was under Luke's protection now.

Trylag's eyes narrowed as he looked between Tiberius and Luke. "And you speak the truth? Tiberius will do the same? He will hide away like a scared rabbit?"

"There is no shame here, Excellency," Luke said, trying to keep the frustration out of his voice. "You have heard the prophecy. We are fighting the hand of fate with every trick in our arsenal."

"You have not answered the question, vampire."

"Yes," Luke snapped. "Tiberius will be locked away as well. As I have already told you."

"He speaks the truth," Tiberius said. "We leave here to go to my cell."

Trylag drew in a noisy breath. "Very well," he said. "I will do as you say." He inclined his head, his hands close to his body. He stood stiffly, his skin turning a burnished orange that seemed to collect at his fingertips.

He was gathering power, Luke knew. Soon, the parademon would reach out, and with his hand, he would rend the very fabric of the universe. That was a parademon's special gift—the creation of a wormhole, and through it, Trylag could travel to his territory in almost the blink of an eye.

The door from the office to the Division 6 hallway opened, and Luke did a double take when he saw Nick walk in. A split second later he shoved Tiberius to the floor and had the tranq gun out and firing—because that wasn't Nick. It was Serge, using the power of the jinn he'd taken from Dirque to throw a glamour—and using his own unique power to drain Tiberius, Luke, and Trylag.

The tranq darts didn't even slow Serge down, though, and he dove for Trylag and began to rip off the parademon's limbs, all while the doomed creature howled in pain.

Luke wanted to simply transform into mist and get

the hell out of there, but Serge had stolen that power. Luke had more strength than he'd had in the warehouse, though, and he had to assume that was because Serge was focused on Trylag, and the draining of power was only a prophylactic measure to protect himself as he attacked the para-daemon.

He considered firing the actual bullets, but it was obvious there was no hope for the para-daemon. And if he fired, he'd just draw attention to himself and to Tiberius.

With Sara filling his thoughts, he urged Tiberius out the door and then pulled it closed.

"Go!" he yelled to Tiberius, who ran down the hall as Luke moved into the next office and shoved aside a lanky weren female so he could get to her phone. "Security," he said, then ordered that they gas Trylag's office, instituting a fail-safe protective measure that existed throughout Division.

The female had watched him with wide eyes, and then pulled up the video feed for Trylag's office, and they watched as the smoky gas poured in . . . and did absolutely nothing to Serge.

Trylag's body lay on the ground, limbless and bleeding. And Serge stood over him, his head cocked, almost as if he was listening to someone calling his name.

Then he tilted his face up, and looked straight into the camera. Luke sucked in air, seeing the depth of dark purpose in the eyes of his friend.

And then Serge reached into the air just as Trylag had done earlier. He whipped his arm in a circle, swirling the air, and soon a hole opened, dark and black.

With one final glance upward toward the camera, Serge stepped inside—and was gone.

◆

Petra curled up in one of the plane's seats, looking out the window at the darkening city disappearing behind them, fighting a trembling that had started deep in her muscles. She wanted to sleep. To forget that Serge was on the loose. That he was some freakish creature who could steal a shadower's power. That she had anything to do with creating this monster that was going to set loose a river of blood.

She wanted to ignore the horrible sensations that filled her head—dark and bitter and full of blood. Had he killed? She knew he must have—that was what the monster did—but she felt only the black pit of evil swirling somewhere deep inside of her. *Serge,* and, dear God, she didn't want to feel it. Didn't want to shoulder the burden of experiencing the evil of what she had made.

And she sure as hell didn't want to do it alone.

But she had no choice. The earth had turned, and she was alone again.

Nicholas.

She wasn't a fool. She knew the way the world worked. Hell, she knew the way *he* worked. He might have said sweet things to her and whispered that they'd be together, but that wasn't something she could hold him to. He was Nicholas Montegue. He wasn't the kind of man who fell for one woman. Especially a woman he could have in his bed for only one night every few years.

So better that she put the walls back up now before the hurt barreled down on her. Because, yeah, she could see the hurt coming. She hated it—oh God, she hated it—but it was absolutely inevitable.

The curtain between the cockpit and the cabin opened and he stepped out, a triumphant grin on his face. "We are safe at cruising altitude, and my friend Mr. Autopilot has the controls. Our cruising time is estimated at ten hours, and we'll reach Paris before the sun rises in the City of Lights."

She wanted to smile at the playfulness in his voice, but couldn't.

He frowned and took a step toward her. "And a good thing, too," he said. "You look like you could use the sleep. Are you okay?"

She wanted to tell him she wasn't. Wanted him to sit near her and caress her with words and let her take some of his strength. But that would be a mistake. She'd already gotten closer to him than she should have. Yes, she'd had the blue moon she'd always dreamed about— too bad she'd never bothered to dream about what would happen after.

"What's that saying?" she asked, tilting her head up to look at him.

"What saying?"

"Be careful what you wish for . . ."

She saw the concern flare in his eyes and gripped the seat next to him as he focused all his attention on her. "Petra, what's wrong?"

"I'd like to be alone now."

"I could sit. We could talk."

"No." She needed to be strong. She'd felt her self-reliance slipping away last night. She needed to grab it back. She already had one man who was prisoner to her, and couldn't bear to have another. Especially not Nicholas, who wasn't a man who would enjoy being trapped by a woman. He was too full of life and joy.

And life with her would be anything but.

She thought about Ferrante. About this mystery alchemist who Nicholas believed could find a cure for Serge. She wished she could put her faith in that hope, too, but she knew more than Nicholas did. There was a cure already, and Ferrante would probably tell Nicholas what Petra already knew. That lifting the curse from Serge was the easiest thing in the world. Petra simply had to die.

No. Once they reached Paris, she'd find a time to slip away. Kiril had to be searching for her. She'd find him. They'd be on the run, but—

"Petra?"

She closed her eyes, gathering strength, wishing the path that lay before her included Nicholas, but knowing it couldn't. "I told you I want to be alone."

She saw a muscle twitch in his jaw, and had to fight the urge to take it all back. To beg him to put his hand beside hers and tell her that somehow, together, they'd find a way through this. She didn't, though, and after a moment he nodded slowly.

"As you wish."

She forced herself not to flinch as he turned and walked away, returning to the cabin and the pilot's seat.

Once again, she was alone. Considering she'd been doing her damnedest to push him away, she was surprised by how much that hurt.

He'd touched her. Dear God, he'd touched her as no one else had. He'd opened her up to pleasure and wonder. He'd made her laugh and feel things she'd never thought she could feel.

Things she wouldn't feel again for a long, long time.

Frustrated, she looked toward the front of the plane and the curtain behind which Nicholas sat. She stood up and took a step in that direction, but she couldn't go all the way, and she ended up merely crossing the aisle.

Behind her, the emergency exit door dominated the hull, and she cast it one suspicious glance before clicking the ends of the seat belt firmly together. She sat, letting the sadness wash over her. Feeling the vibrations of the plane fill her. Then she closed her eyes and willed herself not to cry despite the stabbing, horrible knowledge that no matter what, she wasn't going to feel his touch again.

CHAPTER 25

Nick sat in the pilot's seat, something dark and unfamiliar twisting through him. He tried to analyze it and knew that it wasn't anger he felt. Hell, it wasn't even frustration.

No, it was the unfamiliar ache of loss.

She'd pushed him away and, goddammit, her diffidence had bruised him.

The question was why, and he saw the answer clearly: *She'd* pulled back. She'd usurped Nick's role. Wasn't that his standard approach to a night with a beautiful woman? Thank you very much, but I must be going now? She'd thrust his own goddamned MO back on him, and *that* was eating at him. Not the loss, not the woman herself.

Simply the way she did it.

That was all. Simple. Obvious.

Although, yes, if he was honest he had to admit that there was a measure of irritation arising from the fact that he would, remarkably, have altered his own rules for Petra. Not that his habit of avoiding continued relationships actually constituted a rule. More like the practical ramification of not finding a woman in his bed who intrigued his mind as much as his body. And without that connection, what was the point of bedding her a second time?

With Petra, he would have gone back, though he supposed her diffidence was just as well. Her bed was not
one he could return to. She was like Medusa now, her
touch rather than her eyes capable of altering him forever.

She'd pushed him away almost cruelly, though she
wasn't a woman he could ever believe would be cruel.

A sudden shock of understanding washed over him,
and he sat in the pilot's seat feeling like a goddamned
idiot. His fucking male ego had been so bruised by her
coldness that he hadn't thought to consider where it
came from, much less whether or not it was real. And
frankly, he didn't believe that it was.

He closed his eyes, reaching out for her, searching for
her in the blood they shared. She wouldn't want him
to—but he had to know how she felt, what she was
thinking.

She was thinking about him.

Her body was warm and soft and wanting.

He couldn't read her thoughts—the connection didn't
work that way—but he was certain he understood the
emotions. Desire warring with fear. Fear of what she
was. Fear that he would leave.

By the gods, she was wrong. So very, very wrong.

He stood, intending to go to her, but stopped when
the cockpit radio beeped, signaling an incoming transmission. He frowned; only a few people knew that Serge
had a plane, much less the private frequency. And no
one knew that he and Petra were on this plane.

He considered ignoring the transmission, especially
in light of his overwhelming desire to go to Petra, but
curiosity and instinct for self-preservation changed his

mind. If someone knew they were in Serge's jet, Nick wanted to know who.

He slipped on the headset and pushed the button to talk. "Go ahead."

"Dirque and Trylag are dead," Luke said. "I have Tiberius under guard, but the rest of the Alliance members are targets."

"They've been warned?" Nick asked.

"They have. Whether or not they've gone into hiding, I don't know."

"Shit."

For a moment Luke was silent, and Nick feared that the connection had dropped. Then his friend spoke. "Tariq is on his way to Paris, as is the brother. Be wary."

"I will," Nick said, though something in Luke's voice suggested that was not the real reason for the call.

"It is worse than we thought," Luke said. "This prophecy I told you about—apparently it's coming to pass. Serge is channeling the power of the third. He killed Dirque's guards, so he's not discriminating, but his primary target does seem to be the Alliance."

"The third? The third brother?" He took very little satisfaction from the fact that his theory had been right. "Your message said he drained you and Rand of your power?"

"That's so, although the damage wasn't permanent."

"It fits," Nick said. "If the third seeks revenge, what better way to obtain it than to fill himself with the power that was stolen by the other two brothers."

"Is the girl with you?"

"Of course."

"Then you can end this now."

"What the hell are you talking about?"

"She is the cure, Nick."

Nick tensed, hearing the cool detachment in Luke's words. "What do you mean?"

"Kill her, and Serge will be himself again. The Alliance members have seen it work that way. And Tiberius himself has ordered it."

Nick said nothing, the shock of what Luke said curling around and through him.

"Nicholas? Do you understand?"

Nick swallowed, aware of the way the air seemed to suddenly hang heavy around him. "And if I cannot?"

"You've killed before in service of the Alliance," Luke said.

Nick said nothing.

"I like Petra, too," Luke said, all formality dropping from his tone. "But if Serge is the hand that will destroy the Alliance, and her death can free him—"

"And if it were Sara?"

There was silence on the other end. And then, "Is that the way of it?"

"It is."

"The killing cannot continue," Luke said, and Nick heard the danger in the words. If Nick didn't kill Petra, someone else surely would.

"Ferrante may still yield answers," Nick said, knowing full well that would not stall the Alliance. Before, they wanted her dead to prevent a monster. Now that the monster was out and killing, they would put all their resources toward finding and stopping her.

"Or he may not," Luke countered. "And how many

will die while you avoid certainty to chase a possibility?"

"Does that mean that you intend to tell the Alliance where we're going?"

There was a pause, then, "No. What was said in friendship remains between us. But Nick, they know you're going to Paris. They may well make the connection without me. Think well about what you need to do."

Nick clenched his fists, duty to Tiberius, to the entire shadow world warring with—with what? With desire?

No, it was more than that.

With love.

He closed his eyes and imagined the rage of Sergius. He knew what the monster could do. And he knew where this could end.

"Does she know?" Nick asked. "Does Petra know that her death will end this?" He felt a quick burst of anger at the possibility. But while part of him wanted to lash out at her for hiding from him the very cure that he'd sought when they first started this journey, the practical part knew damn well why she had.

And, he realized, he was glad of it.

Then, he could have taken her life to save Serge.

Now, he knew that he wouldn't. More, he knew that he couldn't.

He didn't wait for Luke's response. "I will do what I must do," he said, and then he ended the transmission. What he didn't say was that what he must do was exactly what he'd been doing all along. He'd find a cure for Serge. He'd find a way to lift Petra's curse.

He loved her, and, dear God, he would not sacrifice her.

He stood, intending to go to her, and only then remembered why he'd returned to the cockpit in the first place. Because Petra herself had pushed him away.

He slammed his fist against the molded plastic wall in frustration, then forced himself to be calm and to reach out again. Once again, he felt her need, felt her silently calling to him despite what her actual words had said.

He had just chosen her above everything else. No matter what she had voiced, he would not stay away.

He'd followed his own heart. Now, he would follow hers, too.

Swiftly, he transformed into mist, then slipped beneath the curtain into the cabin. She'd moved to a different seat, and her legs extended into the aisle. She wasn't asleep, but she wasn't truly awake, either.

They'd melded together before as mist upon mist, but now she was in her human form, and her flesh had power. Because of that, he didn't stroke her skin, but twined himself around her body, over and around, slipping between her thighs and over the swell of her breasts.

He remained only over cloth, and stayed only as mist, but he knew when she felt him. When she realized he was there and that he was touching her, stroking her, *taking her*.

She moaned, a small smile coming to her lips, and he wanted to never see it leave. He wanted to tell her that whatever she'd thought before, she was wrong. He wouldn't leave her any more than he would cut off his own limb.

He'd tell her now, though not with words. Instead with caresses, and soon he sensed the quickening of her pulse. The rise and fall of her breasts. The arousal and the pleasure.

With a soft sigh, she slipped one gloved hand between her legs, stroking herself through her jeans. The other hand cupped her breast, teasing and touching her nipple through the cotton.

He was only mist, but that didn't ease the pull of desire. He craved her, wanted desperately to touch her, and twined sensually around her hand, urging her on, taking his own pleasure by easing her closer and closer to hers until finally—*finally*—her body trembled, and he felt her pleasure ricochet through his consciousness as she cried out with release.

Slowly, he twined away from her, then came back to form in front of her, standing and looking down at her flushed face and full lips. "Wow," she said.

"You're mine now," he said, needing her to understand this fully. "You're mine, and by the gods, I am yours. And I will keep you safe."

He didn't wait for her to answer, but when he reached the cockpit, he turned back around once, and found her looking back with a smile on her face that went straight to his heart.

CHAPTER 26

The thick foliage of the Bois de Boulogne bent under the strain of the wormhole that opened among the trees. Marie, strung out on meth and looking for another quick fuck so she could buy another hit, tottered on nail-point heels and stared, baffled, at the swirling column of wind and color.

In the tallest branches of the trees, birds squawked their protests.

But the girl and the birds didn't run. At least not until the monster came through, its huge form filling the void, its eyes glowing red, its skin tinged crimson, as if it had brushed too close to the fires of hell.

With massive effort, it pushed itself out of the hole, everything about the way it moved suggesting exhaustion. It climbed to its feet, and the birds flew away, their flapping wings echoing the wind in the night.

Marie wavered, part of her mind playing with the pretty, swirling colors, part of her mind screaming for her to run. And part of her wondering if this fucked-up male was up for a twenty-euro blow job, because twenty would get her easily through the rest of the night.

The huge male crawled to its knees, its head rolling like someone stoned or completely wiped out. It held its hands out in front of itself, and the prostitute saw how big they were, and wondered what they'd feel like touching her.

Then it jammed them down, so hard and fast its fingers sliced into the earth like hot knives into butter. It sank in all the way to its elbows, and it closed its eyes as if in ecstasy as power rippled up its arms and shimmered over its entire body.

Marie gaped, her feet rooted to the spot, her mouth hanging open as her chemically charged brain tried to process what the fuck was going on.

She never managed. Hell, she never had time.

The creature was on her in a moment, her death, her blood adding even more power to a creature that was already overflowing.

As it dropped the body, limp and lifeless to the ground, the call filled it, urging it to the next place, the next taking of power.

It lifted its head, sniffing out the way. And as it loped toward the next kill, the blackness within it rose and spread . . . and the daemon—buried deep within what had once been a vampire—curled up and purred.

◆

It was still hours before dawn when they landed in Paris, and as they stepped out of the plane, Petra was struck by the simple fact that as long as she traveled with Nicholas, she wouldn't feel the sun upon her skin. Still, the night sky was open to them, a black void that seemed deep enough to wrap them up and hide them away. Even the stars were hidden, their feeble light no match for the lights of Paris.

"It's like a cloak," she said.

"I've always thought so, too," he said, and she turned, surprised. "What?" he asked.

"Really?"

He laughed, the sound warm and soothing. "I've always thought of the night as protection. Even before I was changed and had no choice but to think of the night as a friend or spend my eternity mourning the loss of the day. Even then, I used to wander the night, slipping from shadow to shadow, observing the world."

"Did you really?" She could imagine him, actually. Hiding just outside of doorways, peering inside rooms, wanting only to satisfy his curiosity for what was going on inside. The world would have been darker then, lit by candles rather than by electric light. "Do you miss the stars?" she asked.

"Sometimes," he said. "But there are still places in the world where you can find the darkness, and then it's like a gift. I'll show them to you sometime."

He smiled when he spoke, and she felt warm. Protected. He'd said from the beginning that was his role, but to offer to show her the stars—that was like offering her the world.

That was, she realized, exactly what he was doing. She remembered his words on the plane: *You're mine now.* He hadn't told her he loved her, but he hadn't needed to. Something had grown between them, something sweet and wonderful, and she cherished it. Maybe that made her a fool, but she didn't care. Maybe her heart and her body were inexperienced and overwhelmed, but she didn't think so. Nicholas was hers.

And while she was still a little fuzzy on the details of how that had happened, she knew that she wasn't about to deny it—and she sure as hell wasn't going to push him away again.

She was still basking when Nicholas hailed a taxi to take them through the center of Paris toward the sixteenth arrondissement. On the way, they passed the Eiffel Tower, and she hugged herself with pleasure, not quite believing that she was actually in Paris. It seemed special. Romantic, even. Despite the fact that they'd come here in a futile attempt to lift a curse and with the Alliance surely nipping at their heels.

"Do you think they're here? The Alliance, I mean?"

A shadow crossed Nicholas's face. "I do. I have reason to believe that Tariq is on his way here. May already be here, in fact."

"An Alliance agent?"

"A tenacious one," Nicholas confirmed. He shifted in the seat to face her straight on. "Have you felt any more of Serge? Do you know if he's here?"

She shook her head. "I've never felt where he is, only the rising of . . . I don't know . . . evil." She drew in a breath and fought a shiver. "And I feel that all the time now. It's like a low electrical hum that spikes sometimes. It spiked not too long ago, about the time we were landing."

"But no thoughts?"

"No." She cocked her head. "Can't you feel it, too? You can feel me, right? Through the blood. Can you feel Serge through me?"

"I can't," he said automatically, but then quieted

himself, and she watched his face go slack as he tried again. She closed her eyes, feeling inside, wishing that she could experience the sensation of him inside her, and frustrated that the blood connection didn't run both ways.

When she opened her eyes, he was looking at her. "No," he said. "There is you, and the warmth you feel toward me, the fear you feel from those following us. But my friend isn't there."

Her throat went dry. "But he is. If you can't feel him, too—what does that mean?"

He shook his head. "I don't know. Maybe that you're feeling him through someone else. A conduit. If there was another to whom I was blood connected, they wouldn't be able to feel you through me. That's the only explanation that comes to mind, but I have no way of testing it."

"Maybe," she said, but she was frowning. She'd *created* Serge, so how could it make sense that she was only a conduit, feeling him through someone else? "Who?" she asked. "Who else could there be?"

"I haven't any idea," he said. "Right now, it doesn't matter. We have larger problems to face."

She heard the tenseness in his voice and matched it with her own. "What's going on? What haven't you told me?"

"He's killing," he said, and her body went cold. "He's started with the Alliance. Dirque and Trylag are dead. We have to assume he's coming after the others. There's a prophecy. I don't know the actual words, but it's about the monster killing off the Alliance members."

"Oh." She tried to process his words. "Oh God. They

know? The Alliance members, they know he's targeting them? They're hiding? Staying safe?"

"Yes. But this is the monster we're talking about, who steals power and grows stronger every day. Is there truly anyplace safe?"

She opened her mouth to say something, but couldn't find words that were adequate.

"Gunnolf is in Paris, Petra. Serge could be here, too. Somehow, I'm going to make sure it ends here."

Somehow.

Serge was killing. He was killing because *she* had made him a killer, and yet she was shying away from the one thing that she could do absolutely. *She could stop him.*

Yes, the idea was scary, but maybe there was a time to surrender to death. To welcome it, even. She wasn't an immortal like Nicholas. Someday, no matter what, she would die and he would live.

If she died today, how many lives would she save?

How unfair that today came now, when she'd found someone to love.

Dear God, could she do it? After having just found Nicholas, did she have the courage to leave him? To step up and do what needed to be done?

She drew in a deep breath. She had to. Somehow, she had to find the courage inside.

They'd arrived outside of le Cimetière de Passy, and Nicholas paid the driver and thanked him in French. Then they were standing in a rough street, facing a stone wall, the Eiffel Tower rising at their backs in the distance.

Nicholas started to take a step toward the gate.

Petra drew in a breath, clenched her hands into fists, and whispered, "Stop."

He turned. "Are you okay?"

"No."

He was at her side in an instant, not touching, but so close that she could feel his comfort. *Dear God, how she would miss him,* she thought, and then wondered if the dead missed anyone.

"What's wrong?"

"Do you have a knife?"

He tilted his head, his eyes seeing more than she wanted. "I do."

She nodded, the gesture more to gather her courage than any sort of acknowledgment. "Will you do something for me?"

She saw his face go wary. "That depends on what you want."

The unexpected response knocked her off her rhythm and she struggled to find her way, the path all the more difficult since she didn't want to walk it. She didn't *want* to die. But if she could save these people . . . hell, if she could save the whole shadow world . . .

"I want you to take my life. Wait," she continued, before he could interrupt. "Do that, and Serge will be free. I'm sorry I didn't tell you before. I was scared. I was . . . I was a coward. But he's killing, Nicholas. He's killing, and I can stop him. *You* can stop him."

"No."

That was it. That was the entire answer. And it was so damned unexpected that she actually stumbled backward. "What?"

The slightest hint of a smile touched his mouth. "No."

"But—" She cut herself off, then searched his face. She'd expected surprise. Anger that she'd kept this from him. Instead, she saw acceptance. More than that, she saw expectation. "You knew. You knew I could stop him and you—how long have you known?"

"Since the flight," he said. "Luke radioed and told me."

"Luke?"

"The Alliance knows, too," he said. "They wanted you dead before so you couldn't create a monster. Now they want you even more so that you can cure a monster."

"And they're right."

He looked at her. "Do you want to die?"

"No." The word came automatically. "No, I don't, but—"

"We *will* find another answer."

He sounded so positive. She wanted to be positive, too.

"We're here to see Ferrante, right? The answer may well be under our noses."

"But—"

"No. We will lift your curse, and we will either cure Serge or recapture him. And that is the way of it."

She licked her lips, something warm and soft filling her up. Hope.

Love.

And then the warmth turned to ice as she remembered the dead. "But the Alliance members—"

"Have known since the day they took office that they

could die at another's hand. Think of the world in which they move, Petra. The shadows and politics, and those make dangerous bedfellows. There are assassins around every corner. Enemies at every curve. They chose a high-risk profession, Petra. And each has known of this prophecy for centuries, and yet none declined their position. They assumed the risk. Let them assume it a little longer."

"You sound like a lawyer," she said.

"Do I? Then let me sound now like your lover. I take the choice away from you, Petra Lang. I will not give you my knife, nor use it on you. I've told you we are in this together. Don't doubt my word."

He reached for her cheek, then halted, as if remembering the danger. As he did, she realized that she was crying, and brushed the tears away.

"Okay?" he asked.

"There may come a time when I have no choice."

"No," he said. "You did not create this curse. These deaths do not hang on your head. And I will not let you pay the price for them. Do you understand me?"

"Yes." There was nothing more to say.

"Good." He cocked his head toward the gate. "Shall we?"

She couldn't help her smile. "Okay."

He tugged on the bars and found them locked. "Well. That's a bit anticlimactic," he said, and she burst out laughing, the tension of the last few moments bubbling out.

"Is a locked gate really that much of a problem for you?" she asked, feeling the wall's rough surface. "Get in however you want. I'll meet you there."

His brows lifted. "Oh?"

She laughed. "Private investigator, remember? Trust me, I've scaled my share of walls." To prove her point, she did just that, using the uneven stones for finger- and footholds, until she reached the top and sat on it, letting her legs swing down. "Easy as pie."

"Apparently so." And then, to her surprise, he followed her up. "And I'm not completely dependent on my vampiric gifts."

She laughed, clutching the side of the wall so she wouldn't tumble off. "No, I guess not. I'm a little surprised, though."

"That I can climb?"

"Not that you can—that you would. Those are nice jeans, after all. And you might accidentally rip your shirt."

"Not to worry. We're in Paris. I'm sure I can find a fashionable replacement for any item I ruin." He looked her up and down. "Actually, it's a shame we don't have more time. I think we could do a lot better for you as well."

She looked down at the jeans and man's T-shirt she'd been wearing since Serge's apartment. "Thanks a lot."

"You look lovely," he said, his voice so soft she almost believed it. "But what woman wouldn't want to haunt the boutiques of the Champs Élysées?"

She smiled, imagining walking hand in hand with him along the streets of Paris, peering in shop windows and sipping café au lait in outdoor cafés while the twinkling lights of the city shone around them. A nice fantasy, but bittersweet, and with a single shove, she pushed herself off the fence and her fantasy out of her head. When she landed on the soft ground, she looked back up at him with what she hoped was a smug, confident grin. "A woman on a mission," she said. "Coming?"

He was beside her with such speed that she never saw him move.

"Neat trick."

"I have many of them."

"You know where we're going. Lead the way."

He began walking, and she had to follow carefully, unable to see the path once they were away from the scattered lampposts. On either side of them, statuary loomed, the polished stone glowing eerily.

She wished she could take his hand.

Around them, the night seemed to curl about the tombs like a living thing, and the more they walked, the more Petra began to feel as if they weren't alone.

Beside her, Nicholas slowed his pace.

"Do you sense it, too?" she asked.

"Someone near," he whispered, stopping at the intersection of two cobbled lanes. "I do. But I've been looking in the dark and I see nothing."

Since that really wasn't reassuring, she turned in a slow circle to have a look for herself. Futile, of course, since her human eyes could see nothing in the dark. If she only had some light . . .

On a whim, she held out her hand. She'd managed a tiny fireball in Serge's kitchen. Could she manage something larger now? Closing her eyes, she concentrated, picturing the earth, summoning the elements. Deep within the molten core, fire burned, and in her mind she drew it up, pulling it to her, willing it to follow her command.

And then . . .

And then . . .

Nothing.

Shit.

Frustrated, she dropped her arm, and saw Nicholas looking at her with a small smile.

She scowled at him, feeling grumpy and ineffective. Magic flowed in her veins, and she should have been practicing all along. If Kiril was afraid that the curse affected her control, then wasn't practice the way to fix that?

Not that she could do anything about it now. What's done was done.

"It's probably better this way," Nicholas said. "If the Alliance is trying to get a bead on your magic, it may not be a good idea to ratchet up that magic."

"I guess," she said, but she still regretted the years she hadn't practiced.

"Maybe he didn't want you skilled at magic, because then you wouldn't need him," Nicholas said.

She frowned. "Kiril? That doesn't make sense."

"Doesn't it? He was bound to you—tightly from what you say—and his life has been defined by his purpose. He is your protector. If you can protect yourself, where does that leave him?"

"No," she said, but the word was weak, because she couldn't truly argue the logic of what Nicholas said. "Kiril loves me."

"The two aren't mutually exclusive."

She didn't answer, thinking of her brother. He must

be going out of his mind with worry. She wondered if he could sense her now, all the way across North America and the Atlantic Ocean. Was he at his desk, writing frantically, working his fears out in story after story? Or was he blocked, unable to lift a pen until she was back with him?

Or was he coming after her?

He was—she was certain of it. The bond between them was intense. More so than with regular siblings, she knew, and she was certain it was the binding spell that kept Kiril so focused on her, so close, sometimes even to the point where she wished that she could slip away from him and hide.

He'd come. There was no question in her mind.

The thought worried her, and she wished that she could sense him like he could sense her. But she couldn't, and she had no way of knowing if he'd somehow managed to follow her. And if he had, was the Alliance following him?

"This one," Nicholas said, stopping in front of a small marble tomb around which bits of chalk had been dropped. Nicholas picked one up, then knelt by a corner and wrote a neat "N.M."

"When will we know?" she asked.

"We'll check back tomorrow night. If he will meet us, the message will be left in the flower vase," he added, pointing to a small metal vase protruding from the concrete. There were no flowers in it. "In the meantime, we'll find someplace safe to wait. How do you feel about a hotel? Blackout shades. Room service. A hot bath and a large bed?"

"I feel pretty good about it."

"As do I." He looked at the sky. "We still have an hour before dawn, but I want to get off the street. Let's hurry."

Since she had no particular interest in hanging around a graveyard any longer than she had to, she fell in step beside him as they headed back toward the front gate. He stopped short after only a few yards, though, and held up a hand. He pointed toward the shadows as he stepped in front of her. She turned to peer into the dark, her pulse pounding as her adrenaline level sky-rocketed.

Nothing. No one.

Just the darkness and the graves, the wind twisting among the tombs.

But Nicholas remained tense, his head tilted, as if he'd found a scent in the air. All things considered, he probably had.

He cocked his head and started moving forward, easing them out of the cemetery.

Fine by her. She was ready to be inside. Someplace safe, where they could regroup. Someplace away from shadows that moved in the night and—

Something grabbed her from behind—a rope! She struggled, but it was no use; the rope simply tightened around her waist. And in front of her, she heard the low, growling laughter of a snarling weren male.

A male who held a stake poised right over Nicholas's heart.

♦

Nick recognized the male who held the stake to his heart as one from Gunnolf's inner circle. Several yards away, Gunnolf himself held the rope that bound Petra, his fiery red hair seeming to spark in the dim glow of the moon.

Around the perimeter stood three other weren, all holding weapons.

Five against two, and considering his vampire gifts and the fact that none of the five would touch Petra, those just might be good odds. The trick was to get the ball rolling without ending up with a stake through his heart.

"I helped you," Petra was saying to Gunnolf. "I helped you and Tiberius, and you both just fucked me over."

"It's nothing personal, lass," he said. "All creatures have a right to survive, aye?"

"This isn't my fault," she said.

"Perhaps that's so," Gunnolf said. "But it changes nothing." He yanked the rope, drawing Petra closer.

Fearing for her, Nick feinted back, away from the point of the stake, then lashed out with a solid punch as the weren regrouped and slammed Nick to the ground.

He kicked up, catching the weren hard in the jaw, then recovered the stake and slammed the weapon into the weren's throat before climbing to his feet and racing toward Petra.

But he was all out of time.

Gunnolf had a knife—a huge fucking knife. So huge that he could easily slice Petra's throat without risk of touching her.

No, no, goddammit, no!

But before Gunnolf could thrust the knife forward, a

wormhole opened, and suddenly Serge was there, grabbing Gunnolf by the leg and ripping him away from the rope, freeing Petra.

And in the process ripping Gunnolf's leg off as well.

"Come on!" Nick yelled, urging Petra toward him as Serge ignored her completely, and turned his attention to the other three weren who had stepped in to help their leader.

She raced toward him, and they turned back to face the monster. In the short time it took for Petra to get to Nick's side, Serge had made mincemeat of the weren.

He was half man/half wolf now, having absorbed more of the werewolf essence, and he snarled as he moved closer to Gunnolf, who lay bleeding on the ground, but still alive.

"Stop!" Petra screamed, which Nick thought was a completely useless thing to do when they needed to be getting the hell out of there.

Or maybe not so useless.

Serge stopped, turning his head to look at Petra from where he stood over Gunnolf, surrounded by bits and pieces of weren bodies.

In the distance, they could hear more weren troops arriving. Serge heard it, too, cocking his head in that direction, and then leaping back through the still-open wormhole.

On the ground, Gunnolf groaned.

"Come on," Nick said, and they raced back the way they'd come, the opposite direction from the troops, until they reached the back wall of the cemetery near Ferrante's tomb.

They were up and over in seconds, then racing down the street.

A Bentley screeched to a stop in front of them, and Nick froze, calculating his odds, weighing his options.

Beside him, Petra stood stock-still, and he could smell the fear on her.

Behind them, the weren troops were coming over the cemetery wall.

The Bentley's door opened, and a man's voice called out for them to "Get in! Get in!"

That voice.

"In," Nick said to Petra, motioning her into the car, then following her, slamming the door and locking it just as the weren reached the car.

He settled back into his seat and sighed. And as Nick met the driver's eyes in the rearview mirror, he could only hope that he hadn't just made a huge mistake.

CHAPTER 27

Petra's heart was pounding as Nicholas slid into the backseat of the car beside her. The driver looked human, about fifty years old, with silver-gray hair that stood up in tufts, as if he spent most of his day running his fingers through it. He'd floored the accelerator, and now they were speeding down the Parisian street, taking corners wildly and quickly losing the weren who loped along, their swiftness no match for a car.

It was because of that as much as the fact that Nicholas had gotten into the car with him that made her trust the man.

But now that they had gotten free of the weren, she wanted to know who he was. No, that wasn't true. She suspected she did know.

Now she wanted to find out if she was right.

"Marco Ferrante?" she asked.

From the front seat, the man banged the steering wheel. "So clever! So clever! I could tell how sharp you were," he said. "From the connection, you know."

He braked at a light, then turned to face them both in the backseat. Nicholas, she saw, sat still and tense, as if he was on guard, ready to bolt if need be. Considering the story he'd told her about their parting, she understood why. But Ferrante appeared to hold no grudge.

"What connection?" she asked.

"Ah! There's the bracelet," he said, his eyes on her wrist. "How lovely it looks on your wrist. I have not seen that bracelet for a long, long time."

She swallowed as a series of small shivers raced up her spine. "You know this bracelet?"

"Manus fati," he said. "The hand of fate," then turned back to the front as the light changed to green.

She glanced sideways at Nicholas, not sure what to make of either Ferrante or the fact that he knew the inscription carved into her bracelet.

"Why are you here, Marco?" Nicholas's voice was tight, making it clear to Petra that he didn't trust Ferrante. She kept one hand on the door latch, just in case. "Why?" Nicholas repeated.

"I was looking for Ms. Lang."

"For Petra?" Nicholas asked, still with that harsh, cold tone, as if he was poised to run. Or to attack. "And how did you know so precisely where to find her?"

From the front seat, Ferrante sighed. "I told you. We have a connection, she and I."

"A connection?" Nicholas repeated. "How the hell do you have a connection with Petra?"

Ferrante looked up, his eyes glancing back at them from the rearview mirror. "Because I am the one who made her the way she is."

♦

"Are you hearing this?" Elric asked. They were in a vehicle borrowed from Division 18, and he had the radio tuned to the local Alliance frequency. "Goddamn, it's a fucking bloodbath, and Gunnolf was barely left alive."

"I hear it," Tariq said, forcing the words out between clenched teeth. The reports blaring out over the radio were almost hysterical, as if procedure and form had been lost to terror. And it took a lot to terrorize Alliance officers.

"The monster is here," Vale said. "Fuck me. I do *not* want to face that thing."

"We don't have to," Tariq said. "Our goal is the girl. Find the goal, kill the girl, destroy the monster." He looked at his teammates. "We walk back into Alliance HQ as fucking heroes." Shit, he just might end up with his uncle's newly empty Alliance seat.

"The brother," Vale said, pulling the small silver tracker from his bag. "We keep our focus on the brother, and he'll lead us to the girl."

"We know he came to Paris," Tariq said. "And we know the girl was right there in the middle of the carnage."

"Sooner or later he's going to hone in on her," Elric said.

Tariq smiled and pulled away from the curb, sliding neatly into the predawn traffic. "And we'll be right there when he does."

♦

"What the hell are you talking about?" Petra demanded, beating Nick to the punch. "You *made* me this way?"

"Do you remember what we sought all those years ago?" Ferrante asked, turning just long enough to look at Nick. "You and I and Giotto?"

Nick hesitated, uncertain if the question was relevant, or if his old mentor was baiting him, laying the groundwork for revenge, long overdue. "I remember."

"Of course you do," Ferrante said. "Forgive me. The question was cruel. That was not my intention."

Nick glanced sideways at Petra, who looked equally baffled. "All right," he said. "Go on."

"I achieved our goal. It took me another ten years of examining the world, traveling to the far reaches of the earth before designing detailed—and often dangerous—experiments. I spent countless hours recording observations, trying to understand the mechanical underpinnings of the universe, of time, of life itself. But finally—*finally*—I achieved that which I'd searched for all my life—immortality."

"Since it has been more than seven hundred years since our last meeting, I had assumed as much," Nick said, making Ferrante chuckle.

"True, my young Nicholas. But what is also true is that my success came at a heavy price."

"What price?" Nick asked, fearing the answer.

It wasn't Ferrante who responded, though. It was Petra.

"Me," she said. "Me, and Vivian Chastain, and others like us."

Once again, Marco met her gaze in the mirror, his smile sad. "Yes," he whispered. "As I said, the price was steep. And, I assure you, unintentional."

"I'm still not following," Nick said, his mind flipping through everything he knew about alchemy, about chemistry and biology. "Tell me how. Exactly."

"The details, no." Nick started to protest, but Ferrante held up a hand and aimed a stern look into the mirror. "I long ago swore never to repeat to another soul what I did, because I see now that my actions were a sin against God."

"Did not God give men minds to explore? And was it not your exploration that led to your immortality?"

"You will not engage me, Nicholas, so do not even try. I will not share the details, but I will tell you the story. Listen, or don't. It's up to you."

Nick glanced sideways at Petra, but she was leaning forward, eager to hear what he had to say. He understood why. Hell, he felt the same way. "Go on."

Ferrante nodded. "The process was complicated, and one that used both mineral and biological elements. It required the extraction, alteration, and reintroduction of various vitreous fluids into a number of subjects."

"Wait," Petra said. "Just so I'm clear. This curse was made in a laboratory?"

"I'm afraid so, although 'curse' is perhaps the wrong word. It's more of a by-product."

"A by-product," she repeated, her voice dry. "Nice."

"As I said, your situation was entirely unintentional. I used assistants. Volunteers. And one was your ancestor. I am deeply sorry."

"But—" She cut herself off, trying to make some sense of what he was saying. "But how can my family's curse be the by-product of something you cooked up in a laboratory?"

"That would require me to go into details, and I—"

"And the blue moon thing," she continued. "How can that be the result of a chemical experiment gone wrong?"

Nick reached out and touched her sleeve, then shook

his head ever so slightly when she looked his direction. He agreed with her—Ferrante was holding something back—but now wasn't the time to push. Ferrante had come with a purpose of his own, and Nick wanted to let him get to it so that he could see the bigger picture of what was going on. "The bottom line is that you figured out a way," Nick prompted.

"And that way created the by-product. The curse," he said to Petra. "Three volunteers assisted me. Three were inflicted by the curse, and I swore to them— *swore*—that I would search for a way to lift it. That bracelet was my bond."

"But what does that have to do with a connection?" Petra asked. "You said it was because you're the reason behind the curse that there's a connection between us. How?"

"I don't know," he said. "It is one of the mysteries of alchemy. But I can summon that connection. Have always been able to summon it, all through these long years."

Nick breathed slowly, reaching out with his own connection to Petra, and could feel within her both belief and wariness. Like him, she could sense that there was some truth in Ferrante's story. And like him, she knew that there were large omissions. Not lies, perhaps, but certainly not the full story.

Ferrante had told them as much at the outset, though, stating outright that he wouldn't tell them the precise method by which he achieved immortality. Was that what he was withholding? Or was there something else? Something more insidious?

Nick considered the question, and as he did, he felt

Petra's thoughts move on as curiosity filled her. Curiosity, and fear.

She was, he realized, thinking of Serge.

"What about the monster?" she asked, as Nick released the blood connection. "Do you feel a connection to it, too?"

"What an interesting question. Why do you ask?"

"Because I do. I can feel its rage and its need to kill. And earlier, at the cemetery, when I told it to stop, it did."

"You controlled Serge?" Marco asked, sounding both surprised and concerned.

"Yeah. I think so. I didn't think that was even possible. I didn't think they *had* control, much less that they could *be* controlled."

"He's changed over time," Nicholas said. "The rage is still there, but it's more intense and focused. Less frenetic. And from what Luke has reported, the monster seems to act with awareness, not the way you've seen it the first few hours out of the gate."

She managed a grin. "I'm not sure if that makes it better or worse. But at any rate, we know he won't hurt me. Kill me, and the monster's done. So the question is, should I do something? Should we try to find Serge? Maybe I can stop him. Control him?"

Ferrante's laugh was coarse. "Perhaps—*perhaps*—you have some level of control, young lady, but can you tell where the monster is?"

"No."

"Then while you are searching for him, the Alliance would surely be searching for you."

"But to be able to call him off. If I'd only known or

been faster, then maybe he wouldn't have destroyed all those people. Maybe Gunnolf would still have his leg."

"In time, perhaps, you could learn to control it. But that won't be necessary."

"What? Why not?"

But the answer didn't come. Instead, a black van slammed into the front passenger door, sending Ferrante's car into a spin.

And when it stopped, Nick saw Tariq and two other agents piling out of the van and racing toward the car with their weapons drawn.

♦

"Stay in the car!" Ferrante shouted. "Stay in the car! The glass is bulletproof. We're safe if we stay in the car!"

As if to prove the point, a bullet slammed into the window, creating an impact mark, but not shattering the glass.

"Move away from the door," Nick said. "The bullets may penetrate metal. And get this damn thing started again," he added, not inclined to sit in the street like a Christmas present for Tariq any longer than they had to.

Ferrante turned the key, and they were greeted with the sound of metal grinding against metal. He slammed his hand against the steering wheel. "Damn this blasted machine!"

"We need to get out of here," Nick said. "For a lot of reasons, not the least of which is that the sun will be up soon."

"It's simply not starting," Ferrante said, trying the key once again.

"The van?" Petra asked. "Do you think we could get to it?"

"No way. They'll put a bullet through your head the second you open that door."

"We have to do something," she said.

"I'll go," Nick said.

"The hell you will!"

"Bullets won't harm me. I have a solid chance."

He saw the fear in her face, but knew he didn't have a choice. He was about to tell her so when the car started to shake as the wind outside picked up.

Beside him, Petra sat up straighter. "Wind," she said. But what she meant, Nick knew, was *Kiril*.

He couldn't see the sorcerer, but the storm raged faster, making their car shake and jump.

Tariq and his team tried to race back to the van, but the wind caught them, lifting them up like puppets. It twirled and twisted, spinning them so fast that Nick couldn't keep focused on them. He found them again only when they burst from the wind tunnel.

Tariq flew through the air, a scream ripping from his throat as he landed—impaled—on an iron fence post. The other two slammed against the stone walls of nearby buildings and lay on the ground, not moving.

"Come on," Petra said as the storm died. She opened her door before Nick could stop her, calling out for Kiril, who appeared from a copse of trees on the far side of the van. She ran to him, stopping only inches from him by the door to the van, and Nick heard her squeal of delight and his relieved response. "Thank God I've found you safe."

In front of Nick, Marco crossed out of his way to go to one of the Alliance agents whose fingers had begun twitching slightly. "Die!" Ferrante said, and then stabbed him through the heart with a knife Nick hadn't even realized the older man had.

Then Ferrante looked at Tariq and the third agent. "Dead," he said to Nick, then spat on the ground. "And good riddance."

"I didn't realize you had such disdain for the Alliance."

"Ha!" Marco said. "They are all of them vile. I have nothing but disdain for the entire shadow world."

Nick tilted his head and looked at his former mentor. "And for me."

He saw Marco's chin lift, then heard his soft, "Ah." He shook his head. "Ah, Nicholas. I should have said the moment you entered my car that there is no animosity left between us."

"You turned me away when I reached out to you before."

"That was almost three centuries ago, and a man can change much in three hundred years." He smiled. "I've had a lot of time to think and study, Nicholas. How can I judge you for taking the path you took? A dark one, for sure, but you were young, and I understand more about the shadow world now than I did then. It wasn't the Nicholas I knew that killed our friend. It was the daemon. And the daemon has no friends."

"Yes," Nick said, humbled by Ferrante's understanding. "You speak the truth."

"I would be a hypocrite otherwise. After all, in the end, my way to immortality was also dark." He nodded toward Petra, still with Kiril by the van. "You didn't intend to bring out the daemon any more than I intended to curse that girl."

Nick moved toward her and heard Kiril's insistent tone. "We're leaving now, Petra. I'm taking you away."

"You're not," Nick said.

Petra shot Nicholas an irritated glance. This was her brother, and she had it perfectly under control.

She turned back to Kiril. "He's right. I'm not leaving Nicholas."

Ferrante hurried over. "This is an argument best left for later. Come, both of you. We are safe now, but soon the Alliance will send more. We must hurry if we want to keep the Alliance off your back forever."

Petra blinked, trying to figure out what he meant. "Forever? How?"

"Why, the reason I sought you out, my dear. I've discovered the way to lift your curse."

"What?" Had she heard wrong? Had he really just said what she thought he said? "A cure? Really?"

She glanced automatically at Nicholas, whose smile was both triumphant and loving. Then she turned to Kiril, who wasn't smiling, but was instead looking at Nicholas, his expression harsh.

"I cannot be sure until we try it," Marco said. "You are the last of your kind, my dear. But I am cautiously optimistic."

She'd worry about her brother later. This was too important. "Will it cure Serge, too?"

"It will."

"Is it dangerous?" Nicholas asked.

"There is some risk," Marco said. "But—"

"I don't care," she said. "I'll take it."

"You will *not*," Kiril said.

"Petra, you—"

"I can't live like this," she said, facing Nicholas square on. "I want to finally be free of this curse. And if this is a chance to do that, I have to take it."

CHAPTER 28

Marco's house was exactly what Petra would expect from a man who'd had centuries to gather wealth. A sprawling mansion with carved marble columns, topiaries dotting the manicured lawn, and a smattering of outbuildings, their silhouettes rising in the distance.

"This is incredible," she said, as he pulled into a circular driveway, the massive staircase leading to the entrance rising before them.

The foyer was tiled with slate, a huge room with high ceilings that echoed as they walked, the sound only partially muffled by huge vases of colorful, fragrant flowers. Petra stopped walking, then looked at Nicholas beside her and grinned. "Wow. I like hanging in these new, more luxurious circles. I think I'm going to have to keep you."

On her other side, Kiril was watching Nicholas, not her. She sighed at the disapproval on his face. With Ferrante waving her cure like a carrot, this really wasn't the time to get into it with her brother. She had a feeling, though, that she didn't have a choice.

"There is little time to waste," Ferrante said. "But some things cannot be prepared in advance. The laboratory is right there," he said, pointing to a door on the far side of the foyer. "Fifteen minutes, and then I will come for you. Okay?"

She nodded, nervous about the danger, but more excited about the possibility of being able to move freely through the world.

Of being able to touch Nicholas.

Ferrante looked at Nicholas. "Perhaps we could talk while I set up? I think there are things left between us that should be said."

Nicholas caught her eye, and she nodded. Only then did he turn and follow Ferrante into the next room.

"You left," Kiril said. "You chose that one over me."

"Chose?" she repeated. She knew how overprotective Kiril could be, but this was beyond unfair. "Kiril, I want to be cured, and that's what Nicholas wanted, too. And look where we are. Standing on the precipice of that very thing."

"So they say. How do you know the two of them aren't even now plotting your demise? Perhaps this was a ruse, designed to lure you in and make you trust. You'll go through those doors, and they will kill you to free Sergius."

She blinked at him. "Whoa. Do you need a tinfoil cap to go with all those conspiracy theories?"

"Don't play games with me, Petra."

"I'm sorry," she said. "I know you're genuinely worried for me. I do. I get that. But Nicholas isn't going to kill me. He's already had that chance. He *knows*, Kiril. He knew and he let me live."

Kiril snorted.

"It's true." She licked her lips, not wanting to admit the next part to her brother, but knowing she had to. "And after I heard that Serge was free and killing, I wanted to. I wanted to end my life in Paris. Nicholas wouldn't let me."

"Nicholas," he repeated, flinching slightly as he said the word. He drew in a breath, then closed his eyes. When he opened them, he was Kiril the protector, the twin who'd always acted as though he was older and wiser. "What have you done, Petra?"

"What are you talking about?"

He crossed his arms and started to circle her. "We just came off a blue moon," he said as the air in the room seemed to swell and gust. "What exactly did you do?"

She bristled. "That is exactly none of your business."

"The hell it's not."

"How?" she demanded. "How is my personal life your business?"

"You're my—my *sister*," he said in a voice that wasn't yelling, but was so firm and precise he might as well be. The wind picked up, whipping through her hair. "You're my *responsibility*. What you do, where you are, who you are with. All of those things matter to me."

She wanted to yell right back at him. Hell, she wanted to pick up one of the vases of flowers and smash it on the ground at his feet.

She didn't. Instead, with Herculean effort, she reined her temper in. "It isn't your business anymore."

He tilted his head to the side, his eyes narrowing at first, and then going wide. "Oh no," he finally said. "You think you're in love with the guy?"

"I don't *think*," she said. "I am."

Something close to despair brushed over his face before his features hardened, anger firing in his eyes. "He's a vampire, Petra, in case that little detail escaped your attention. A bloodsucker. And on top of that, he's immortal. You'll get older and he'll continue to look like a poster boy for an action-adventure movie. You want that?"

"Yes," she said. "I do."

Kiril scoffed. "This is so fucked up." He ran his fingers through hair that was dancing in the wind, a small gale moving now through the foyer and tottering the vases on their stands. "Massively and completely fucked up. That is no life for you," he said, his voice rising. "You deserve better than ending up an old lady with a vampire."

"Stop it," she said.

"He'll dump you when you turn wrinkled and gray."

"*Stop it.*"

"You know it's true."

"It isn't," she said, but she had to admit, if only to herself, that she hadn't thought about the immortality thing. Kiril was right. She'd grow older. And Nicholas would stay exactly the same.

No. That didn't matter. Not right then. Right then, the only thing that mattered was the cure. Everything else would follow. They'd find a solution. Somehow, they would.

"Dammit, Petra. Haven't you read all those stories I've written for you? Your life is special. We—you deserve a better happily ever after."

"The stories shouldn't even be about me. They should be about other people. Other friends. Kiril, don't you see? You should have some experiences that don't center around me."

"I protect you."

"If I'm cured, I won't need protection anymore." She took a step closer, then reached out and put a gloved hand on his clothed shoulder, something she never did. "And even if this cure doesn't work, Nicholas can protect me now."

"No."

"Yes, dammit. You're an incredibly strong sorcerer for Christ's sake! Break the binding spell and live your life. I swear to you, Nicholas will protect mine."

"I can't leave you like that."

"You can."

Something hot flashed in his eyes. "No, you don't understand. Dammit, Petra, you're more than my sister. You're—"

"What?" She stepped closer, worried by what she saw in his face. "What am I?"

He didn't meet her eyes, and the wind stopped suddenly, as if in defeat. "You're my obligation," he said, and then stepped away.

She watched him go, certain that wasn't what he had intended to say.

♦

Nick glanced around the room, breathing in the scent of sulfur and acid, taking in the scrubbed work surfaces and Bunsen burners glowing softly in the corners. Fluorescent lights hung from the ceiling, and speakers mounted in the corner pumped in music, but in many ways the lab remained familiar. Welcoming. *Home.*

"I have missed our talks," Ferrante said. "I deeply regret that I rejected your overture when you last tried to make contact with me."

"I will admit that your refusal hurt, but I understood. After what I did—"

"We have already spoken of it. Let us consider that part of our lives closed and move on to the next."

He stopped pouring chemicals and checking settings long enough to turn and face Nick, his face reflecting nothing but sincerity. "I want that more than you can know."

Relief flowed through Nick, and he realized how much he'd missed Ferrante. And how intense—upon seeing him again—the need to make amends had grown.

"She is a lovely girl, isn't she?" Ferrante asked.

"She is," Nick agreed.

"I am so happy that I found you two in time. I was terrified I would be too late." He shuddered. "Damned Alliance puppets. You must hate them, the way they slapped her with a death sentence. The way they chased after you as if you were bugs to exterminate."

Nick tensed, unable to avoid the feeling that this was thorny ground. "They have been a nuisance," he said.

Marco shook his head. "Such corruption. Have you not seen evidence of that yourself?"

He had, of course. Over the years, he'd seen more acts of corruption than he could count. "But is any government perfect?"

"Probably not. But the Alliance is diseased from the inside. The infighting among the vampires and the therians, for example. Can the time spent on such petty concerns truly be good for the whole?" He tossed a hand up into the air. "But I'm babbling like the old man I've become. I'm afraid that after so many years there is little for me to do but watch and listen."

"Petra is beside herself about the possibility of a cure," Nick said.

"I imagine she would be."

"I'm optimistic as well. But we need to talk, Marco."

Ferrante turned to him. "What is it?"

"I love this woman. I'm not going to let you poke her or prod her or inject her or do whatever you intend to do until you have first taken me through the process step by step. You don't want to reveal the details of how you obtained immortality? Fine. I can live with that. But not this. This I need to see beforehand. This, *I* need to understand."

For a moment, Ferrante only stared at him. Then the older man nodded. "Of course. Of course. Good Lord, I should have offered that myself. I spend so much time within my own mind that I forget the needs of others."

"Now," Nick said, nodding at the lab table.

"Do you not think Petra and her brother deserve to understand, too? Go get them. We will have wine to toast our impending triumph, and while we drink, I'll explain. You will understand, and then we'll begin." He reached over and took Nick's hand in his. "Soon, you will be able to touch your woman."

Nick nodded, the prospect that her touch lay only moments away filling him with an almost unbearable feeling of longing.

He found Petra in the foyer, holding one of the flowers in her hands. She looked up as he walked in, then started to pluck the petals, murmuring, "he loves me, he loves me not, he—"

"Loves you," Nick said, taking the flower and brushing the soft petals over her cheek.

"Hang on. I can't trust you with these things." She took the flower back, ending on, "he loves me," then looked up at Nick with a mischievous grin. "I guess you know what you're talking about after all."

"Apparently," he said, moving to sit beside her on the step. "You're a dangerous woman, Petra Lang."

"Oh, thanks a lot. Rub it in."

"Not to the world. To me."

"Am I? How?"

"You hold in your hands the power to break my heart." He spoke without reservation, surprised not by the feeling, but by his own forthrightness. Was it because it was true? Or because what they were about to undertake was dangerous, and he feared he wouldn't again have the opportunity to say it?

He didn't know. All he knew was that he meant it.

"I would never," she said, and he knew she meant it, too. Her mouth quirked into a sad smile. "That's not fair, you know."

"What?"

"To say something like that to me when I can't kiss you."

He glanced toward the closed laboratory door. "Soon."

She licked her lips. "So how is Ferrante's supersecret lab? Does it make you want to give up advocacy and go back to being a man of science?" She spoke casually, but he could hear the nervousness in her voice.

"It's quite impressive, and yes, I suppose it does a bit.

Actually, I thought I would use my astounding scientific skills and vet Marco's process."

"What do you mean?"

"I mean I won't let you do this unless I am entirely sure that I understand the process and it's safe. Not certain," he said, holding up a finger to ward off her protest. "But I want to understand the theory and check Marco's calculations and equipment. I want you there, too. You should understand the nature of what you're about to undertake."

"Of course. You're right." She stood up. "Now?"

"Kiril?"

"He's in there," she said, pointing to the formal living room on the other side of the foyer. "Sulking."

Nick laughed. "About what?"

"You. He's jealous. Apparently he thinks you're usurping his life's work."

"I suppose I am," Nick said.

"If only I could convince him that was a good thing."

CHAPTER 29

"Come in, come in!" Nick stood beside Petra as Marco ushered them into the lab, her brother on her other side, sending the occasional dark and disapproving look Nick's way.

"Come. Drink." Marco led them to the end of one of the lab tables where four glasses of wine sat among beakers of colored liquids and burlap sacks holding who knows what. He distributed the glasses, then raised his into the air. "To the reunion of old friends and the promise of better days."

"I'll drink to that," Petra said.

They clinked glasses and drank as Marco began to speak. "I know only Nicholas is fully versed in the scientific underpinning of what I have discovered here, so I will try to couch my explanation in layman's terms."

"I appreciate that," Petra said.

"I want you to understand how long I have been working toward this day. I created the first generation of those inflicted with the Touch over seven hundred years ago, but it's only been in the last, oh, five hundred years that I recognized the possibility of control and began to hone that potential."

"Control?" Nick repeated, suddenly wary. "You want to explain what you mean by that?"

Marco lifted a hand. "Goodness! Please! Forgive an

old man his excitement. I'm telling my tale all out of order."

"Did we come here for a story? Or to examine a formula?"

"The two are intertwined. Please. Indulge me. I assure you I will get to the relevant details as quickly as possible."

He gestured to Petra. "The first step involves an electromagnetic charge. Don't worry, the generator isn't yet on. But come here, my dear," he added, grabbing one of the small burlap sacks off the lab table, and then taking her to a corner of the lab.

The area had a floor not of stone but of a dark metal. "An alloy of my own invention," Marco said when he noticed Nick's curiosity. "Through the use of low-voltage electricity, it focuses the power of the earth." He grinned, as happy as a child with a new toy. "Of course, with Petra, she already has the earthen power inside her. The magical bloodline, you see. That is the key."

"The key?" Petra asked, running the toe of her shoe along the alloy beneath her feet.

"The truth is that much of what I have worked out here today would not be possible without your bloodline."

Petra frowned. "What do you mean?"

"Magical ability runs in your family, does it not? I saw what your brother did to those Alliance agents."

Nick saw Petra glance toward Kiril, as if expecting him to answer, but her brother only stood there, his eyes narrow slits, as if he was so bored by the whole thing that he could take a nap right then.

"Yeah," Petra said. "Are you saying that if I were

someone else—like Vivian Chastain—that you couldn't cure me?"

"Not at all. I'm saying that if you were Vivian Chastain, there would be no need to keep you."

Warning bells clanged in Nick's head. "Keep her? What the hell are you talking about, Marco?"

"I've done you a favor, Nicholas. You love the woman, do you not? Now she can be at your side forever." He smiled thinly. "However long your forever may be."

Cold, hard fear bubbled within Nick and he felt the daemon twisting inside. "What have you done, Marco?"

"Her wine," he said. "I added a particularly potent elixir to her wine. She won't die, Nicholas. She's as immortal as you. I need her for a long time, you see."

"What the fuck?" Petra said, echoing Nick's thoughts precisely. She took a step toward Nick, and was immediately thrown backward.

"Force field," Marco said, and the word was still hanging in the air as Nick launched himself at his old friend, the daemon inside snapping and ready for a fight. Ready to rip the fucking head off this man—this monster—who had tricked and trapped the woman he loved.

Nick was ending this now—Marco died *now*.

Except Nick never made it.

Instead, Marco swept his arm out, sending a storm of dust from the burlap sack into the air.

Hematite.

Nick faltered, stumbling as the hematite powder coated his body. He sagged to the ground, realizing he'd breathed some of the dust. Hematite prevented a vampire from changing to mist or animal, though speed and strength were usually retained, albeit lessened.

But Nick had *breathed* the hematite, which meant his strength was reduced even more. Now that the shock of the hematite assault had worn off, he had about as much strength as a human, and considering he was in a lab with a madman, he really didn't think that would be enough.

He looked at Petra, who was staring at him with wide eyes, her hands pounding against what appeared to be pure air. He started to go to her, but Marco pulled a gun from a nearby lab table and pointed it at him.

"It won't kill you, but in light of the hematite, I think it will take you out of the game. And I'm certain you don't want to leave now, do you?"

Nick stayed put, although he did shift around just enough to look for Kiril, certain Petra's twin would raise a gale force wind, whip that gun out of Marco's hand, and level the lab. But Kiril was on the ground, eyes closed, chest rising and falling.

"Sedative," Marco said. "I considered killing him, but I didn't want to get off on the wrong foot with Petra. And, frankly, he will make a fine specimen for study."

"Why are you doing this?" Petra asked. "*What* are you doing?"

"I am creating an arsenal. With it, I will change the world and make it a better place. And you, Petra, are the lever I need."

Petra shook her head, still confused, still terrified. All she knew was that she was trapped and he'd hurt Nicholas. She needed to understand what was going on.

More, she needed to keep him talking. He'd said that he'd given Kiril a sedative, and she was hoping—*please*—that he didn't realize that her brother's magical constitution required more than the usual amount to knock him out for any length of time.

"What arsenal?" she asked. "What do you mean?"

"I'll show you," he said, then pushed a button. A tile in the wall slid open, and a cage rolled in. A cramped cage holding a naked, raging vampire, its mouth sewn shut with sloppy stitches, its arms and fists battering the hematite bars that encased it.

"One touch," Ferrante said. "One touch from you and we get another weapon. Another creature to do my bidding. Don't worry, I'll shoot it first. Not to kill it, but to knock it out so that you can safely get close enough to touch."

"You're insane," Nicholas whispered, which was exactly what Petra was thinking.

"What do you mean, do your bidding?" Petra asked, hoping that Marco was hyped up enough on his freakish plan that he'd keep talking about it. And talk and talk.

"How do you think I managed to already eliminate two members of the Alliance? I control the monster. I speak to Serge. I speak, and he obeys. And soon the rest of the Alliance will fall."

"Oh dear God," Petra whispered.

"At first, centuries ago, my control over these beautiful creatures was sporadic. And there is none when the monsters are young, still raging about from the change. But over time, whenever one of my cursed created a monster, I was able to hone my skill. To use subtle bits of magic to focus the connection between me and the monster. And then the damned Alliance began killing the monsters off as well as the cursed who made them. Bastards!"

"Magic?" Petra said. "You use spells to connect?"

"There is a bit of magic involved, yes. I think that is why you are so precious to me."

"Precious? How?" Petra glanced toward Nick, who was eyeing the room, as if looking for a weapon. Kiril was still on the ground. But she saw his fingers twitch and hoped that meant he was waking up.

"With Serge, I have more control than ever before. I am certain that it is because your magical heritage concentrated the power of the curse, rendering control simpler. It makes sense, don't you see, since both the magic and the curse come from the earth."

"Fine," Nick said. "But you already have Serge. You have your all-powerful whipping boy. So do this one thing for me. Because you once loved me as a son. Free the girl from the curse."

Marco turned slowly toward Nick, every movement signaling danger. "First of all, as I have explained, I seek to build an arsenal, and for that I need Petra. Now that I know she creates a monster that I can control, I would be foolish to afflict the curse on another and simply hope for the best."

"Afflict the curse?" Nick repeated, his mind spinning as he tried to put together a plan that would get them out of there, and alive.

"Second of all, there is no cure." He spoke harshly, his words cutting Nick to ribbons, and surely doing the same to Petra. "None that I have found, anyway.

"And finally, my darling Nicholas, I did once love you. At one time, you were my prodigy, my student, my friend. But that ended long ago. And if keeping this girl from you will cut you deeply, then I will joyfully strike that blow against you who destroyed my work and murdered my friend."

"You bastard," Nick whispered, ignoring the way Marco's words stung. It had been the daemon, he told himself. And it was a long time ago.

"Giotto had the answer, you know. He truly did." Ferrante tapped his temple. "Right there in his head. And it would have worked. But you struck him down, and I was never—*never*—able to reproduce the formula he had developed."

"Were you upset I'd killed your friend, or crushed because you had to work harder to find immortality?"

"I had to seek another avenue," Ferrante said, ignoring him. "Another way to draw upon the eternal flow of life. It took over a decade of study and experimentation. Of failure and of death. But I finally found the way."

"I see where this is leading, you hypocritical prick," Nick said. "You didn't find immortality through alchemy. You found it through black magic. The dark arts that you supposedly disdain."

"Through the power of the earth, Nicholas. Through the earth, and through the blood."

"Sacrifices," Nick said.

"Very good! You are as clever as I remember. Yes, sacrifices. But not blood sacrifices."

"What then?"

"For my longevity, I must present a sacrifice willing to carry the curse of the Third."

"My family," Petra whispered, and Marco pointed a finger at her.

"Yes, yes. The young lady has been listening. The sacrifice is the center of the ceremony. The sacrificed takes the curse, and I am rewarded by the Third for presenting the sacrificed with the gift of life. Each monster created extends my life, too. It's all a beautifully symbiotic relationship."

"That's insane," Petra said, the edge of hatred in her voice. "You didn't get volunteers. What did you do? Did you drug my ancestor?"

"The sacrifice must be willing," Marco said. "I merely offered what the person needed. Most often money." He nodded at the bracelet Petra wore. "Payment for a sacrifice. I'm surprised your family kept it. I had expected they would sell it for food or rent."

"You sick son of a bitch," she said, then slammed her hand hard against the force field.

"And the Third?" Nick asked. "It's playing this game for revenge? Through the monster your sacrifice creates?"

Marco shrugged. "Who knows the mind of a god? I speak only of my own revenge. A vampire destroyed my ambitions without retribution. The Alliance destroys my monsters and my cursed ones. The shadow world preys on humankind, Nicholas. It is vile. Corrupt. A plague, a blight, and I have the power to erase that scourge forever. I knew this when you first came to me with talk of a dark lady. And with every year that passes I see how insidious the shadow world truly is."

If he rushed Marco, he would undoubtedly suffer a gunshot wound, but unless Marco got him in the head or the heart, Nick should be able to continue without needing extraordinary time to heal. He had only human strength now, though. Could a wounded human overtake an immortal? If only Kiril were awake.

He clenched his fists, frustrated, and worked to keep the madman talking. "You would do better? What do you think you're accomplishing with all this?"

"Eradication. A new beginning." He smiled, slow and scary. "You have heard of the prophecy? I consider myself the hand that guides it." He glanced at Petra. "As the inscription on your bracelet suggests, we are all of us moved by the hand of fate."

"By fate?" Petra said. "*You're* the one that sent Serge after Dirque and Trylag."

"And the others as well," Marco said, without a hint of remorse.

"You said you sacrifice for your *longevity*," Petra said. "Not for your immortality."

"She is such a clever girl. We will become great friends, I am certain."

"Each sacrifice only gets you so many years, doesn't it? That's why my family line only goes back a couple of centuries."

"It is so. And soon, I must sacrifice another. But that is none of your worry. You need only touch those I bring to you."

"Not happening,"

"I think it will," Marco said, and as he spoke the air shifted, colors swirled, and a tunnel opened.

And right in the middle of it stood Serge. He burst from the wormhole and scooped Nick up so quickly and like so much garbage that Nick had no time to react at all. And then the monster thrust Nick up and held him aloft, the pressure on Nick's head and spine such that with the subtlest flick of his wrist, Serge could rip Nick's head right off.

"You will touch the creature in the cage, Petra dear. Because if you don't, your Nicholas will die."

CHAPTER 30

"*You hurt him,*" Petra yelled, "and the first opportunity I have, you better believe I'll slit my own throat. I die, and you're all out of luck, you freakish son of a bitch."

"I'm quite sure I can manage to keep you alive," Ferrante said, though Nick thought he looked a bit worried. "Of course my methods might prove unpleasantly constrictive when extended over the centuries. If you find them too unpleasant, I'm sure a medically induced coma would work just fine."

"You bastard," she whispered as Nick searched for something, anything, that would get him out of Serge's grasp—and hopefully kill Ferrante in the process. Right then, he wanted nothing more than to see Ferrante dead.

Dead . . .

He thought about what he and Petra had discussed once, about how it seemed as though she was a conduit between Serge and an unknown.

Well, that unknown had made itself known in a very big way.

But what if it was more than that? Not a conduit, but a full-fledged connection. A symbiotic relationship.

If Petra died, Serge was cured. Petra created Serge. Ferrante created Petra. Or created her curse, at any rate.

Did that mean that if *Ferrante* died, Serge was cured? More than that, did it mean that *Petra* was cured?

Dear God, it made sense. He had to be right.

It was hardly a perfect plan. For one thing, he could only assume that Ferrante had stopped the aging process, not made himself indestructible. He would continue to live so long as no one cut out his heart or put a bullet through his brain.

Nick couldn't be certain that was the case, but it was a fair assumption.

Still, even if they managed an attack on Ferrante—and how the hell they would manage that under the circumstances he didn't know. Unless the attempt succeeded with absolute perfection, Ferrante would surely kill both Nick and Kiril right then, and Petra would be at his mercy.

But if it worked . . .

He craned his head, trying to see Kiril, but his vision was blocked by lab equipment.

"Petra," he called. "It's Ferrante. It's Ferrante as much as you."

Her forehead crinkled, and he realized that she didn't know what he meant. Ferrante did, though. Either that or he was simply hedging his bets, because he snarled out an order to Serge. "Kill him."

And right away, Serge's hands tightened on Nick's head.

"Stop!" Petra's cry filled the room, and to Nick's amazement, Serge stopped. He remembered the way she'd managed to make Serge stop at the graveyard. And recalled what Ferrante said about her bloodline playing a part in controlling the monster.

"It's the magic," Nick called. "Focus. Keep your focus tight. It's the only way to compensate for his years of practice."

From behind the force field, Petra clenched her hands into fists at her sides as Ferrante, his face red with fury, muttered under his breath, urging Serge to hurry up and kill Nicholas.

Petra was amazed that she had any control over Serge at all, but the effort was exhausting her, and she wasn't sure how long she could keep it up.

She had to do something else, and Nicholas's words echoed in her mind: It's Ferrante as much as you.

Oh dear God, he was right! He had to be!

She glanced toward her brother and saw that he was moving. She cried out for him, screaming loud and sharp, and then alternated, silently focusing her energy on Serge.

As Nicholas had said, she thought of it as conjuring fire. Pulling it up. Focusing. Holding.

Pushing Serge back with her mind and calling for Kiril with her voice. Over and over, until she feared it wasn't working and he wouldn't wake. And then—

"Petra?"

His voice, low and groggy, had her almost sagging in relief, but she didn't let up the mental chant to Serge.

Stop. Don't. Stay.

"Wind!" she cried aloud.

Her brother, thank God, understood.

It started slow—too slow, she feared—but before she could alter her chant and beg him to increase the wind's fury, he did so himself. Papers whipped around the room, faster and faster as the wind kicked up and up, a tornado gathering at the center among the five of them, the tight wind dark with dust and debris.

And then bits of debris came flying out.

A book, surging across the room to batter Nicholas. A broken beaker, barely missing him.

"No!" she cried, but she couldn't say more, not and keep up the chant, and if she didn't keep up the chant then she would be the reason Nicholas died, not Kiril.

On the far side of the windstorm, Ferrante stood firm, his hands out, as if he was gathering magic. That was exactly what he was doing, she realized, and if he gathered enough, he'd be able to override her inexperienced control over the monster, which now stood, frozen immobile by the warring commands being thrown at it.

But not immobile for long.

She was running out of time. *Nicholas* was running out of time.

A few feet away, Kiril shifted to look at her, and this time she saw the jealousy on his face unshielded. And the desire.

Oh dear God. She finally understood. It was more than a brother's love she saw in his eyes. It was the love of a man for a woman, and the realization made her shudder with sadness and despair.

"*Kiril, no!* If you love me, no!"

He blinked, his expression confused. "You love him?"

Tears streaked her face. "I do. Please, Kiril. I do."

He turned away slowly, as if in a trance, and she kept up the mental chant against Serge, infusing it with all the hope she had in her.

A knife burst from the tornado, heading straight toward Nicholas.

She screamed out in agony and frustration, but then its trajectory changed and Kiril was using the wind to hurl it straight toward Ferrante.

"You will not!" Ferrante howled, lifting his arm. Pointing the gun.

Pulling the trigger.

The bullet shot out, the report deafening.

And then Kiril was on the ground, and the tornado was fading, and Petra was certain that all was lost.

"It's over," Ferrante said as she frantically, tearfully, took up the chant again, trying to counteract his order:

"Serge, *kill*."

But then a final gust of wind burst through the room, shooting shards of broken glass toward Marco. One lodged in his throat, and he fell, the gun falling from his hand as he staggered backward to grasp at the glass even as the wind died . . . and as Kiril died with it.

But still, Serge held Nicholas.

And Petra realized that although her brother had managed a final assault—a final attempt to help save the man she loved—he hadn't managed to kill Marco.

Serge remained a monster.

Held above Serge, Nick saw their chance. "Have him drop me," he called to Petra.

With Marco injured, it should be easier for her, but Nick could see the fatigue on Petra's face. And now that Serge had no warring commands controlling him, his own monstrous urge to rip and destroy was coming out. Nick could feel the hands tighten, and he called down, yelling Serge's name. "I'm your friend, dammit. If you're in there at all, Serge, it's Nick!"

He had no idea if it worked, but he did know he wasn't being ripped in two, so that was good.

Across the room, Marco lay in a pool of blood. But he was still breathing. Worse, he was crawling.

The gun.

In the force field, beads of sweat gathered on Petra's forehead, her hands clenched at her sides.

Silently, he urged her to hurry.

And then, as if she'd pulled into her all the magic she could find, she boomed out a loud, imperious command. "Drop him!"

Serge did, and Nick scrambled toward the gun, Serge behind him.

Nick tossed himself forward, his fingers almost grasping the weapon, but Serge grabbed his leg, pulling him down, still inches from the gun.

"No!" Petra screamed. "Serge! Stop!"

The hold relaxed. Nick jerked his leg free. He had the gun and in seconds he was up. In seconds he fired.

And he put a bullet right between the eyes of his old friend and mentor.

Marco was dead.

It had worked.

Behind Nick, Serge collapsed to the ground.

And on the far side of the room, Petra cried out.

Nick raced to her, then found the controls that operated the force field.

"Petra," he cried, and then hesitated before pulling her into his arms.

"It worked," she said, smiling through tears. "Killing

Marco—it cured me. I can feel it. I can tell." She slid into his arms and held him close as he stroked the back of her hair. "It worked."

They stayed that way for an eternity, until Serge stood and came to them. Nick looked up at his friend. This wasn't the creature that'd destroyed Dirque and Trylag and so many others. But neither was it the same old Serge. The scent of him was different. His skin was different. And Nick tried very hard not to fear what else might be different.

"Thank you," Serge said, focusing on both Nick and on Petra.

"Serge," Nick said, then stopped, unsure what else he wanted to say.

"I must go. The Alliance seeks me for my crimes."

"That wasn't you," Petra protested.

Serge faced her square on. "Wasn't it?"

"Stay," Nick said. "We'll get you back to New York. I'll get this worked out with the Alliance. You don't need to be out there. Not now."

The corner of Serge's mouth lifted. "Worried about what I am now, Nicholas? Don't be. I'm more than I was before. But I'm not a plague upon the earth, and my daemon sleeps. Give me time. I will return."

"Serge—"

"Good-bye, Nicholas," he said, and then he turned and walked out of the lab.

"Should you let him go?"

Nick considered the possible responses. He could run after Serge and beg, but unless Serge wanted to stay, he was going. And because of the hematite, Nick was in no position to fight him. What would be the point, anyway? "It's okay," Nick finally said. "He'll be back."

She nodded, and for a moment, they simply looked into each other's eyes, both overwhelmed by everything that had transpired.

Then slowly—so very slowly—she pressed her palm to his cheek.

A shiver ran through her and a single tear spilled down her cheek. Nick brushed it away with the pad of his thumb, and before he could pull his hand back, she caught it, and pressed her face against his hand.

She looked up at him, and he trembled from the depth of emotion he saw there.

"I love you," he whispered.

"I love you, too," she said. "Forever."

EPILOGUE

Petra lay naked in bed, her body twined with Nicholas's, flesh upon flesh, so intimate that when she closed her eyes she couldn't tell where she ended and he began.

Heaven.

The Ritz Paris was huge and beautiful, wonderfully appointed, but Petra didn't much care. The bed was firm, the sheets were clean, and room service was awesome.

As far as hotels went, those were her only current requirements.

Beside her, Nicholas shifted as he woke up, now fully healed from the hematite dust. He propped himself on his elbow and smiled at her. "You look beautiful."

"I have bed head," she countered, and leaned over to kiss him, taking it slow and savoring the feel of her lips against his. "You're going to have to deal with it, because I'm not getting up."

He stroked a hand down her side, over the curve of her hip, and she practically purred. "Really not a problem."

She sighed. It had been a full week since she'd been freed from the curse, and the first two days had been a whirlwind of official activity. She'd been checked out by Division 18 and Alliance doctors and scientists and pronounced curse-free, which she already knew, and immortal, which she hadn't been sure of. She'd told the medical team about the elixir that Marco had put in her drink. They'd found traces of it in his lab, and a series of magic and scientific tests had confirmed that the elixir—in combination with her magical bloodline—rendered her immortal.

Amazing, but she supposed she had to thank the murderous freak for giving her a very long life with Nicholas.

She ran her bare toes up Nicholas's calf. *Forever.*

She liked the sound of that.

"I got a text from Luke a few hours ago. Gunnolf's being fitted for a prosthetic today."

"Good," she said. She wasn't feeling all warm and fuzzy toward the werewolf, but in the end he and Tiberius had come through for her. All charges had been dropped against her and Nicholas. She was a free woman. It felt pretty damn good.

"Are he and Sara coming for the funeral tomorrow?"

"They are. Sara's hearing was yesterday and all charges were dropped. They said they'd see us at the service."

Petra had debated whether to take Kiril's body back to the States, but in the end she'd decided to stay in France. His favorite author was French—Flaubert—and she thought he'd like it here. The funeral was scheduled for tomorrow, just after sunset.

Nicholas stroked her cheek. "Are you okay?"

She nodded. "It'll get easier."

"He loved you, and in the end he proved to you just how much."

"I know." Although she hadn't told Nicholas just how much Kiril had loved her—because that was Kiril's secret that should die with him—Nicholas was still right that Kiril had acted out of love. She only wished she'd understood how he felt earlier, wished she hadn't completely missed all the signs. She would have tried to help him. Tried to break all the binds between them, and not just her grandmother's spell.

But it was over, and in the end, her brother had saved her life and Nicholas's. And that was one hell of an epitaph.

Rand and Lissa were coming, too, and Petra and Lissa had already planned the world's most massive shopping day in Paris. She'd never had a girl's day, complete with a massage, and she was looking forward to it with almost absurd anticipation.

She rolled over and spooned up against Nick, then sighed with pleasure as he curled his body around hers, the sensation familiar and yet still deliciously new.

She closed her eyes, warm and safe and happy.

But underneath it all, she felt something else. Faint stirrings. Hints of unease. *Serge?*

She frowned and slid off the bed.

"Petra?"

"I'm fine," she said. "I want to see Paris."

She pushed the curtains aside and looked out, taking in the lights and the bustle of the amazing city. Below them, crowds surged, a river of humanity that she could join now, whenever she wanted to.

Nick came up behind her and slid his hands around her waist. "Want to go down and rub shoulders with the masses?"

She laughed and turned in his arms, the feeling of unease fading against the glow of the man.

"Absolutely not," she said, tilting her face up for a kiss. "Right now, I only want you."

Can't get enough of
J. K. Beck's sexy Shadow Keepers?

Get ready to sink your teeth into
the next book in J. K. Beck's
hot new series

WHEN PASSION LIES

Coming soon from Bantam Books

Turn the page to take a peek inside. . . .

CHAPTER 1

◗ *Zermatt, Switzerland*

The bar was dark, so dark that it was hard to see the faces of the men and women huddled around tall tables or leaning against the centuries-old bar, looking for a drink or a good time or both.

Caris stood in deepest shadows, back in the far corner, beyond the dartboard and the karaoke stage where a Teutonic male croaked out the Beatles' "Help!" in broken English.

He spread his arms wide, gyrated his hips, and mangled the chorus. Caris cringed, and in a moment of rare charity hoped that he hadn't come to get laid, because no woman in the bar looked drunk enough to take him home. And that said a lot, since most of the people in the small bar smelled of sex and lust and pure animal heat. So much so, in fact, that the power of their passion seemed to cling to her, making her skin burn and her hunger build.

But she hadn't come for sex. She'd come for something entirely different.

Caris had come to kill.

Slowly, she scoured the faces of the men in the bar, the darkness no hindrance to her vampiric vision. She'd never seen his face, and during her captivity he'd taken care to mask his scent, yet she knew exactly who she was looking for. His description was set out in excruciating detail in the dossier she'd received that morning from a particularly resourceful PI she'd retained in Zurich.

She sighed. For decades she'd followed so many leads, only to find that she'd been stalking the wrong prey.

This time though . . .

By the gods, this time she had to be right. One more false lead and she feared she would snap. Orion had told her over and over she should simply quit. Pack it in. Throw in the towel and all those other cutesy sayings for giving up. But she couldn't. She *wouldn't*. That would mean that *he* would have won. That he'd taken her perfect life and ripped it into tiny pieces.

And that was unacceptable. There was a price for pain.

Tonight, he'd learn just how heavy a price her pain had borne.

One by one, she examined the faces in the bar, ignoring the two blond male vampires hunched in a corner. She wasn't interested in other vamps. Not tonight.

She let her eyes pass over the females, focusing only on the men. The breadth of their chests. The cut of their shoulders. Searching for a man with a bulky frame and the same dark hair and thin mustache reflected in the dossier picture.

He wasn't there.

Goddamn it all, he wasn't there.

With a series of curses burning her tongue, she whirled around. Maybe he was in another bar. Maybe he was hiking the damn Matterhorn. Maybe the universe was playing one big nasty trick on her.

Didn't matter. Ultimately, she'd find him. Ultimately, she'd—

Tiberius?

It wasn't him, of course. Not the man she'd once loved with every breath in her body. But the midnight-black hair and infinite eyes had caught her attention as surely as Tiberius's had that first night when he'd strode into her father's court, a stranger offering his services as a warrior and a strategist. The resemblance was striking, and for the briefest of moments, her throat tightened and her pulse burned, violent anger warring with the deepest of desire.

It wasn't her father who had held the stranger's interest. It was her. He'd walked with her in the moonlight, his touch making her blood simmer and her pulse quicken.

She'd looked out over her father's land and seen nothing but Tiberius, wanted nothing but him. His touch. His kiss. His everything.

And eventually, he had told her his secret. Had told her about the dark kiss. About the shadows.

He'd told her what he was.

His gaze had never left her as he spoke, searching her eyes for fear or loathing. He hadn't found it. How could she ever be scared of him? Instead, she'd been intrigued, certain that she was looking destiny in the face. That he was her destiny.

Tiberius. Her mate. Her love.

"Buy you a drink?" the man in front of her asked, and when he spoke the illusion faded. His was the voice of a man who picked up women in bars. Definitely not Tiberius.

She paused, looked him slowly up and down, then continued toward the door.

He fell into step beside her despite the brush-off. Apparently, he was either stubborn or stupid.

"You're alone," he said.

"Your powers of perception are mind-boggling." She kept on walking.

"A woman like you shouldn't be alone."

She stopped, then slowly turned to face him. "And what kind of woman is that?"

"A beautiful one."

"Trust me," she said. "It's a deadly beauty."

"I know." He was looking at her hard, and she could smell the truth on him. He knew what she was, and damned if that didn't excite him. The prospect of blood teased her daemon, the dark malevolence that lived deep inside every vampire, and her hunger grew.

The wolf stirred, too. The secret beast inside her. *He'd* made her this way, and she'd come to kill in payment for his dirty little tricks. For turning her into walking death. An outsider in her own damn world.

Can't go there, Caris. Don't even think it.

"I want what you can give." He looked at her with eyes wide and wild, like a junkie staring into a candy jar filled with meth.

"Death?"

"The rush." His chest rose and fell with his breath, the scent of desire wafting off him. He licked his lips and took a step toward her. "I know what you are," he said, then tilted his head to the side. "Feed."

Something raw and angry welled inside her. "You have no idea what I am," she said. "You don't have a goddamned clue."

"You're a vampire."

The word hit her with the force of a slap, and she stepped closer, so close she could feel the heat of his excitement rising from his bone-pale skin. "I'm not," she said. "Not anymore." Not fully, anyway. If she were, Tiberius wouldn't have kicked her out. Now she was something new. Something horrible.

She looked into those dark eyes and saw the fear growing, a fear that fed and fueled her, that primed her up and begged her to take, take, *take*. To get revenge. Against the man she hunted, yes. But more against the man who'd loved her up until the day he'd dumped her. She wanted to give Tiberius the big Fuck You. And right now . . . right now it was this guy standing in front of her. This guy, waiting for her to take his blood, his life . . .

She fought it down, fought it back.

Not now. Not when she was on the hunt.

"Go," she said, pressing her palm against his chest and pushing him away from her. "Find yourself a less dangerous game to play."

She left him gawking in her wake as she strode outside. She'd hit the next bar. She'd find her quarry. She'd come to this town with a purpose, and she didn't intend to be distracted. Not even by the goddamned memories of Tiberius.

They'd ruled together for centuries—first in the human world until the rumors had begun, the people whispering about the king and the queen who lived in the night and never aged—and then in the shadow world. A dark warrior rising to power within the Alliance, working to strengthen the power of the vampire race. Fighting to defend their kind against the ancient enemies—the therians. Werewolves and other shifters. Shadowers, yes. But not of their kind.

She'd stood with him shoulder to shoulder. His woman, his confidante, his heart. And his secret weapon. A warrior as fierce as he, hiding beneath the soft curves of a woman.

Never once had she doubted Tiberius's love or his admiration. His strong arms would always be around her. His soft words would always whisper to her. They could spend eternity walking the earth, filling the night with conversation and never tiring of each other. She was as certain of it as she was of the inevitable sunrise.

Until she'd been ambushed.

Jumped in the forest. Tied up. Tormented and tortured as a full moon leered overhead.

And bitten. The wolf had sunk his teeth into her, and the weren curse had poured into her veins.

She'd changed.

She'd changed and the nightmare had begun.

Her world had turned upside down, and her love had betrayed her.

She hated him, yes.

But she blamed the weren who'd stalked her.

Blamed him . . . and would kill him.

A scream ripped through the night as if echoing her own need to rend and tear. She told herself to ignore it— not her problem. But the smell of fear permeated the air.

Whatever was happening, it was close. And, damn it all, she was already heading in that direction.

She found them in the alley behind the bar—the two vamps and the idiot patron with Tiberius's eyes. One of the vamps leaned lazily against the rough-hewn wooden wall while the other held the human in a mockery of a lover's embrace, his teeth sunk deep into the male's flesh.

She started to turn away—she wasn't the PEC. It wasn't her job to arrest vamps who ran around feeding on humans, even dumb-ass ones who'd been begging for trouble. Especially not dumb-ass ones who reminded her of Tiberius. And wasn't there some sort of sweet justice in seeing the life sucked out of him?

She watched for a second, breathing in the scent of fear, the aroma of death. She watched, and then she cursed.

Goddamn it all.

Three long strides and she was right in front of them. "Funny," she said, speaking to the one with his fangs buried in flesh. "He doesn't look like a licensed faunt."

"Not your business, little girl," the one with his mouth free said. "Not unless you're interested in sharing."

She faced him, her hand going to her hip, pushing the leather of her coat back, revealing the knife she habitually wore there. "I don't think we've been introduced," she said. "I'm Caris."

"Caris?"

She actually saw him swallow, and she had to bite back a smile. Apparently her reputation was worth something even up here on the Matterhorn.

"You should go if you want to live."

She didn't have to repeat herself. The one who'd been holding up the wall cut and ran. The other dropped the human, wiped the blood off his lips with the back of his hand, and then backed out of the alley, his eyes fixed on her as if she might just jump him for spite.

Any other night, and she might just have done that.

The human slumped to the ground, his cheek pressed against a slush of dirty snow. She could hear his pulse, weak but steady. She walked away, leaving him to the cold, but she pulled out her cellphone and called the pub. Told the bartender who answered that there was a man in his alley bleeding from the neck. Just her little charitable contribution for the day.

On the *bahnhofstrasse,* she paused to look up and down the street. She lifted her chin, sniffing the cold air out of habit. She expected nothing—so far her luck hadn't exactly been stellar—and was surprised to catch a scent. Musky. Animal.

Weren.

Not necessarily the one she hunted, couldn't get her hopes up yet. But she turned left, following the scent up the hill, through twisting streets, and finally out of the village and up a hiking path into the mountains.

The trail was stronger now, and she increased her pace, realizing she was gaining on him. The moon hung heavy in the sky—seventy percent waxing gibbous—and the animal within was relishing the hunt. The daemon—primed from the blood and charged from the memories—wanted nothing more than the kill.

Melting snow and fallen leaves littered the path, but she moved in silence, twisting around a copse of trees and then stopping short—he was there. And he hadn't yet realized she was behind him.

Her hand went to her knife. She had a gun, too. A small revolver tucked in at the small of her back. Five silver bullets. They'd kill a werewolf dead enough, but this was one kill Caris wanted to make with her hands. Not her fangs—the thought of her mouth closing over this pile of flesh made her ill. But with a blade. One quick motion across his throat—face-to-face so she could see his expression, and watch as he understood that the time had come to pay for his sins.

She stepped forward, no longer caring about stealth. She wanted a fight. Craved it, in fact. Her daemon wanted to play. And so long as the weren ended up dead, she was more than happy to let her daemon get out and stretch its legs.

According to the dossier, the weren's name was Cyrus Reinholdt. She didn't much care—to her he was simply the enemy, the hated, the bastard who'd fucked her over. But right then, Reinholdt turned, and a flicker of joy passed through her as she saw the recognition—and the fear—in his eyes.

She tensed, but didn't lunge. Didn't move forward, didn't attack, and for a split second she wondered at her hesitation. This was the weren she'd been looking for. The son of a bitch who'd destroyed her life, her love.

Inside, the daemon growled, wanting blood. Her body itched to leap, the wolf within wanting to rip this cousin to shreds.

Still, though, she didn't move, and as the blood boiling in her head calmed, she realized why. It wasn't the kill she wanted—not right away. It was answers.

Why the hell had he done this to her? Why the hell had he changed her into a goddamned leper?

"Why?"

The question came out as a whisper, but she knew he heard it.

"I heard you were coming to find me," he said, and at first she thought he meant in the past, that he was answering her question. "News travels fast in the mountains."

"And here I am. Tell me what I want to know, and maybe I'll let you live." It was a lie she didn't regret telling.

He didn't answer. Instead, he reached into his coat and pulled out a gun. Not something she usually feared, but this was the one man in all the world who would know what type of bullet would hurt her. Wooden bullets coated in silver. A weapon designed to kill either a vampire or a werewolf. Or both.

"Abomination." He held the gun steady. "I should never—"

"Why?" This time the word ripped from her throat, and she hated her own lack of control, but dammit, she'd been waiting decades to face this man and she wanted answers. "Why did you do this to me?"

His finger moved on the trigger, and in that same instant, she launched herself sideways. The bullet sang out, burning through the leather sleeve of her coat, slicing into the flesh of her arm. But no kill shot. He'd fucked up there big-time.

She fell back into the snow and rolled, and when she came up, she had her own gun in her hands. He was about to get off another round, but she fired one shot at his head, and he stumbled backward, a neat little hole in his skull. She stood, aimed, and put another through his heart, knocking him to the ground.

The man she'd come to kill was dead.

Somehow, she didn't feel any better.